SURROUNDED!

It had been a long, hard day, but now the children were asleep in the wagons and Abbie and the others had gathered around the fire. Suddenly a coyote howled. Another answered. Save for the coyotes, there was complete silence. Silence—except for a faint sound of shivering grass. The group around the fire seemed suddenly too small to be alone in the still vastness, too inadequate and helpless.

What if—? Even as her fear formed itself into thought, Abbie saw through the shadows a figure—and another—and others steal with panther-like tread between the wagons and the creek bed. . . .

A LANTERN
IN HER HAND

You'll Love These New Titles from Vista

(0451)

☐ **PLEASE DON'T KISS ME NOW by Merrill Joan Gerber.** With her mom into self-fulfillment and her dad remarried, life for fifteen-year-old Leslie is getting pretty confusing. And when Brian Sweeney, the senior-class heartthrob starts getting interested in her she tries to forget her troubles and find security in his arms ... (115759—$1.95)

☐ **CALL ME MARGO by Judith St. George.** Margo Allinger's family moved around so much that the shy teenager could never make any lasting friendships. But now she was going to be living at Haywood for three whole years. At first everything goes well, but when the going gets tough Margo realizes that it is up to her to conquer her fear and learn to speak up for herself. (118502—$2.25)

☐ **TWO POINT ZERO by Anne Snyder and Louis Pelletier.** If Kate Fleming hadn't desperately needed the money for college, she never would have agreed to write papers for the football team's star kicker. Everything goes smoothly until she gets involved with handsome Doug Hollis, whose exposée on cheating for the magazine threatens to ruin her chances for getting into law school. (114760—$1.75)

☐ **TWO LOVES FOR JENNY by Sandy Miller.** When Jenny and her boyfriend Doug both enter the statewide music competition she is faced with a tough choice: should she let Doug win, or should she play her best, and possibly lose his friendship instead? (115317—$1.75)

Prices slightly higher in Canada

A LANTERN IN HER HAND

Bess Streeter Aldrich

Because the road was steep and long,
And through a dark and lonely land,
God set upon my lips a song
And put a lantern in my hand.
— JOYCE KILMER

A SIGNET VISTA BOOK

NEW AMERICAN LIBRARY

PUBLISHER'S NOTE

This novel is a work of fiction. Names, characters, places, and incidents are either the product of the author's imagination or are used fictitiously, and any resemblance to actual persons, living or dead, events, or locales is entirely coincidental.

SIGNET VISTA TRADEMARK REG. U.S. PAT. OFF. AND FOREIGN COUNTRIES
REGISTERED TRADEMARK—MARCA REGISTRADA
HECHO EN CHICAGO, U.S.A.

SIGNET, SIGNET CLASSIC, MENTOR, PLUME, MERIDIAN and NAL BOOKS
are published by New American Library,
1633 Broadway, New York, New York 10019

First Signet Vista Printing, May, 1983

4   5   6   7   8   9   10   11   12

PRINTED IN THE UNITED STATES OF AMERICA

Introduction

Cedartown sits beside a great highway which was once a buffalo trail. If you start in one direction on the highway— and travel far enough—you will come to the effete east. If you start in the opposite direction—and travel a few hundred miles farther—you will come to the distinctive west. Cedartown is neither effete nor distinctive, nor is it even particularly pleasing to the passing tourist. It is beautiful only in the eyes of those who live here and in the memories of the Nebraska-born whose dwelling in far places has given them moments of homesickness for the low rolling hills, the swell and dip of the ripening wheat, the fields of sinuously waving corn and the elusively fragrant odor of alfalfa.

There are weeks when drifting snow and sullen sleet hold the Cedartown community in their bitter grasp. There are times when hot winds come out of the southwest and parch it with their feverish breath. There are periods of monotonous drouth and periods of dreary rain; but between these on-slaughts there are days so perfect, so filled with clover odors and the rich, pungent smell of newly turned loam, so summac-laden and apple-burdened, that to the prairie-born there are no others as lovely by mountain or lake or sea.

The paved streets of Cedartown lie primly parallel over the obliterated tracks of the buffalo. The substantial buildings of Cedartown stand smartly over the dead ashes of Indian campfires. There are very few people left now in the commu-nity who have seen the transition,—who have witnessed the westward trek of the last buffalo, the flicker of the last burnt-out ember.

Old Abbie Deal was one of these.

Just outside the corporate limits of Cedartown stands the old Deal home. It was once a farm-house, but the acreage around it has been sold, and Cedartown has grown out to meet it, so that a newcomer could not know where the town ceased and the country began.

The house stands well back from the road in a big yard with a long double row of cedars connecting the formal parlor entrance and the small front gate, However, in the days when the Deals lived there, scarcely any one used the little gate, or walked up the grassy path between the cedars. All comers chose to enter by the wide carriage-gate standing hospitably open and beckoning a welcome to the lane road which runs past a row of Lombardy poplars to the sitting-room porch.

The house itself is without distinction. There were no architects in the community when the first of its rooms were built. "We'll have the living-room there and the kitchen here," one told old Asy Drumm. And old Asy, with few comments and much tobacco-chewing, placed the living-room there and the kitchen here. The result was weatherproof, sturdy and artless. When the country was new, homes, like dresses, were constructed more for wearing qualities than beauty.

Twice, onto the first wing-and-ell, old Asy, a little more glum and tobacco-stained, added a room, until the house had attained its present form. That form, now, is not unlike an aeroplane which has settled down between the cedars at the front and the cottonwood wind-break in the rear. The parlor, protruding toward the road, might contain the engine. The sitting-room to the left and a bedroom to the right seem the wings, while the dining-room, kitchen, and a summer kitchen beyond, trail out like the long tail of the thing. If one's imagination is keen he can even fancy that the fan-shaped colored-glass window in the parlor may some day begin to whirl, propeller-like, and the whole house rise up over the cedars.

The interior of the house, during Abbie Deal's lifetime, was a combination of old-fashioned things which she had accumulated through the years, and modern new ones which the grown children had given her. A dull-finished, beautifully-proportioned radio cabinet stood opposite a homemade, rudely painted what-not. A kitchen table, with a little declivity in one corner, in which old Doc Matthews had rolled pills in Civil War times, stood near a white enameled case which was the last word in refrigeration. A little crude oil-painting of a prairie sunset, which Abbie Deal had done in the 'seventies, hung across the room from a really exquisite study of the same subject, which a daughter, Mrs. Frederick Hamilton Baker, had done forty years later.

Abbie Deal kept everything that had ever come into the house. Every nail, every button, every string, was carefully hoarded. "This would make a strong bottom for one of the kitchen chairs some day," old Abbie Deal would say, when in truth the bottom of the chair was as strong as its legs. Or, "Save those stubs of candles from the Christmas tree. I can melt them and run them into one big one." The characteristic was a hang-over from the lean and frugal days when the country was new, when every tiny thing had its use. As a consequence, there was in the house the flotsam of all the years.

One of the daughters, Mrs. Harrison Scannell Rhodes, on her annual visit out from Chicago, protested once: "Mother, if the house only represented some one *period!* But it's such a jumbled combination of things. They're not antique. They're just *old.*"

"And why should it?" Old lady Deal flared up a little. "*I'm* no one period. I've lived with spinning-wheels and telephones . . . with tallow-dips and electric lights. *I'm* not antique. I'm just *old.* It represents *me,* doesn't it?"

You will infer from the retort that old Abbie Deal was a strong personality. And you will be quite right. The fact that she lived there in the old home until her eightieth year, over the protests of children and grandchildren, attested to that. At the time she was seventy, they began trying to pry her away from "The Cedars." They talked over various plans for her—that she should go to Omaha to live with Mack,—to Lincoln to live with Margaret,—that she should have rooms at John's right there in Cedartown,—that Grace should give up her teaching in Wesleyan University temporarily and stay at home. When they had quite definitely decided on the Lincoln home with Margaret, old Abbie Deal spoke "I will do nothing of the kind,'' she said with finality. ''I am going to stay right here. And kindly let me alone. Because a woman is old, has she no rights?''

After that they did not press the matter. They ''let her alone,'' but they drove in frequently, for only the Chicago daughter lived far away. Sometimes, on Sundays, the lane road contained a half dozen high-powered cars parked there through the dinner hour and the afternoon. But not one son or daughter could ever become reconciled to the idea of driving away and leaving her there.

''When I think of fire . . . .'' one of them would say.

''Or of her getting sick in the night . . .''

''Or falling . . . and no one to help her . . .''

''Or any one of a dozen things . . .''

''Yes . . . something will happen to Mother some day.''

And they were quite right. Something happened to Mother. Last July on a late afternoon, while suppers cooked and children of the north end of town played ''Run, Sheep, Run,'' in her yard, old lady Deal died. A neighbor woman found her lying across the foot of the bed, fully dressed, while the slice of meat which she had been cooking, burned to a crisp.

Of the five middle-aged children, seven grandchildren and three great-grandchildren, not one was with her. They all came hastily in response to the messages. Within two hours' time, a shining limousine, two big sedans, and a roadster all stood in the lane road. For the first time, when the cars turned into the driveway by the Lombardy poplars, no little old white-haired woman with bright brown eyes, had come hurrying out to give cheery greeting. That queer, solemn hush of death hung over the whole place. It was in the quivering droop of the cottonwoods,—in the deepening of the prairie twilight,—in the silence of the star-filled summer sky.

They all gathered in the parlor with its modern radio and its old-fashioned what-not, its elaborate new floor-lamp and its crude oil-painting. All of the children and several of the grandchildren were there. Mackenzie Deal, the Omaha banker, was there. John Deal, the Cedartown attorney and state legislator, was there. Mrs. Harrison Scannell Rhodes of Chicago, who had been visiting in Omaha, was there. Mrs. Frederick Hamilton Baker, of Lincoln, and Miss Grace Deal, of Wesleyan University, were there. They were people of poise, men and women not given to hysterical demonstration, but at the first gathering they all broke down. For a brief quarter of an hour there in the old parlor with its familiar objects, they let their grief have sway. For a little while there in the farm-home of their youth, they were but children whose mother had left them lonely when night was coming on.

When they had pulled themselves together, their greatest grief seemed to be that she died alone. In deepest remorse they blamed themselves. Standing there together in common sorrow, they said the same things over and over to each other:

"Didn't she seem as well as ever to you last week?"

"I'll never forgive myself that I played bridge all afternoon."

"Do you suppose she suffered much?"

"Or called for us?"

"Isn't it *dreadful?* Poor Mother! So many of us . . . and not one of us here just when she needed us . . . and after all she's done for us."

Only one,—Laura Deal,—a twelve-year-old granddaughter, turned away from the window where she had been looking down the long double row of cedars, and said in a clear, steady voice: "*I* don't think it was so dreadful. I think it was kind of nice. Maybe she didn't miss you." She looked slowly around the circle of her elders. "When you stop to think about it, maybe she didn't miss you *at all*. One time Grandma told me she was the very happiest when she was living over all her memories. Maybe . . ." She hesitated, a little shy at expressing the thought in her heart, "Maybe she was doing that . . . *then*."

This is the story of the old lady who died while the meat burned and the children played "Run, Sheep, Run" across her yard.

Chapter 1

Abbie Mackenzie was old Abbie Deal's maiden name. And because the first eight years of her life were interesting only to her family, we shall skip over them as lightly as Abbie herself used to skip a hoop on the high, crack-filled sidewalks in the little village of Chicago, which stood at the side of a lake where the bulrushes grew.

We find her then, at eight, in the year 1854, camping at night on the edge of some timberland just off the beaten trail between Dubuque and the new home in Blackhawk County, Iowa, to which the little family was bound.

Abbie and a big sister of fifteen, Isabelle, were curled up together under two old patchwork quilts in one of the wagons. Another sister, Mary, and a little brother, Basil, were in the other wagon with their mother. Sixteen-year-old James and eleven-year-old Dennie, the men of the party, were sleeping near the oxen, so that the warmth of the animals' bodies would keep them warm.

Because she had propped up a small section of the wagon's canvas cover, Abbie could see out into the night. The darkness was a heavy, animate thing. It hung thickly about the wagon, vaguely weird, remotely fearsome. It seemed to see and hear and feel. It looked at Abbie with its stars, heard her whispered words with its tree-leaves, felt of her warm little body with its cool breeze fingers. Something about the queer closeness of it almost frightened her. Something about the hushed silence of it made her think of her father who had died two years before. She summoned a picture of him into her mind, now,—recalling the paleness of his long, thin face, the neatness of his neckcloth, the gentle courtesy of his manner. Thinking of him so, she punched Isabelle with an active elbow. "Belle, tell me about Father and Mother."

The big girl was a little impatient. "I've told you everything I remember."

"Tell it again."

"I should think you'd get tired of hearing the same thing."

"Oh, I *never* do."

"Well . . . Father were what they call an aristocrat. He lived in Aberdeen, Scotland, and his folks, the Mackenzies, had a town house and two country houses. He belonged to the landed gentry."

"What's landed gentry?"

"It means he were a gentleman and didn't have to work."

"Will James and Dennie be gentlemen?"

"Of course not. We lost all our money."

"Tell how we lost it." Abbie settled herself with complacence. There was an element of satisfaction in having had such a foreign substance at one time, even if it was long before her birth.

"Well . . . Father were a young man and never had to do nothing but enjoy hisself, and he were out one day following the hare and hounds . . ."

"Tell about that."

"That's hunting . . . a pack of hounds after a rabbit . . . and he got away from the rest of them and were lost."

"The rabbit?"

"No, dunce-cap, . . . you know I mean Father. And he came to the peasant's cottage."

"What's peasant?"

"Awful poor people that have to work. But don't stop me every minute. I always forget where I were. Well . . . and he wanted a drink. And a sixteen-year-old peasant girl come out of the house. They were Irish, but I guess they were working for some folks in Scotland. Anyway it were Mother and she got a drink for him . . . were pulling up the rope and he took the rope and pulled it up hisself. Just think! A *gentleman* . . . and Mother were sixteen . . . just *one* year older than me. Abbie, do you suppose there'll be an aristocratic landed gentleman out in Blackhawk County where we're going?"

"No . . . I don't think so. Go on."

"Well, Mother were pretty . . . Irish girls about *always* are . . . and there were a rosebush and Father asked her for a rose and she pulled one for him. Abbie, don't you tell anybody, but I've got a little rosebush done up in a wet rag in the wagon and I'm going to plant it out in Blackhawk County."

"Ho! Ho! It takes years and years for a rosebush to grow big enough to have flowers to pull off for a-*ris* . . . for a-*rist* . . . for gentlemen. Go on."

"Anyway, Father took his rose and went away and the next day he came back."

"Were he lost again?"

"No, dunce-cap! He came back to see Mother a-purpose. And he come other days, even after that, and they would walk over the heather hills together."

"What's feather hills?"

"Not feather! *Heather!* . . . a little kind of weedy grass. And all the neighbors shook their heads and said they'd seen *that* thing happen before from the gentry . . . and . . ." Isabelle whispered solemnly, *"no good ever come of it."*

"What did they say that for?"

"I can't tell you now. You wouldn't understand. When you're as old as me, you will. But just the same, Father *did* marry her and took her to Aberdeen to the big Mackenzie house. Mother wore her best dress and her best head-shawl, but even then, all fixed up that nice way, the Mackenzies didn't like her. Father's mother were Isabelle Anders-Mackenzie and she were awful proud and I hate her for not liking Mother. I hate her so bad that I'm sorry I'm named for her. If Mother would let me, I'd change it to Rosamond. I read about a Rosamond and she . . ."

"Go on about her . . . not *you.*"

"Well . . . she were ashamed of Mother, but she had to take her in because she were Father's wife, and she dressed her up grand and tried to make her different. But when Mother would go back to see her folks, she'd put on her peasant dress and wear her shawl on her head and slip away. And Sundays when the Mackenzies would go to the kirk . . ."

"What's kirk?"

"Church. Where were I? Oh . . . the aristocrats set down below and the peasants all set up in the loft . . ."

"Like a hay loft?"

"No. Stop interrupting, or I won't tell you one thing more. And Mother wouldn't leave her folks, the O'Conners, so Father went and set with them and the Mackenzies were just *sick* with shame. Then Grandfather Mackenzie died, and a long time afterward . . . after Janet and James and Mary and Dennie and I were all born, Grandmother Isabelle Anders-Mackenzie . . ."

"I just *admire* to hear that name . . ."

"There you go again. Now I'm through telling it."

"Please . . . I won't stop you again."

"Well. . . . Grandmother died, too. Then Father come to America on a sailing vessel, just for a pleasure trip, and he were gone so long and folks thought he weren't coming back at all . . . and Mother cried something terrible . . . and Father had signed a note for a man . . ."

"What's signed a . . . ? Oh, . . . go on."

"And it made him lose all his money. Men come and put cards up on the house and stables while he were gone and the signs said there were going to be a roup there."

"What's . . . ? Go on."

"A roup's an auction sale. There were fifteen saddle-horses in the stables, but after the roup cards went up Mother were not allowed to touch one on account of the law, and so her and James and Janet walked twenty-seven miles to have her father and mother come and bid in some of her things. She's got 'em yet in that little wooden chest with calf-skin all over it. It's in the other wagon and I know just what's in it because I saw 'em. There's a white silk shawl with big solid roses in the corners . . . all *four* corners . . . and a jeweled fan . . . and a breastpin with lavender sets and a string of pearls. There are just as many things as there are girls in our family and Mother says each girl are to have one for a keepsake. I know which one I want . . . the silk shawl. I tried it on once when Mother were gone and I looked a lot like the painting of Isabelle Anders-Mackenzie that hung up on the landing of the stairway in the great hall. Course, you understand, Abbie, I never said I hated her *looks* . . ."

"Which one is Mother going to give me?"

"I don't know. She aren't going to give 'em to us until our wedding days. Of course, Janet didn't get hers on *her* wed-

ding day because she got married out here in Blackhawk
County before we come, but Mother'll give it to her to-
morrow when we get there.''

"Go on . . . you're forgetting the end of the story.''

"Oh, well, you know it anyway. When Father got back to
Liverpool he heard all about the money and the property
being lost, and the things being sold, and he never even went
to Aberdeen but sent for Mother and all five of us children to
come to Liverpool and we all crossed the ocean. I were seven
and I can remember just as well . . . and when we got to
New York, you were born.''

Abbie breathed a sigh of relief. It was a welcome respite
after a narrow escape. With every telling of the story, almost
it seemed for a time that she was not to be born.

"Now tell about the painting of Isabelle Anders-Mackenzie
that hung on the landing of the stairway in the great hall.''
Abbie rolled the magic words from her lips in delicious
anticipation. This was the part she liked the best of all.

"Well . . . it were beauteous. It were in a great heavy
gold frame . . . and as big as life. I can remember it just as
well. In the picture she were young, you know . . .''

"And beautiful . . .'' prompted Abbie.

"And beautiful. She had reddish-brown hair like yours . . .
and she were standing by a kind-of . . . a table-thing, and
she had on a velvet dress that swept down and around her . . .
and she had a hat in her hand with a plume . . .''

"A flowing white plume . . .'' corrected Abbie.

"A flowing white plume,'' repeated the more matter-of-
fact Isabelle. "And she had pretty hands and long slender
fingers that tapered at the ends.''

Abbie held her hands up to the opening of the canvas on
the wagon and peered at them in the moonlight. The fingers
were long and slender and they tapered at the ends. She
sighed with satisfaction, and slipped them under the old
patched quilt.

"And nobody knows what become of the picture?'' It was
half statement, half question, as though from the vast fund of
information which Isabelle possessed, she might, some day,
suddenly remember what had become of the picture.

"No. It were sold at the roup. I don't know who got it.''

Abbie sighed again, but not with satisfaction. Of all the

beautiful things that were sold, she felt that she could have missed seeing any of them with better grace than the portrait. In her immature way, she resented the sale more than any other thing,—the passing of the lovely lady into other hands. Jewels, money, furniture,—they seemed lifeless, inanimate things beside the picture of the woman who was flesh of her flesh. It ought to have been saved. It was their own grandmother who stood there forever inside the heavy gold frame, in the dark velvet dress that swept around her,—and with the flowing white plume—and the long slender fingers that tapered at the ends.

"Well, I wish we had it here with us, Belle. We could have it all wrapped up in quilts in the wagon . . . and then some day out in Blackhawk County when we get rich, we could build us a grand house with a wide curving stairway and hang the picture on the landing . . . and everybody that come . . ."

"Abbie! Belle!" A voice came suddenly from the other wagon. "Sure 'n' you're the talkers. Settle yoursel's now. We want to get a good early start by sunup."

Abbie started. From a dreamy journey into the fields of romance she had been drawn back to the prosaic world of reality by her mother's voice. She could not quite reconcile good fat Mother with the romantic figure of the pretty girl at the well, picking a rose for an aristocratic gentleman. But then, Mother was almost an old woman, now,—thirty-seven.

Abbie turned to the opening in the canvas cover and looked out again at the night. Yellow-white, the moon rose higher over the dark clumps of trees. A thousand stars, looking down, paled at its rising. An owl gave its mournful call. The smell of burning maple boughs came from the fire. A wolf howled in the distance so that James got up and took out the other gun from the wagon. There was a constant tick-tacking in the timber,—all the little night creatures at their work. It was queer how it all hurt you,—how the odor of the night, the silver sheen of the moon, the moist feeling of the dew, the whispering of the night breeze, how, somewhere down in your throat it hurt you. It was sad, too, that this evening would never come again. The night winds were blowing it away. You could not stop the winds and you could not stop Time. It went on and on,—and on. To-morrow night would come and the moon would look down on this same spot,—the trees and the grass, the wagon-tracks and the dead campfire. But she would not be here. Her heart swelled with an emotion which she could not name. Tears came to her eyes. The telling of the story always brought that same feeling.

"Isabelle Anders-Mackenzie," she said it over until it took upon itself the cadence of a melody, the rhythm of a poem. "I shall be like her," she thought. "I have hair like her now and hands like her. I shall be lovely. And I shall do wonderful things . . . sing before big audiences and paint pictures inside of gold frames and write things in a book." She wondered how you got things put in a book. There were some books in one of the wooden chests over in the other wagon. A man with a long name that began *S-h-a-k-e-s* . . . had made some of them. They had been Father's. Mother didn't read them. She didn't read anything but her Bible. Even that was hard for her, so that she read the same verses over and over. Yes, she would be like Father and Isabelle Anders-Mackenzie, not like Mother's family with their cottage on the side of the hill and their dark shawls over their heads. She would be rich and lovely . . . with a velvet dress and a long sweeping plume . . . under the moon . . . and the night wind, . . . that felt of your body with its long . . . slender fingers . . . that tapered at the ends . . .

Abbie Mackenzie slept,—little Abbie Mackenzie, with the mixture of the two strains of blood,—with the stout body of the O'Conners and the slender hands of the Mackenzies, —with the O'Conner sturdiness and the Mackenzie refinement. And she is to need them both,—the physical attributes of the peasant and the mental ones of the aristocrat,—the warm heart of the Irish and the steadfastness of the Scotch. Yes, Abbie Mackenzie is to need them both in the eighty years she is to live,—courage and love,—a song upon her lips and a lantern in her hand.

Chapter 2

The sun, shining through the propped-up canvas of the wagon, wakened Abbie. Wide-eyed, she looked out through the aperture upon the same setting of the night before. But now it was changed. The child lived a life in each of two distinct worlds and it is not possible to say which one she most enjoyed. One of them was made of moonbeams and star-dust, of night winds and cloud fancies, of aristocratic gentlemen and lovely ladies. The other was the equally pleasant one of boiled potatoes and salt pork, of games with Basil and Mary, of riding a-top old Buck or picking wild flowers at the edge of the timber.

Just now the prosaic world of everyday seemed the more attractive of the two. James had replenished the night fire and Mother was cooking breakfast, with the odor of frying pork and corn-cakes strong on the air. The team of horses and the oxen were eating close by, the horses guzzling their grain noisily, the oxen chewing slowly and stolidly.

Maggie O'Conner Mackenzie was a heavy, dumpy woman, her body the shape of a pudding-bag tied in the middle. One shawl was wrapped around the shapeless figure and a smaller one, over her head, was knotted under her fat chin. Strands of heavy black hair showed around the edges of the head-shawl, and the face enclosed in its folds was round and smooth, fat and placid. Only her dark Irish eyes, the color of the blue-black waters at Kilkee, and a dimple in the middle of her rolling chin, gave a touch of reality to the old romance of the peasant girl.

This was the last day of the journey which had been of three weeks' duration. (Six decades later James Mackenzie was to make the journey back with a grandson in one day.)

Breakfast over, the little cavalcade set out with much noisy chatter,—reminders not to forget this or that.

"Did ye put out the last o' the fire, Dennie?"

"Fasten that buckle on Whitey's bridle, Belle."

The mother drove the horse team,—James, the oxen. Walking along beside the latter, James' boyish "Gee" or "Haw" or "Whoa How" rang out with valiant attempts to make the notes stentorian. Buck was a red and white animal, Boy a brindle. As they walked, they swung their huge heads rhythmically from side to side, the brass buttons a-top their horns shining in the morning sun. Almost at the first rod's length of the journey little Basil had to stop the procession to change from one wagon to the other. Belle rode on the seat with her mother, but, because it was early and cool, Abbie, Mary and Dennie walked behind, darting off the trail to gather Mayflowers or wild Bouncing-Bets. Sometimes they jumped over the young rosin-weeds and wild blue phlox and occasionally they caught on the back of the wagon, clutching onto the household goods and swinging their feet off the ground for a few moments.

About nine, they forded a stream. The oxen ahead crossed slowly, lumberingly, with many stops in that foolish, stolid way they had. When they were across, Mother Mackenzie drove her team into the creek bed. As the horses were going up the bank, one of them stumbled, crowding against its mate. There was a creaking, and backing, a shouting and a tipping. One sack of flour began falling slowly, and then another and another. Eight sacks of flour, pushing against each other, slipped slowly into the water like fat, clumsy, old men reluctant to wet their feet.

Maggie Mackenzie was out and managing her horses by way of their bridles, while James, running back from his own wagon, assisted in bringing order out of the catastrophe. Then some one called excitedly, "Look out for the bedding," and two great pillows started floating down stream with majestic motion, as though the geese from which their contents had been plucked, were suddenly coming to life.

"Och!" And "Och!" The mother wrung her hands in distress. Eight sacks of flour and two pillows were a fortune.

Abbie and Dennie and little Basil, their laughter high with excitement, all ran along the side of the creek bed after the pillows. In the meantime, James and Belle were wading into the stream and pulling out the sacks. To the mother the disaster seemed more than she could bear. "Och! If I ever get there," said Maggie O'Conner Mackenzie, "sure 'n' I'll never l'ave the spot." Sure, and she never did. Many years later she died a quarter of a mile from the place where she first stepped out of the wagon.

When the last sack was retrieved, the entire family, with much dire foreboding, crowded around James, who was opening a sack to see how the contents fared. It was as though the whole of life's future hung on the outcome. To their extreme relief the wet flour had formed but a thin paste, which, with a few moments drying in the sun, now high and hot, would form a crust and keep the precious contents unharmed.

In spite of the delay the family reached the settlement on the Cedar River by the middle of the afternoon and stopped near the log cabin of Tom Graves, the man whom the older sister Janet had come out to marry. Janet, herself, hearing the creaking of the wagons, came hurrying down the grassy trail to meet them, a three-weeks-old baby in her arms. The baby was something by way of surprise to the entire group of relatives, his arrival having taken place after the family had started westward.

Maggie O'Conner Mackenzie, with much clucking and chirping and adjustment of clothing, welcomed her first grandchild.

"Sure 'n' he's the big one. How did ye get along? Is he good? Did ye have a doctor or a neighbor woman?"

Janet answered them all even while her mother was still talking. Oh, yes, there was a doctor,—Doc Matthews over at town. Cedar Falls was quite a place. It had a sawmill and a hotel and a store, a dozen log cabins, and a few frame ones. The school-house had the only tower bell in the state. For pay Tom was to haul in a load of wood for the doctor's office stove,—he had a two-roomed house, part log and part frame.

The oxen behind them slathered and snorted. There was the smell in the air of newly-cut chips. The woods back of the cabin looked thick and impenetrable beyond the short arrows of the sun. And then Tom Graves, himself, came out of the timber, his ax, the insignia of the fight, on his shoulder.

"Here is my mother, Tom, and this is Belle and that one is Mary. And that boy is James and this one Dennie and here's little Basil. And over there with the reddish-brown hair is Abbie,—we almost forgot her."

So much was to be said, and all at once. "We've got a house all ready for you, Mother. It was Grandpa Deal's sheep shed. The Deals have been here for three years, but they've moved down farther on the prairie now in a fine big log house, and you can have this until you get your own cabin done. We've cleaned it all out for you and hung a thick quilt over the opening, and if it storms you can come in with us."

And so Maggie O'Conner Mackenzie, who had lived in the great Aberdeen town house and on the two Scotch country estates, was to make her bed now in a sheep shed.

Every one turned in to help with the settling. From the wagons they took out the walnut bedsteads and the bedding and the highboy. They brought in the heavy, cumbersome guns and the powder-horn and the splint-bottom chairs. Maggie Mackenzie brought in her flat-iron into which one put glowing hickory embers through an iron door, and she hung up the iron tallow-lamp with a homespun wick hanging over the side like a tongue hanging grotesquely from the side of a mouth. If she could have foreseen that two granddaughters, Mrs. Harrison Scannell Rhodes and Mrs. Frederick Hamilton Baker, were going to stage a polite but intensive campaign over which one could have the old tallow-lamp in her sun parlor, a half century later, she would have shaken her fat sides with laughter.

Everything was out of the wagon now,—everything but one. Abbie, standing in the grassy trail in front of the old sheep shed, was watching for it. On tiptoe there in her ankle-length starched dress, her red-brown hair wound around her head and tucked into a snood, she was the picture of watchful waiting. She might have been carved in marble as "Expectancy."

"Let me! Let me!" she called, when her mother was bringing out the calf-skin-covered box from under the wagon seat.

"If ye'll carry it carefu'."

No need to caution Abbie to be careful. In a warm feeling of pleasure over the temporary possession, she clasped her arms around its hairy sides and the "M.OC." initials formed by nail-heads.

Inside the box lay all the accouterments of another life. In its skin-covered depths was all the equipment of an entirely different world. They were symbols of things in life to come. They represented the future in which she would some day live. She got down on her knees on the dirt floor, with its earthy odor, and pushed the little chest into the far, dark corner under her mother's bed. Lovingly and lingeringly she relinquished her hold upon it. For a few moments she saw herself in that future, her red-brown hair in curls, over her shoulders a white silk shawl with roses in the corners, its folds held together with a lavender breastpin. There was a string of pearls around her neck, and she was waving a jeweled fan with long, white fingers that tapered at the ends. There was soft music playing. She came out on a high stage ready to sing. Lovely ladies and courtly men were clapping their hands. Some of them stood up. She smiled at them and waved her jeweled fan. . . .

"Abbie . . . Abbie . . . where are you?" Quite suddenly, the gorgeous trappings fell away. She was back in the everyday world, hearing loud voices calling her.

"Abbie! . . ." The voices were raised high in fright. She scrambled out backward from under the bed.

"Abbie . . . Abbie . . ." Dennis and Mary were running toward her, their faces white with fear. "The Indians are coming. A man here on horseback says the Indians are coming down the river."

Abbie scrambled back under the bed and brought out the hairy chest in her arms. Not to any wild and heathenish Indian was Abbie Mackenzie intending to relinquish the only tangible tie that bound her to the lovely lady.

Chapter 3

In the midst of the hurry and confusion and fright, Abbie gathered that they were all to get back into the wagons and "go down to Grandpa Deal's," wherever that was.

Everything that could be handled easily was thrown into the wagons. Janet rolled a fresh batch of bread and raised doughnuts into a homespun tablecloth. Tom tied old Whitey to the back of his wagon and put her new calf in the end of the box so she could see her offspring and not bellow for it. Abbie clutched the hairy chest in protecting arms. The cavalcade started lumberingly down the river road. Through the dark timber they drove, over spongy moist leaves, past thickets of sumac and hazelbrush, their hearts pounding in alarm, their bodies tense with fear, every tree the potential hiding place of an Indian.

Out of the cool river road and onto the hot, flat prairie they came as suddenly as one opens a door upon a bright, heated room. For two miles they drove over the faintly marked prairie trail, coming then to another wooded section and to the largest house in the community,—a big log structure which looked palatial to Abbie's eyes after Tom Graves' one-roomed cabin and the sheep shed.

Other horse and ox teams were hitched to the straw-roofed log stable. Other families were scurrying into the house with smoked hams and batches of bread and valued possessions in their arms. Not far from the back door of the big log house, Abbie, still grasping the hairy chest, stopped to watch a boy of twelve or thirteen caressing the sleek, quivering head of a young deer, tied to a tree by a strap around its neck.

A small, severe-looking woman in a black calico dress, with a black netting cap tied under her sharply pointed chin, was scolding nervously. "No, Willie, you can't. I won't have it. It's bad enough to have the whole kit 'n' bilin' in the country comin' 'n' trackin' up,—all the rag-shag 'n' bob-tails bringin' their stuff."

"But, Mother," the boy plead, "I'll keep her by herself. I'll get her up the loft stairs."

"No,—you sha'n't, Willie Deal."

And then a big, powerful man came out,—a man with only one arm, his left sleeve pinned to the side of his coat. He had a shock of wiry black hair, and an equally wiry beard which gave him an unkempt look. But his eyes were blue and twinkling and kind,—they held the calmness of blue ice, but not its coldness.

He put his one hand on the boy's dark head, now, and said quietly, "You'd best let her go, son. She'll take care of herself,—and it's only fair to give her her freedom."

Without a word the boy cut the strap at the fawn's throat, and even while he was unloosing the piece around her neck, she darted from him lightly, gracefully, into the hazel-brush.

Inside the big log house where all seemed confusion, Abbie, after a time, sought out the dark-haired boy.

"Do you think you'll ever get her back?" she asked shyly.

"Get what?"

"Your little deer."

"Naw, . . . never." The boy turned his head away.

Abbie's heart seemed bursting with sorrow for him. There was that word again,—*never*. It was the saddest word! It made her throat hurt. Willie Deal would never, never have his little deer again.

With his head still averted, the boy said tensely, "I found her . . . 'n' raised her . . . myself."

Abbie put her hand out gently and touched the boy's arm.

"I'm sorry." Her voice held deep sympathy.

"Aw . . ." He threw up his fine dark head. "I didn't care."

But Abbie knew it was not so. Abbie knew that he cared.

It seems precarious business to take time to describe Grandpa and Grandma Deal, when a band of disgruntled Indians is reported on its way down the Shell Rock, but, pending its arrival, one ought to know a little of Gideon Deal and his wife. They were not yet out of their forties. Indeed, their youngest daughter, Regina, was only nine, but through older offspring scattered about the community, several grandchildren had been presented to them, and so, to differentiate them from other and younger Deals, the titles "Grandpa" and "Grandma" had been bestowed early upon them.

To the other settlers Grandpa Deal seemed as substantial as the native hickory timber in whose clearing he had built his house. He was both freighter and farmer. Two of the grown sons worked his place, while he himself drove the six-ox-team over the long trail to Dubuque and back, with freight for the whole community. For this,—and for his reputation as a wit,—he was known far and wide. To fully appreciate his wit, one must have taken Grandma Deal into account, for she was the background against which his droll sayings stood forth. The little wiry woman, fretful, energetic and humorless, was intolerant of wasting time in fun-making. Grandpa Deal, kind, easy-going and jolly, was always picking up every little saying of his partner's to bandy it about with sly drollness. There was never any loud laughter on his part, just a twinkle in the sharp blue eyes appreciative of his outlook on life. Grandma Deal spent her time hustling about, darting in and out, scolding at Grandpa, finding fault with the children, the well-sweep, the weather, everything that came under her eagle eye or into her busy brain.

Just now, however, Grandma was not scolding. Grandpa was not joking. The news of impending disaster had brought them to a common ground of fear. Most of the other families of the community had gathered now in the larger and stronger Deal home in response to the rumor of the Indian uprising. Already the men were stationing guns near windows and barring and barricading doors. Several women were running bullets in the little salamander stove, a queer affair whose short legs in front and long legs in the back, gave it the appearance of an inverted giraffe. One woman was hysterical; another a little out of her mind from fear, kept wanting to go back out doors where there was air.

All night they waited for whatever Fate had in store for

them. In the morning, a man rode up on horseback, a young
boy, about Willie Deal's age, behind him in the saddle. It
was Doc Matthews, who had come to bring word that the
hostile band of Indians had gone north.

Immediately there was the confusion of getting ready to
leave. Grandpa Deal told those who lived farthest away to
stay and make a visit for the day. Abbie could hear Grandma
Deal sputtering about her husband's freehanded hospitality.

The boy who came with Doc Matthews was his son Ed. He
had been east all year to a boys' boarding school. He was
dressed in a nice suit and a flat white collar and a little round
hat.

He stood and looked at Willie Deal in his homespun suit.
Willie Deal stood and looked at Eddie Matthews from the
Philadelphia boarding-school. Their contempt seemed mutual.

The Indian scare, then, had gone into nothing. The wagons
went lumbering back across the prairie and through the damp,
dark river road where the hazel-brush and sumac knotted
together under the native oaks and hickories.

All summer long, the Mackenzies lived in the sheep shed,
while their own log house was being built. James and Tom
Graves were building it, and Dennie was helping, battening
the inside with long split saplings and filling the chinks with
mud.

All summer long, Abbie went happily in and out of the
sheep shed with the patchwork quilt in front for the door.
There were so many lovely things to do that one did not know
how to find time for them all. There were flowers in the
deep, dark recesses of the Big Woods,—wild honeysuckles
and Bouncing-Bets and tall ferns that one could pretend were
long, sweeping, white plumes.

Sometimes Abbie would take one of the longest of the
ferns and, with a slender twig, pin it on a wild grapevine leaf
or a plantain for a hat. Then she would drape one of her
mother's dark shawls around her sturdy little body, and standing on a grassy hillock in the clearing, pretend she was
Isabelle Anders-Mackenzie, the lovely lady.

And then she had a whole set of dishes hidden in the
hollow of an oak at the edge of the timberland. James had
made them for her from acorns, removing the nut and whit-
tling little handles for the cups. And she had a child for which

she must care constantly. It was an elongated-shaped stone with a small round formation on the end for its head. She put little Basil's outgrown dress on it and a knitted bonnet. She liked the feeling of the stone against her breast. It seemed heavy and like a real baby. Sometimes in carrying it about, her heart would swell in potential mother love for it. But sometimes there was no need to pretend about a baby, for there was Janet's real, live one to hold and rock. Janet had a low, wooden trundle-bed for him that pushed under the big bed. It was rough on the outside and the ends were made from the sawed round disks of a tree.

One afternoon, Willie Deal came up to the Big Woods with his shaggy-haired father to see Tom Graves. Willie Deal had remembered Abbie and brought her a plant in a clay jar he had made. The plant was a green, lacy, fernlike thing, and there were three little, round, scarlet balls on it.

"Whatever are they?" Abbie wanted to know.

"They're love apples," Willie told her. "But don't you ever dare put one up to your mouth. They're tremendous poisonous."

Abbie promised that she never, never would so much as touch the poison. For how could Willie Deal and Abbie Mackenzie in the 'fifties know anything about vitamin-filled tomatoes?

And then, in the fall, Janet's baby was not quite well. No one seemed to know what the matter could be. Maggie O'Conner Mackenzie doctored him with castor oil and peppermint. Grandma Deal sent word by Tom Graves to give him sassafras tea and tie a little bag of asafetida around his neck. When he seemed no better, Janet, pale and worried, said maybe they ought to send for Dr. Matthews. Abbie was frightened beyond measure when she heard that, for she well knew that a doctor was the last resort for saving one who was sick. Tom went out immediately to saddle a horse and go for the doctor. Janet told Abbie to hold the baby while she went out to the lean-to kitchen for warm water. Mother Mackenzie had gone over to her own home for flannel cloths.

And then, Abbie was calling them and crying all in the same breath, "Janet, . . . Mother, . . . come quick . . . oh, come . . ."

Janet was in the room like a flash, a wild bittern at the call of its young. Abbie could scarcely talk for crying: "I was just holding him as steady. He acted queer, . . . and threw up his arms. He got kind of bluish. What ought I to 've done?"

Doctor Matthews came with Tom. He said, yes, the baby was dead. Janet was wild with grief. Sitting on the edge of the bed, she rocked the little cold form back and forth in her arms and would not let them take him from her. Rachel, who lives again in every grieving mother, was crying for her child and would not be comforted.

Over in their own cabin, Abbie sobbed aloud on the bed. Suddenly she sat up, "I hate God," she said. Maggie Mackenzie hushed her quickly and told her it was tremendous wicked to say that.

"But he made death. I hate death. I *hate* it."

"The poor colleen," her mother said to Belle. "She's smart like the Mackenzies, . . . but faith . . . an' she has the Irish heart."

Chapter 4

By the time Abbie was eleven, she was doing more work. Life was not all play now. One of her tasks was to thread the wicks into candle molds, for her slim fingers were more agile than her mother's short, thick ones. She had to poke the long wick-string through all of the six molds, and carefully loop the tops over a stick to keep them from slipping. Her mother would then pour the hot tallow into the molds and set it away to harden. Abbie was always anxious to see the finished product slip out. She would watch her mother plunge the molds into hot water to loosen the hard grease, and then, "Let me, . . . let me," she would call, and sometimes Maggie Mackenzie would let her carefully work the shining cream-colored candles out of their containers.

There were a dozen other tasks for her to perform,—drive the cows to drink, gather eggs from the chickens' stolen nests among the sheds and stacks, and the daily one of going to school.

But even work could take upon itself a mask of fun. One could pretend, when threading the wicks into candle molds, that one was stringing pearls accidentally broken at the ball, —that the long walk through the hazel-brush to the school-house was between rows of admiring spectators who, instead of a mere rustling in the wind, were whispering, "There she goes,—there goes Abbie Mackenzie, the singer."

For Abbie was always singing from the elevation of her grassy knoll in the clearing. It made her happy to walk up the little incline, turn and bow to an unseen audience, throw up her head and let forth her emotions in song. Her heart would swell in a feeling of oneness with Nature and the Creator of it, and there would come to her a great longing for things she did not quite know or understand.

The log school-house sat in a clearing of timber just out of the river's high-water line. The hazel-brush and sumac tangled together under its windows and there were butternut and black walnut trees behind it. The desks were rough shelves against the walls on three sides of the room, and in front of them were three long benches of equal height, so that a strapping six-foot boy or a tiny six-year-old girl could, with economy, use the same seats.

While studying, the children sat with their backs toward the teacher, but when it was recitation time they had to put their legs up over the benches and turn to face him. Abbie always crawled over slowly, holding modestly on to her dress and three petticoats. But Regina Deal would flip over daringly in a whirlwind of skirts and pantalets. The cloaks and bonnets were hung on nails on the one side of the room which contained no desk-shelf. The water-pail and dipper were on a bench by the door, which made a sloppily wet corner, excepting on those winter days when the dipper froze in the pail. The room was heated by a stove in the center, and one unhappily roasted or froze in proportion to his proximity to the stove.

Sometimes the contents of the dinner buckets were also frozen and one had to thaw them out before eating. On fall days, a few of the more adventuresome of the squirrels and chipmunks whisked in and out of the window-opening in the logs, purloining the crumbs for waiting families.

In the spring, when the maple sap ran, every one crossed the river in flat-bottomed boats and helped in the little sugar camp. Louise and Regina Deal showed Abbie and Mary Mackenzie how to make maple eggs. They took tiny pieces of shell off the small ends of eggs, carefully removed the raw contents, ran the maple sap into the hollow molds, and after it had hardened, picked off the shells,—and behold, there was a platter of candy ready for the winter parties.

The fall in which Abbie was eleven, the entire crowd of young people on the north side of the river was invited to the Mackenzies'. Already there was a social distinction being drawn between the north, or country side, and the south, or town side, of the river. The party was for Belle, who was soon to be married. Belle had planted her rosebush by the log cabin, but the chickens had pecked at it, and the pigs had rooted under it, and no aristocratic gentleman had come by,—only a plain farmer boy who had hired out to Tom Graves.

The young folks came in lumber wagons along the river road under the full moon. The few pieces of furniture were set out of doors to make room for the party, and there were tallow candles lighted and placed high up on shelves. In an iron kettle there was taffy cooking to be pulled later, and platters of pop-corn balls and dishes of maple drops, into which hickory nuts, butternuts, hazelnuts or walnuts had been stirred.

The crowd played dancing games to their own singing and hand-clapping:

> *"I won't have none of your weevily wheat,*
> *I won't have none of your barley,*
> *I won't have none but the best of wheat,*
> *To make a cake for Charley."*

When the fun was at its height, a horse and rider drew up at the door, and some one called out, "Hey there, . . . you." The young folks, upon going out to see who it was, found Ed Matthews there with a deer carcass, which he had been pulling behind him with a rope. Ed, who was sixteen now, was dressed in "city" hunter togs, a leather looking coat and pants and a cap with a long bill in front. His boots were almost hip-high and fitted snugly to his legs.

When they were crowding around to look at the deer, Abbie first saw the strap drawn taut on its neck. Immediately, she was looking up into the face of Will Deal,—a darkened, flashing face. The young folks all discussed the queer fact of the strap being on the deer's neck. But Will Deal said nothing. And Abbie, sensing that Will did not want to tell about it, said nothing.

Regina and Louise and Mary Mackenzie all invited Ed Matthews in to the party. He accepted, and immediately became the center of the games and dancing. But for some reason the party was not so pleasant. For some reason,

Ed Matthews, in his city hunter togs, had spoiled the party.

When the horses were hitched to the wagons and the young folks were all leaving, Abbie touched Will Deal on the arm.

"It was your little deer, wasn't it?"

"I 'spose so."

Something intuitive made Abbie say, "I'm sorry *he* was the one who shot it."

Will's face flashed darkly, "Aw, shucks! . . . I don't care."

But Abbie knew that it was not so. Abbie knew that Will Deal cared.

Two years later, Grandpa Deal was sent by the county to the General Assembly. Word trickled back to the settlement that he was well liked by his constituents, and that he was called "Old Blackhawk" and "the wag of the House."

Will Deal, eighteen now, had done the freighting from Dubuque all fall during his father's absence, but when spring came, an older brother assumed the business while Will took over the farm work. Once when Abbie came by, he stopped the team and sat on the plow-handle and called out to her to come and hear a letter from his father. It began, "Dear Friend," and ended, "This from your affectionate father." It said that he hoped Will could comfortably till the fields, that there was some talk of dividing two of the counties, that board was tremendous high,—three dollars a week,—that his sister, Harriett, had left on the stage, that the Pikes Peakers were beginning to run, and that he looked for quite a rush this spring for the gold regions. Abbie felt quite proud of the fact that a young man like Will Deal would read his letters to a thirteen-year-old girl.

It was only a few weeks later, that an old Springfield friend of Grandpa Deal's was nominated for the presidency of the United States. When Grandpa Deal came home, he said that if you'd known Abe Lincoln as well as he had, you'd never in the world think that he'd have been picked for the nomination, but just the same there was hoss sense inside his long hide.

All summer long one heard political talk here and there, —about slavery and secessionists and the outcome of the fall election. Men would stop in wagons on the river road and talk so long that their teams would amble a short way into the woods, cropping at the juicy ferns. Grandma Deal scolded all summer about it. Abbie heard her say that she kept dinner hot so many times for Grandpa, who was talking to groups around the store over in town or on the schoolhouse steps, that she had a notion to quit cooking for him altogether.

All winter the talk grew thicker and more heated. While Abbie did not fully understand it all, she knew in February, when the Southern Confederacy had been established, that things were at some sort of a crisis. But from hearing Grandpa Deal talk, she felt confident that when Abe Lincoln would take his seat in March, everything was going to be all right. And Grandpa Deal was to have plenty of time to talk, for his old job of freighting from Dubuque was to be taken from him. Slowly, but surely, the construction of the Dubuque and Sioux City road was being carried westward.

Abraham Lincoln took his seat in March, but everything was not going to be all right. Twenty-seven days later the first iron horse from Dubuque shrieked its triumphant way across the Deal farm, and on into Cedar Falls, and the old-time freighter's task was finished. The train's arrival was timely for the community, inasmuch as events were to follow which would suspend construction and cause Cedar Falls to remain the western terminus of the road for four years.

Abbie had now passed her fourteenth birthday. On an April afternoon, with the river high and clods of snow still at the roots of trees, she went into the timber to look for anemones and Dutchmen's breeches, for dog-toothed violets and the first signs of Mayflower buds. Coming out on her own particular grassy knoll in the clearing, she went up to the hillock, in one of those moments of desire to let out her feelings in song. To the squirrels she may have seemed an ordinary girl clothed in a green-checked gingham dress, with reddish-brown curls twisted up into a snood but the squirrels were not seeing correctly. For Abbie knew that she had a dark velvet dress that swept around her feet, a string of pearls on her neck, and in her hand a hat with a sweeping plume. She was holding it carelessly at her side with her long, slender fingers that tapered at the ends.

At the top of the knoll she turned. A sea of white faces looked up at her. To the casual observer it might have seemed a mass of wild plum-blossoms. Even before she sang, the audience applauded vociferously and a few people stood up. An onlooker, who was not magic-eyed, might have thought the wind merely blew the blossoms. Abbie bowed, smiled,— waited for her accompaniment to begin. She fingered her pearls, and smiled at the girl at the reed-organ. All at once she realized that the girl at the organ was a talented orphan whom she had been befriending. It made her feel happy, light-hearted. She threw back her head and began singing:

> *"Oh! the Lady of the Lea,*
> *Fair and young and gay was she,*
> *Beautiful exceedingly,*
> *The Lady of the Lea."*

The song embodied for her all the enchantment of the Arabian Nights. It opened a door to a magic castle. It smelled of perfume and spices. It stood for wonderful things in life to come.

> *"Many a wooer sought her hand,*
> *For she had gold and she had land,"*

Her voice rose melodiously high and sweet and true.

> *"Everything at her command,*
> *The Lady of the Lea."*

Her heart seemed bursting with love of the trees, the sky, the melody.

> *"Oh, the Lady of the Lea,*
> *Fair and young and gay was she,"*

There seemed a gleam ahead of her,—a light that beckoned, —a little will-o'-the-wisp out there beyond the settlement in the Big Woods. It was something no one knew about,—Mother nor Mary nor Belle. Only for her it shone,—for her, and other lovely ladies.

"Fanciful exceedingly,
The Lady of the Lea."

When the song had died away and Abbie was bowing to the invisible audience, she heard it, "Abbie, . . . oh, Abbie . . . hoo-hoo!" Mary's voice was calling and crying in the distance. She slipped out of the clearing, climbed the stake-and-rider fence, and saw Mary coming,—calling and crying and coming toward her. "Abbie, they've just got word out from Dubuque that Fort Sumter was fired on."

Abbie clutched her. "What, . . . what does *that* mean, Mary?"

"It means, . . ." Mary's voice whispered it hoarsely, "Grandpa Deal says it means *war*."

Chapter 5

Yes, it meant war, with James leaving at the first call, and Belle's young husband enlisting without her knowing his intentions. Abbie thought she could not stand it to see them go. It seemed that life was doing something to her which she could not countenance. She had a queer sensation of wind blowing past her,—of wind that she could not stop. She stood in front of the Seth Thomas clock on the shelf in her mother's cabin and watched the hands moving above the little brown church painted on the glass of the door. *Oh, stop Time for a few minutes until we can do something about the war.*

But the winds blew past, and the clock hands went around, and James and Belle's husband and several of the neighbor boys had gone to war.

And by 1862, when Lincoln's call for additional volunteers came, Dennie, who was nineteen now, went into the Cedar Falls Reserves, a group of one hundred stalwart fellows. And Abbie again went all through the torn emotions of parting with Dennie and hating war.

And then she learned that there was one thing worse than going to war. And that was not going to war. Will Deal told her so. To be twenty-one and able-bodied, and see the Reserves entrain and not go! He was ashamed, and miserable. But his father, with his one arm, and in the Assembly as he was,—and no one to farm,—and Regina and Louise and his mother all depending on him,—he could not go. It seemed queer that of all the people in the community, Abbie Mackenzie, who was only sixteen, should be the one in whom Will Deal confided. And because Will Deal had done this, Abbie told him some things she had never told a soul,—that some day she was going to be a big person. She could feel it in her,—that she was going to do great things, sing before vast audiences, and paint lovely pictures in frames and write things in a book.

"You know, Will, I don't want people to laugh at me,— and I don't believe you would. But sometimes it all comes over me, that I can do these big things. It's ahead of me, . . . kind-of like a light in the woods that shines and stays far away. And when I read verses, . . . or hear music, . . . or sing, . . . it beckons me on, . . . and my throat hurts with wanting to do something great."

Will did not laugh at her, but instead, looked at her queerly for a moment, noticing for the first time that her skin was as creamy-white as the May-flowers that grew in the Big Woods, that her lips were of deep red tints and her eyes of deep brown ones, and that her mop of curly hair held them both, —the reds and the browns.

And then, the next year, Ed Matthews, who had been east to college, was drafted. And Doc Matthews called Will out of the field where he was cutting wheat with a cradle, and told him he would give him five hundred dollars to go in Ed's place.

Will walked to the house, laid the sack of gold pieces in his mother's lap and said, "I'm going, Mother. There's the money to hire the work done."

He left from the new Dubuque and Sioux City station two miles from his father's place. Grandpa Deal was there, sick at heart, joking the boys. Grandma Deal, in her black cap tied under her wrinkled face, was there, scolding that Will was going, that the coach would be crowded,—scolding and sputtering in her little nagging way. Why didn't they stand back? Why didn't they go to-morrow? What made every one so noisy? Maggie O'Conner Mackenzie, in her white cap tied under her plump, placid face, was there. And Abbie Mackenzie, in a sprigged delaine over hoop skirts, and with a little pancake flowered hat tipped over her forehead, was there. *Oh, God, stop the wind blowing by,—the wind that blows Time away. Stop the clock hands until I can think whether Will Deal ought to go to war.*

And then, something happened. The train was ready to start. There were good-bys and noise and tears and confusion. Will Deal shook his father's one hand, and kissed his mother's little wrinkled cheeks and Regina and Louise,—and started to shake hands with Abbie Mackenzie, but suddenly kissed her instead. And if battles have been lost and kingdoms have fallen over less, who is there to blame Abbie Mackenzie, that her own little kingdom was in a state of revolution when she left the station and drove home in the lumber-wagon across the prairie and over the damp, dark river road?

In the fall of '64, when she was seventeen, Abbie herself was teaching the home school,—in a new white schoolhouse with green blinds, but standing in the same spot where the hazel-brush grew in tangled masses down toward the river bank. There was only one big boy in school that autumn, a harmless unfortunate, whom Grandpa Deal termed a "three-quarters wit." The others were "with Sherman." And Sherman was before Atlanta.

Abbie's thoughts seemed always with them, those boys in shabby blue: James and Dennie and all the old neighborhood schoolmates. Through the monotonously droning reading of the McGuffey readers, the ciphering and the tramped copy-book work, she thought of them. "God bring them all safe home. Please bring them home, God, . . . James and Dennie and Will Deal." There were other friends and schoolmates, but no one so big and fine and clean as Will Deal, and so understanding. Whenever she craved understanding, she always thought of Will Deal, who did not laugh at her fancies, but gave her sympathy instead.

Ed Matthews, who had paid his way out of the draft, came home that fall for a few days. Ed was going to be a doctor like his father. Several times he had stopped his horse at the schoolhouse door and, with the reins over his arm, talked to Abbie. She was a little proud of the attention. It was rather complimentary to be singled out from all the girls in the neighborhood for attention from Ed. She could not quite make up her mind whether she really liked Ed or not. Will Deal didn't like him,—had never liked him. But Will was prejudiced. And it was nice to see a young man dress as Ed did. In his riding outfit he certainly looked tony. There were some rumors around about Ed,—something about his drinking at times, and riding at dusk down a by-road which decent people avoided,—but no one had verified them, so far as Abbie knew, and, anyway, people were probably jealous of him and his opportunities.

In that week of October on a Friday afternoon, when the hazel-brush was as brown-burnished as Abbie's hair, and the Big Woods a mass of scarlet and bronze and crimson she closed the schoolhouse and left for home.

In the distance she could see the new, stylish, high-top buggy of Doctor Matthews going down the lane road where the honey-locusts, yellow now, bordered the north side of the Deal place. She was thinking that she could have ridden home with the doctor if she had been out a little earlier. Not that she cared, for it was pleasant walking. Who could believe that the guns of the war were booming in the South this Indian summer day? When nearly home she paused, turned abruptly, and climbing the stake-and-rider fence, walked through the oaks into the clearing where the October sun flecked down through leaf shadows. Not for several years had she visited the old grassy knoll between the huge trees. She went up to the top of the knoll now and faced an invisible audience in that old intangible dream which she always had with her. Half amused at her own childishness, half earnest in her actions, there in the seclusion of the woods, she unloosed from its binding ribbons the reddish-brown mass of her hair. She unbuttoned the top buttons of her lavender-sprigged delaine dress and pulled it down over the creamy whiteness of her shoulders, tucking in the edges to hold it. Then, with her reddish-bronze hair, with its overtones of gold, framing the Mayflower petals of her skin, and with her warm brown eyes half closed, Abbie Mackenzie threw back her head and sang:

> "*Oh, the Lady of the Lea,*
> *Fair and young and gay was she,*
> *Beautiful exceedingly,*
> *The Lady of the Lea.*"

The notes rose like the nuptial flight of birds, notes of desire and a longing for their fulfillment.

> *"To her bower at last there came,*
> *A youthful knight of noble name,*
> *Hand and heart in hope to claim*
> *And in love fell she."*

They throbbed with the joy of life and the pathos of it, with the beauty of peace and the sadness of war.

> *"Still she put his suit aside,*
> *So he left her in her pride,*
> *And broken-hearted drooped and died,*
> *The Lady—"*

A twig snapped and the note snapped with it. Frightened, Abbie whirled to the sound. Ed Matthews stood near her, his blond face aflame. Abbie gave a startled cry, and in fright and embarrassment, clutched the neck of her gown. But Ed Matthews had her in his arms, was kissing her full red lips and creamy Mayflower petals of her neck, burying his flushed face in the red-bronze of her hair.

"Abbie, . . . Abbie, . . . you coquette! . . . You're wonderful, . . . gorgeous. I love you. I never knew . . . I want you. . . . You're going with me. . . . You'll marry me. . . . I'll take you east . . . to New York. . . . Your voice . . . I didn't realize . . . You can have the best teachers . . . I have to go back to-morrow . . . Abbie . . . you *coquette* . . . ! And we have to-night left . . . to-night is ours . . ."

Swept away on the tide of Ed's passionate words, she seemed to be without thought of comprehension. When she could speak, she found herself saying almost without her own volition, "Don't, Ed, don't *touch* me. You've no right. *You've no right*." She was trying to button the high neck of her dress, pushing Ed's protesting hand away, twisting up the red-brown curls of her hair. Ed's laughter disconcerted and frightened her. He seemed so very sure of himself,—and of her.

It was sundown when they reached the Mackenzie cabin. For a long time they stood in front of it, talking. Ed's flushed face bent to Abbie's.

"I *think* so, Ed, . . . but I'm not sure. It's sudden and, . . . when you come in the spring I'll know my own mind."

"You're playing with me. You *are* a coquette."

"No, Ed, . . . I'm *really* uncertain."

"Uncertain about marrying me?" Ed's opinion of himself was not what one would term feeble. "Uncertain about going to New York, . . . with *that* voice? . . ."

"Oh, Ed, *if* I went, . . ." Abbie was suddenly childish, wistful, "would I be a lovely lady?"

Ed Matthews' banter and his high-handedness were stilled, his passion and his ardor quieted. He bent and kissed Abbie's pretty tapering hand. "You would be a lovely lady," he said gently.

When he had gone, Mary and Mother Mackenzie drew Abbie in to tell them what it was all about.

Importuned to secrecy, Mary was excited beyond the completion of sentences. "Abbie . . . *you* . . . Doctor Ed Matthews . . . to go to New York . . . your voice . . . teachers in New York . . . it might be in the opera . . ."

Mother Mackenzie asked gravely, "Do you *love* him, acushla?"

Abbie turned burning cheeks to her Irish mother and clutched her plump shoulders. "I don't know. Tell me, mother, what *is* love?"

"That," said Maggie O'Conner Mackenzie, "I canna tell ye. An' no one can tell ye. Sure, an' I mind an' I knew it though, mysel'. I look for you to know it, yoursel', Abbie."

Abbie went up to her loft room. She wanted to be alone. Love? Was this love? To be able to go to New York and study? Her voice . . . a new world . . . the world of courtly men and lovely ladies . . . of silken shawls . . . of strings of pearls . . . of flowing plumes. But that world also held Ed Matthews with his eyes that were not quite steady, with his disconcerting laugh and the vague, unproven rumors. But he loved her, that was certain. Or . . . was it so certain? His kisses . . . Abbie's face burned with the memory. She thought of Will Deal and the day he had left for war two years before. Will had kissed her, too—

Quite suddenly she wished she could talk the whole thing over with Will Deal. Will would help her know her own mind,—help her understand what love was. Of all the people she knew in the whole world, Will was the most understanding. He was so steady,—so dependable. "Oh God, bring Will Deal safe home soon to help me know."

Chapter 6

And then the presidential campaign of '64 was on in full swing. Over in town there were parades and banners and torchlights and much bombastic oratory. General Sherman was close upon Atlanta and Grandpa Deal was close upon General Sherman. For he had been delegated by Governor Kirkwood to go to the first division of General Logan's Fifteenth Army Corps to bring the vote of the Iowa contingent back to the state. Many weeks elapsed before his return. Atlanta fell. All communication to the north was severed, for General Sherman had started on his wearisome march to the sea. And with the tramping columns rode Grandpa Deal on a horse whose mane was as black as Grandpa Deal's own bushy head. A veritable old man of the sea he looked upon his return, grotesque appearing, with the bag of ballots swung over his shoulder by a strap, a faded carpet-bag in his one hand,—in the bag the government's pay to many of the Iowa boys.

Abbie was "boarding around," and was at the Deal house for the week when Grandpa came. He told his experiences to the family in high glee, his ice-blue eyes twinkling behind the bushy brows. "I'd al'a's throw the old bag down," he would relate with silent chuckles, " 'n' give it a kick for extra measure, so's nobody'd allow the' was any val'e to it,—'n' all the time the' was two thousand four hundred and twenty-two dollars in its old insides."

"Did you," Abbie moistened dry red lips, "did you—happen to see Will?"

The chuckles died. Yes, he had seen Will, had in fact kept as close to Company B, 31st Iowa Regiment as he consistently could. He had tried to make Will ride the horse a few times when he was exhausted. He had sat around the campfire with him a few nights, when the boys sang and joked and told stories to keep up their spirits. "Was the awfulest dense pitch-pine smoke from them campfires ye'd ever see. Boys used to kinda apologize to me about 'em, bein' as how I was a sort o' guest on the march. But I'd al'a's tell 'em black smoke didn't interfere much with my complexion."

In a few minutes he said soberly: "Will's been caught stealin'."

"Stealing?" A sharp pang of apprehension went through Abbie. She and Grandma Deal turned to each other in mutual fright.

"Yes, sir, . . . stealin'." Grandpa Deal's forehead was puckered in agony.

"My boy stole?" Grandma's little worried face took on an added anxiety.

" 'Twas at Savannah. Provisions was one ear of corn to the man. There was transports layin' right out there in sight off the coast with food on for our boys. Couldn't get in 'til fortifications fell. 'N' then my boy . . ." His voice shook in mock sorrow. "My boy went to the corral," the eyes began to twinkle, " 'n' stole two ears of corn from some army mules 'n' boiled the corn for supper."

Grandma was provoked. "You ain't got no call to be scarin' me that way," she sputtered. "You ain't got no call to spend your life jokin'."

"Oh, come, now, Ma. Better to laugh than to cry. Will maybe'll be remorse-stricken all the days o' his life,—to hear the brayin' in his conscience of them poor, helpless, skinny, mouse-colored government mules."

When Abbie was starting for school, Grandpa casually followed her out. "Had a good visit with Will." He cocked one eye up at the well-sweep.

"Did you?"

"Yep. He wanted to know how all the Iowa folks was."

"Did he?"

"Yep. More specifically, he wanted to know how all the Blackhawk folks was."

"Did he?"

"Yep. Collectively, he wanted to know how all the folks in our community was."

"Did he?"

"Yep. Individually, he wanted to know how *you* was."

"Oh, . . . did he?"

"Yep. He says to me," . . . Grandpa carelessly picked up a handful of snow and threw it at a rooster. "If I can rec'lect his words exact, they was, 'How's my Abbie-girl?' "

Abbie walked over the crusted snow in a maze of conflicting emotions,—behind the hard little stays of her waist a burning letter from Ed Matthews and plans for her future,—in her heart, the memory of Will Deal's one kiss, more poignant than either.

A new minister and his wife came to the growing town that fall and made a round of calls among the country folk. They were Vermont people. The Reverend Ezra Whitman was dignified, pompous, a little pedantic. Mrs. Whitman was refined, soft-spoken, a graduate of a girls' seminary. She took a great interest in Abbie, so that the young teacher began going into town to see her. She found that Mrs. Whitman was something of an artist. The little new frame house in which the couple lived held several oil paintings that seemed the acme of art to Abbie, and there was always an unfinished canvas on an easel. The paints fascinated the girl. She longed to get her hands on them. Something in her eyes must have flashed its unspoken message, for one day Mrs. Whitman asked her if she would like to try her hand with the brush. It thrilled her beyond words. Crudely enough, but with some intuitive knowledge, she did a little clump of trees on a piece of waste canvas.

"I'll never be satisfied until I can do it well," she said. From that time on, at Mrs. Whitman's invitation, she began painting with her, riding over to town when she could, tramping the two and one-half miles through slush or mud when there was no other way to go.

"It's your voice, though, that shows the greater promise," Mrs. Whitman told her. "I wish I could help you with that, too. Mr. Whitman's sister will know what to tell you when she comes. She teaches voice in my old seminary."

And when the sister came, and heard Abbie, she was

enthusiastic. "It's good," she told them all. "It's more than good. It's splendid. You can do really big things with it. You must try sometime to come East for lessons."

But Abbie was too bashful to tell her that already she had an opportunity to go to New York to study. Her praise had its influence in Abbie's decision. If her voice was really as good as Mrs. Whitman thought—— And so, on the day in April that Lee surrendered, Abbie Mackenzie surrendered, too. She wrote the letter to Ed Matthews that she would marry him. When she had sent it over to town to be mailed she went to her old grassy knoll in the clearing to sing. But she did not seem to sing well. Something seemed lacking. The melody sounded flat, unlovely, like a song from which the soul had fled.

In the weeks that followed, Abbie felt restless, nervous and a little sad. She told herself that it was on account of Lincoln's assassination. And indeed, some of it was, for the whole settlement mourned. But not all of her mood was due to the President's tragic death.

On a day in May, with the honey-locusts all in bloom, she stood at the door of the schoolhouse, and watched the train from the east shriek its way across Grandpa Deal's newly planted corn-fields. She washed her blackboard, set her desk to rights, locked the schoolhouse, and started home. And, quite suddenly, she saw some one coming down the lane. Abbie stood still, her heart pounding tumultuously with the uncertainty of the figure's identity. The world was a lovely painting of sunshine, blue skies, honey-locusts, bees on the blossoms,—a palpitating, throbbing world of spring.

Will Deal in his blue soldier's suit was coming toward her. She could not take her eyes from his face. He was smiling, questioningly, a little quizzically, and with something that was infinitely more tender. He slipped the knapsack from his back and held out his arms. Swiftly, lightly, Abbie went to him.

"Oh, Will, don't let me, . . . don't let me do it," Abbie began sobbing a little wildly, almost hysterically. For two years Abbie Mackenzie had not shed a tear and now she was crying wildly in Will Deal's arms. Will held her close, smoothed her hair back from her creamy-white forehead.

"Do what, Abbie-girl?" He was all gentleness, all desirous of understanding.

"Marry Ed Matthews."

Will caught her fiercely, held her closer, kissed her red lips, laid his face to her cheek that was like Mayflower petals. And Abbie thought of ships that come home to the harbor.

"I should say I won't. He could buy me in the draft . . . but he can't buy my Abbie."

"I was afraid all the time, Will."

Will held her close,—smoothed her red-brown hair.

"Afraid of what, Abbie-girl?"

"I don't know. Just afraid."

"You're not afraid with me?"

"Not with you, Will. Why is that?"

"Because I love you and you love me."

"Yes, that's it . . . and I'm not afraid."

"Of life with me, Abbie-girl?"

"Not of anything, Will, with you."

"And you'll always love me?"

"Always, Will, . . . in this life and the next."

The afternoon sun rays lengthened across the fields. The honey-locusts dropped in the lane. The bees made noisy forages into the hearts of the blossoms. Will and Abbie lingered, all the melody of life a-tune, all the heaven that they desired, there in the lane under the honey-locusts.

Chapter 7

They were married on a winter's day of 1865, when Abbie was not quite nineteen and Will was twenty-three. The day was mild, even warm, a phenomenon for that time of year. "A weather-breeder," every one called it. A few men shed their coats and worked in their shirt-sleeves during the middle of the day, so that they might tell of it in years to come.

Maggie Mackenzie and Abbie and Mary set the furniture out of the log house, so there would be room for the guests. Janet's two children were designated as a committee to keep the chickens off the various pieces, but so excited were the youngsters over the elaborate culinary preparations, that during a period of the abandonment of their posts, an old hen flew up on top of the high boy and laid an egg in the work-basket.

Abbie had made two new dresses from cloth sent out from Chicago. One was a wine-colored merino, the other a brown alpaca, both made fashionably full over hoop-skirts, with panniers at the side. A new little hat, the shape of a butter-bowl, with ribbon bows on it, added much to her pride.

Toward evening of the great day, Abbie was all of a-flutter because there were so many things to do. There was still water to be heated in a boiler on the stove and the washtub to be brought in for her bath. She had to skim a pan of milk, so that she could make the skin of her face and hands soft with cream. And she nearly forgot the flour she was to brown in the oven with which to powder her body. Basil, fifteen now, helped take the hot water on its perilous journey up the loft ladder with the saplings nailed across for steps, and lifted up the wooden tub on his strong young shoulders.

In spite of the unusually warm day, it was a little chilly for one's ablutions in the loft room, but Abbie was young and vigorous and used to it. She put on her muslin chemise and pantalets and her tight little stays, holding her breath until she could lace them so that her two hands could almost span her waist. Into her bosom she slipped a little netting sack of dried rose petals, which smelled faintly and tantalizingly of by-gone Junes. Then over her head she dropped and fastened the long collapsible hoop-skirt, with its nineteen bands of white covered wires. There were three white muslin petticoats, starched almost to chinaware stiffness and ruffled to the knees. Abbie and her mother had hemmed seventy-two yards of ruffles by hand. Grandma Deal had one of the Howe stitching machines, but not all families could afford one. Then, at last, she put on her wine-colored merino with its countless rows of flutings of the same material and side panniers.

She was patting her hair into place and pulling out the long shoulder curl, when her mother came puffingly, slowly, up the loft ladder. Mother was getting old now. She was forty-seven,—heavy and placid. Her fat round face in its white cap with strings tied under her two chins, appeared in the loft opening. Abbie went over to her and took her hand, so that she would not fall. She saw that her mother had the calf-skin covered box in her hand.

It was several moments before Maggie Mackenzie could talk, puffingly, after the climb. "Abbie, I want ye to have the pearls. I'm savin' the fan for Mary. Janet has the breast-pin, you know, and Belle the shawl. Belle always stuck 'n' hung fer the shawl. And the pearls are fer you. Ye'll ne'er starve as long as ye have 'em." She opened the little hairy-skinned chest and took out a small velvet box and from it the pearls themselves. She twined them through her short stubby fingers, their creamy shimmer incongruous in the plump peasant hand. "They were Basil's fine mother's. After she died, . . . Basil gave 'em to me in the days of wealth. Sure, but it wasn't the wealth that brought us happiness. Many's the time I've hated it . . . longin' for a little house somewhere, . . . out of the wind 'n' rain, . . . 'n' not many things at all, at all. . . ."

There were tears in Abbie's brown eyes when she took
them. She held their creamy luster in the palm of her
firm young hand. Into her mind came that old admiration
for Isabelle Anders-Mackenzie. The touch of the jewels
seemed to bring her near, to call up the vision of the lovely
lady who was wearing them in the wide gold frame,—the
lovely lady with the sweeping velvet and the long flowing
plume and the fingers that tapered at the ends. Some day
she was going to be like her. Some day she, too, would
be lovely and gracious and wealthy. All of life was before
her. All the future was hers. And that future now held
Will, with his steady gray eyes,—Will Deal who was like
a quiet harbor. Song, soft and meltingly tender came to
her lips:

> *"Oh, the Lady of the Lea,*
> *Fair and young and gay was she,"*

She held the pearls up to the wine-colored merino and
looked in the small oblong glass.

> *"Beautiful exceedingly,*
> *The Lady of the Lea."*

Then she turned to her mother. Her face was flushed,
tender. "Thank you, Mother, . . . so much, . . . I'll keep
them always. But with the dark dress and the high neck, . . .
I'll just not wear them to-night. After awhile when Will and I
are wealthy, I'll wear them. And maybe we'll have, . . ."
Some reticences existing at the time, the blood swept Abbie's
face, ". . . maybe we'll have a daughter some day and *she*
can wear them on her wedding night, . . . in white satin . . .
and all the things that go with it . . ."

Abbie swept across the dingy loft room, her hoops swinging in wiry bounces. She knelt down by her mother's chair,
her skirts forming a huge circular mound, and laid her head
against the older woman's. "And besides, Mother, *you*
understand, don't you . . . when you follow your heart you
don't need *pearls* to make you happy?"

It was time now. Abbie went down the ladder with the
saplings nailed across for steps. She had to go backward so

that her hoops could navigate the descension with some degree of modesty. The fiddlers were playing, "The Girl I Left Behind Me." Will, looking big and fine and handsome, was there in the black suit Grandma Deal had made him. Grandpa Deal, with his one arm and the kindly twinkle in his ice-blue eyes, was there,—joking. Grandma Deal, in a black cap with black strings tied under the face that was covered with the faint tracing of hosts of wrinkles, was there. She was nervous, fretful, scolding. Why didn't the men stand back? Why didn't they shut that door? Where was that preacher keeping himself? A thousand mental worries like a thousand gnats irritating the peace of her mind. Whole families had come in wagons. Regina Deal and her beau and Dr. and Mrs. Matthews were the only ones who had come in high-top buggies. When the doctor and his wife came in there was a little buzz of excitement, some whispering that they wondered whether or not it was true that young Dr. Ed had wanted Abbie.

A solemn hush fell on the company.

"Inasmuch as we are gathered here together in the sight of the Lord." Suddenly, Abbie wanted to halt the ceremony. There seemed nothing in her mind but that odd thought of a wind rushing by, a wind she could not stop,—Time, going by,—time which she could not stay. Stop Time for a minute, until she could think what queer thing was happening to her.

"Do you take this woman, . . . sickness, . . . health, . . . 'til death, . . ." What a queer thing to talk about now,—death,—when it was life that was before them. ". . . this man . . . lawfully wedded husband . . . ?"

"I do." *But, oh Will . . . Will . . . who are you? Do I know you?*

And then, quite suddenly, Abbie Mackenzie was Abbie Deal. The fiddlers played "Money Musk," and "Turkey in the Straw." The company danced,—square dances of intricate design. Grandpa Deal wanted to take a partner, but Grandma Deal said no, it was foolish for an old man, fifty-five. But Maggie O'Conner Mackenzie danced,—alone, lightly and puffingly, in the middle of the floor, to:

> "*Oh the days of the Kerry dancing,*
> *Oh the days when my heart was young.*"

There were biscuits and chickens and cakes and cider to be eaten from tables formed by putting long boards over saw horses. And then, more dancing.

Will Deal's dark serious face bent low above Abbie's creamy-petaled, flushed one. A long row of love-apples stood in the window.

Chapter 8

Will and Abbie drove to Grandpa Deal's in a two-wheeled cart behind an old white mare. So slowly did they drive that several passed them on the river road,—Grandpa and Grandma Deal and Louise in a lumber-wagon with a fine big team, and Regina Deal and her beau in the new high-top buggy. Grandpa laughed and called out some saucy jokes, but Grandma told him to hush his foolishness and 'tend to his driving.

Will and Abbie had the front bedroom of the big five-roomed log-house for their own. In the weeks that followed, Will went about the regular farm work for his father, and Abbie put her young shoulder to the wheel of the housework. For Will's sake she tried to meet his mother's petty nagging with forbearance. But it wore on her like the constant dripping of water on a stone. Grandma Deal was a chronic grumbler and a born pessimist. She saw bad signs in Nature's most ordinary activities. If a dog ate grass, if a bird flew through the house, if the moon rose from a cloud, the direst things were about to happen. And life meant nothing to her, apparently, but work. The first break of day and the last ray of sunlight saw her at the hard tasks of the housework. And when all other duties seemed done, she immediately brought out a box of intricate quilt blocks, The Rose of Sharon and The Star of Bethlehem, The Rising Sun or the Log Cabin. For Grandpa Deal, Abbie had nothing but love. His Yankee drollness could always bring a bubbling laugh to her lips and his stump of an arm gave her added tenderness toward him.

Looking at the two, she used to wonder how he could keep so cheerful. He never crossed Grandma, never argued with her in any way but jovially, never lost his temper. "Now, Mother," he would say, "can't you see the funny side of that?"

"No, I can't," she would retort, "and neither could you if you'd stop your foolish jokin' and keep your mind on your work."

It never went into a quarrel. When it approached one, Grandpa would go whistling out to the barn to work. Yes, Abbie loved Will's father better than his mother. In the same way did she enjoy and dislike Louise and Regina. Louise was energetic, pleasant, peace-loving. Regina was selfish, a mischief-maker and a shirk. The young farmer with whom Regina was now keeping company had come first to see Louise. Although Abbie knew little of the circumstances, she felt quite definitely sure that Regina had maneuvered the transposition with adroitness.

All spring, Abbie, fearful that the family might think she was not doing her part, took more than her share of the household duties. She helped boil the maple sap down into sugar, swept and dusted, baked and cooked, and took over the entire care of the chickens. Louise worked with her faithfully, but Regina slipped out from under the tasks with all the agility of an eel.

And then Abbie was not well, . . .

"She's not doing her share," Abbie overheard Grandma's sputtering. "I told you it was too good to be true. I said all the time it wouldn't last."

"Now, Mother," Grandpa's voice came gently, patiently, "I think I know what's the matter. You wouldn't want her to overdo."

"Overdo, nothing. I brought eight babies into the world. And I ain't ever seen the time anybody cared if *I* was overdoin'."

"Now, Mother, I wouldn't say that. It was hard, but you was healthy and I always got help for you."

"Yes, a passel o' neighbor girls that wasn't worth their weight in salt. Now, I s'pose it'll fall on me to take care o' Abbie. Nobody cares if I die or not."

Abbie heard Grandpa go whistling down to the barn. Then

she threw herself on the bed and cried tears of sensitiveness and discontent.

More and more she wanted her own home. If it were no better than the old sheep shed that she lived in one summer when she was a little girl, at least it would be their own. Will was good to her,—so kind and understanding, but he did not seem to sense how much she wanted a home of her own.

Abbie's baby was born in January of 1867. Roads were drifted and Doc Matthews, in a coonskin cap with the tail down his back, came on a horse, his saddle-bags full of quinine and calomel.

Nature had to take its course without much aid from its handmaid, Science—and Nature took a fiendish course with Abbie. Two days and a night she wrestled with Nature, as Jacob wrestled with the angel. And then she had a son. Lying there after her ordeal, with the baby on her arm, she knew the age-old surge of mother-love. All her old love of life seemed to concentrate on one thing,—the little soft, helpless bundle. The world of romance, of courtly men and lovely ladies was a world of unreality,—and only Will and the little son were worth her thoughts.

Mackenzie Deal, they named him, but it was too big a mouthful for so small a bit of humanity, and it was not long until every one had shortened it to Mack. Will was inordinately proud of him. Grandpa Deal and Louise came in several times a day to see him, but Regina was not overly interested. Grandma Deal sputtered about the care of him. Why didn't Abbie keep more shawls around him? Why did she let the sun shine across the bed that way? Why did she ask the doctor all those questions when he didn't know as much about babies as a mother?

When Abbie was up, life grew richer, more full. Her voice took on a mellowness. With the baby in the high-backed wooden rocker, she crooned old lullabies which Maggie O'Conner had brought from the whins of Bally-poreen.

As little Mack grew that year and crept and then stood on fat wobbling legs by the chairs, Abbie's desire for a home of her own reached gigantic proportions.

"You know, Will," she brought up the subject in the spring, a little shyly, half hesitatingly, "I wish we could have a home of our own. Your folks . . ." She dropped her eyes that Will might not see the telltale evasion in them,—''are good to me, but I'd so like my own little house. It needn't be half as big . . . or nice . . .''

To Abbie's surprise Will turned on her in a sort of suppressed fury. "I don't like it either, you needn't think. I'm thinking every day what to do. What am I here? A hired man for Father. I'll never get anywhere. And now we've got the baby . . . I'm glad you've been the one to bring it up. It decides me. We're going out to Nebraska to start for ourselves."

"*Nebraska?*" It had the sound of South Africa.

"Yes, . . . there are too many settlers here. And as long as I'm anywhere around here I'd always have to work for Father. It ain't right, I tell you. And another thing, Abbie, our boy sha'n't be tied down. He can do what he wants. And we're going to Nebraska,—you and I and little Mack."

"Oh, no, Will, not out there. Anywhere around here, but not to that far-off place. Why, Will, . . . my mother . . . my brothers and sisters . . . your folks . . . they're *all* around here . . .''

"You can come back to visit them, I promise you that, Abbie, whenever you want to. It's a wonderful opportunity. It's the poor man's country. We can get railroad land dirt cheap . . . or lease school lands near the river or even push on farther west and homestead."

"It's dangerous, Will. There are Indians."

"Well, so are there Indians here. A whole camp of 'em over by Fisher's Lake."

"But they're peaceable, . . . and those out there . . . Oh, Will . . .''

"It's been fourteen years since the government made the treaty with the Indians out there . . . fourteen years ago, they gave up their title to all that land out there bordering on the Missouri. I guess when it's been that long settling, we'll find it in pretty good shape. . . .'' Will was talking definitely, stubbornly, as though the question were settled. Abbie was so frightened at the turn the argument was taking that she studiously kept her voice calm.

"The baby, Will, . . . we have to think of him. There won't be good schools . . . or doctors . . .''

"It *is* of him I'm thinking . . . the big future for him out in the newer country. He'll be a farmer. All the Deals have always been for the land. . . ."

Fathers have always thought it,—that their sons belong only to them. Small wonder that Will Deal made the mistake of forgetting something, forgetting that the baby was also a Mackenzie, that his mother held her head as Isabelle Anders-Mackenzie had held hers in the wide gold frame—that her hair had the gold-brown tints of the lovely lady,—that her long slender fingers tapered at the ends.

"But, Will . . ." Never had Abbie so thoroughly felt that queer sensation of being swept along by the wind which she could not stop,—of Time, which she could not stay. "Will . . . my voice . . . Mrs. Whitman . . . Everyone thinks I ought to do something with it. And my painting, Will . . . to go away out there . . ."

"Oh, we'll find you good teachers out there. No, Abbie, I've been thinking it over a long time and it's my chance. We're going in the summer. I'll be getting everything ready. The army money will buy the wagon and oxen and the land, . . . and I'll make up my mind soon about it, . . . whether to buy near the river, or homestead farther out."

So Will had said he was going West. The era of this freedom had not dawned. Abbie Deal's man had said he was going to Nebraska, and Abbie had to go too. It was as simple as that, then.

They began preparations, with Abbie still protesting that Nebraska was too far away and too uncivilized.

"It's been a state since March of last year," Will gave equal arguments in its favor. "They've got the site all chosen for the new capital. It's named Lincoln. Queer when you stop to think about it that an old friend of Father's should ever get big enough to be president and have a town named after him—ain't it?"

But Abbie was not thinking of the recently martyred President. "Yes, but they say the place they've chosen is away out on the prairie with just two or three log houses." She was not so willing to believe the best of the infant state as was Will.

He sought out all the good news he could find to cheer her. Once he brought an Omaha newspaper. "Talk about a new country, . . ." he was enthusiastic. "Everything's as citified as can be in Omaha, . . . and we won't be so far from there. The paper says it has fifteen thousand inhabitants, . . . a regular city. How's this for you, eleven churches and five schools, and five banks. It says, 'Dealers in gold dust, bullion, coin and exchange.' And the Union Pacific's got an overland mail route clear to Laramie, with two trains every day.''

"Yes, and you read on a little farther. You're leaving out some things. I saw that paper myself, Will Deal.''

Will laughed. "Oh, five breweries and sixty saloons, . . . that ain't so bad. And besides there's a hoop factory.''

"Well, I don't care about that. They might even go out of style some day, although Regina thinks they never will. I wouldn't care if they did. Even if they do make you look stylish, they're not comfortable.''

And all the time Abbie was getting together her little possessions, and Will was preparing the outfit. He had intended to make a new ox-yoke, had in fact already cut the maple, and some pliable hickory for the bows, when Mother Mackenzie gave him the sturdy yoke that she had used fourteen years before on the trip out from Illinois. He painted the names of his ox team, "Red" and "Baldy," on it and in the center, "Nebraska, 1868.''

After some correspondence with an old army friend, Will bought his land, "sight unseen." He was pleased with his purchase. It was railroad land and he paid two dollars an acre for it. Some people from Michigan by the name of Lutz were getting two quarter-sections near him.

"It's only thirty-five miles from Nebraska City and about ten miles from Weeping Water. The county seat, Plattsmouth, has a hotel and some houses and a grist mill . . . It only takes a couple of hours to grind a sack of corn.''

"Yes, providing you've got the *corn*." Abbie could not yet enter heartily into the plans.

"Oh, we'll have the corn all right. They say the soil is the finest and blackest you ever saw.''

And then, before they were ready, Abbie knew that she was to be a mother again.

On a morning in July they started. Red and Baldy, in front of Grandpa Deal's, stood hitched to the prairie-schooner in their stupid, stolid way. All the possessions were in the wagon, covered now with its new white canvas. Every one was there to see them off. Mother Mackenzie, with her pudding-bag-shaped body and her blue-black Irish eyes and her white cap, brought the calf-skin-covered box and the Seth Thomas clock with the little brown church painted on the glass.

"You take the chest, Abbie . . . I want ye to have it. You can keep the pearls in it. And the clock, too, . . . it seems like it's yours. I mind how ye was al'a's sayin' no one could stop Time."

The Reverend and Mrs. Whitman came. Mrs. Whitman had a box of paints and some canvas for Abbie. "Keep on with your little painting talent, Abbie," she told her.

"Yes," the Reverend Whitman said, a little pompously, "and with your music. We can do with our lives whatever we will, you know."

"Yes, I know," agreed Abbie.

Grandma Deal, in her black cap, was sputtering because she had not had time to put her bread in loaves. Why didn't they tie the chicken-coop on better? Why hadn't they started the day before? The weather looked as though it might storm. What did they bother with a dog for? There, a bird flew in front of the oxen,—that was a bad sign.

Doctor Matthews stopped in his new top-buggy.

Grandpa Deal's ice-blue eyes were clouded with sadness "Good luck to you, my boy. And Abbie, a real daughter couldn't have been kinder."

Abbie's heart was in her throat. Oh, stop the wind rushing by. Stop Time for a few minutes, until she could think whether this move was the thing to do. Life was not right. It was not meant that you should leave your own this way. It was not meant that weeks and weeks of travel should separate you from your folks. The baby, little Mack, would forget Mother Mackenzie and kind old Grandpa Deal. And the next baby would never know them.

Only one thing gave her strength for the parting. Only one thing gave her courage to make the long journey to the raw new state. Her love for Will. Abbie's love for her husband had retained its sweetness and its ardor. And in her heart she knew that as much as she cared for her people,—as dear as were her mother and sisters and the old settlement to her, —they did not outweigh her love for him If being with Will meant making a new home in a far, unsettled country, why, then, she chose to journey bravely to the far, unsettled country.

Abbie threw up her head fearlessly. "Well, we're ready."

"Good-by . . ."

"Take good care of little Mack."

"Oh, Abbie, Abbie . . ."

"Mother . . . good-by . . ."

"Janet, dear, . . . Mary . . . Belle . . . Louise . . . Thank you all for all you did . . . Good-by . . . Yes, we'll write as soon as . . . Kiss Grandma, Mack-baby . . ."

Will was boyishly gay. For the first time he felt free from "the folks,"—his own master.

"Well, here we go." He cracked the long black snaky looking whip. "We'll come back rich." He laughed in excitement.

The wagon lurched,—steadied,—moved on.

"Good-by . . . good-by . . . good-by . . ."

Hands were in the air,—a sunbonnet waved,—an apron was thrown over some one's head. There was sobbing. Abbie's hand was on her hard, dry throat. It felt as though it must burst. Stop the wind. Stop Time for a minute. The wagon lurched ahead.

Far back in the road Abbie could still see the little group, painted flatly against the white of the fence and the green of the honey-locusts.

Will's eyes, full of the light of hope and courage, looked to the west. But Abbie's, tear-misted, clung to the east.

Chapter 9

It was three weeks later, on a hot morning, that Will and Abbie and the other two families, whose land was to join theirs, broke camp, twenty miles out of Plattsmouth, where they had crossed the Platte on the ferry. The journey over western Iowa had been one endless lurching through acres of dry grass and sunflowers, thickets of sumac, wild plum and Indian currant. And now, save for the little clump of natural growth near the wagons, there was still not a tree in sight, not a shrub nor bush, a human being nor any living thing, nothing but the coarse prairie grass.

The heads of the two Lutz families were brothers, Oscar and Henry. Oscar had a wife and three small children, Henry, a young bride and her little six-year-old orphaned nephew. Grandpa Lutz, a mild-mannered, gentle old man, had also come into the new country with his sons. They had traveled from Michigan, the two younger men by wagons, several weeks prior to the others. The women, children and the old gentleman had gone by train to Quincy, Illinois, where they had taken a river steamer to Hannibal, Missouri, crossing the Missouri to St. Joseph and taking a boat up the Missouri to Plattsmouth. There the men, having preceded the party, had waited a week for the boat to appear.

"I'd go down every day and kick the post the boat was goin' to tie up to," Oscar Lutz was telling Will.

Will laughed. "What for?"

"Oh, I don't know. Had to take all the delay out on

57

somethin' or somebody, so I kicked the post instead o' Henry, here.''

Sarah, the bride, was a pretty girl. Her hair was crow-black, her cheeks pink as prairie roses, her little black beady eyes had merry wrinkles of laughter around them. Life seemed a joke to her. This forenoon she had decorated the wagon with Indian paint brush, which burned like flames of fire against the dingy white of the canvas cover.

Abbie, in her illness from heat and fatigue and pregnancy, could only sit and wonder how young Sarah Lutz could be so happy and active. Nothing seemed to worry or frighten her. Apparently she had not even been disturbed by the story of the graves at Eight-Mile Grove,—the seven graves under the little clump of trees fenced around with slabs which the blacksmith there had told them were brought from the saw-mill at Rock Bluff. They had asked him innocently enough who was buried there. Abbie almost shivered now at the thought of his answer.

"Claim jumpers 'n horse thieves 'n sich," he had said indifferently. And, shifting his tobacco, had added definitely, "Hung. Vigilance committee." And more grimly specific, "To that there tree."

"Hung?" Some one had repeated in the silence that followed.

"Yep. Hang 'em in summer," he had explained cheerfully, " 'n' pike 'em under the ice in winter."

Abbie shuddered again at the memory of the grim voice.

The journey on from camp was across the vast prairie itself. As the morning passed, the heat rolled over Abbie in waves like the rippling of the grass. She looked out from the canvas to see Will plodding along, his shoulders drooping. He had not called back any gay cheery thing all forenoon. The grass out there,—would it never cease to wave? There were four rhythmic beats like music, but music which irritated rather than soothed one: *Blow . . . wave . . . ripple . . . dip.* It beat upon her brain, so that she turned wearily away from the sight. And then, as one fascinated by something distasteful, she looked again. Yes, it never ceased from those four beats: *Blow, . . . wave, . . . ripple, . . . dip, . . . blow . . . wave . . . ripple . . . dip . . .*

Little Mack was sleeping, and Abbie dropped over beside him. She closed her eyes and kept her mind on the lane beside Grandpa Deal's with the honey-locusts and the maples, on the black walnut grove back of his house and the hazel-nut thickets around the schoolhouse. How cool and pleasant the schoolhouse looked with the green shutters against the white siding! How good it would seem to draw water from Grandpa Deal's well. In fancy she pulled up the bucket with the windlass and put her face into its cold, dark depths.

She slept,—and sleeping, walked in the cool of the maples and oaks in the Big Woods, picked anemones and creamy white Mayflowers. She dropped down in a bed of cool ferns behind Janet Graves' house in the timber. Suddenly, the wagon creaked and lurched and she opened her eyes. Hurriedly sitting up, only half cognizant of where she was she looked out through the canvas. The sun shone hot on the flat prairie. *Blow,* . . . *wave,* . . . *ripple,* . . . *dip.* . . . An intense nausea seized her,—the *mal de mer* of the prairie-schooner passenger lurching over the hot, dry inland sea.

Later in the forenoon they sighted a fringe of trees against the unclouded sky. It seemed an oasis,—or was it a mirage to vanish when they should come to it?

"The Weeping Water," Henry Lutz called back. And they knew they were getting near to the new home.

They crossed the shallow, winding stream not far from a stone mill. A man with milk-pails in his hands paused to watch the cavalcade. Will, walking by his ox team, was wet to the boot-tops.

The man grinned and called out jovially: "You've got your baptism of the new country now. You're branded. You'll never go back."

"I don't want to go back," Will called out with equal jocosity. Abbie in the wagon almost moaned from nausea, heat and homesickness.

On the other side of the stream there stood a team of oxen hitched to a covered wagon so odd-looking, that even Abbie sat up in interest. The wagon-box was a rowboat painted a gaudy blue, the bow curving toward the stolid oxen's buttocks, the stern forming the base of the rear canvas doorway. A man with his wife and two babies waited for the others to come up. Gus Reinmueller, he said his name was, and jerking an indifferent thumb toward his wife, he gave a laconic, "My voman, Christine."

Christine seemed as stolid as the oxen, her face as patiently expressionless. One could not have told whether she was old or young. Her colorless hair was braided in small braids and wound flat from ear to ear, looking like a small oval-shaped rug pinned on the back of her head.

This was the third family, then, to be going up into the same section with the Deals. And together, after a lunch, the wagons journeyed on to the west. In a long, straggling line they journeyed stolidly and silently toward the sun. Of them all, only Sarah Lutz sometimes called out a cheery comment. Abbie lay on the wagon bottom, so ill with nausea and heat, that it seemed she could never again take any interest in life.

Toward evening another long fringe of trees penciled itself against the dipping sun.

"Stove Creek," Henry Lutz called back. And they knew they were at their destination.

There were old buffalo wallows along the creek banks, shallow declivities, where the huge beasts had rolled and stamped out the mud. The sight of buffalo chips, too, reminded them that the time was not long past since the shaggy fellows had ambled leisurely along the creek bed. They crossed the creek, which was little more than a ravine now, with its few inches of water. And then Henry Lutz, who was in the lead, stopped.

"Well, here we are," he called when Will and Abbie had caught up with him. "This is yours." He had a rude paper plan in his hand. "Mine lies over there to the west. Oscar's is to the north of mine, and Reinmueller's,—" Gus and Christine had come up in the ridiculous boat wagon. "Reinmueller's is exactly south of Deal's."

Abbie crawled out of the wagon-box. She was stiff and ill and her head ached from the blinding sunlight. Sarah Lutz, with her round rosy cheeks and her beady black eyes, was out of her wagon, too, and over to Abbie's.

"Well, you're home." She was chuckling in her merry way. "This is where you live,—and my good gracious, —you've got callers." She shook hands with Abbie in mock formality. "May I come in and sit a while? Yes, thank you, I'll take the rocking-chair, Mrs. Deal. Yes, thanks, I'll have a cup of tea."

It made Abbie laugh a little, too, the nonsense of it at such a time. And then, "Boo!" Abbie squealed and jumped and ran for the wagon. A little dark, lizard-shaped thing had darted close to her feet with the speed of lightning.

"They're just swifts," Will told her, "as harmless as mice."

"Yes, and just as horrid," Abbie called back.

They camped in a group for the night. It made quite a party: Will, Abbie and little Mack, the Oscar Lutzes with their three children, Henry and Sarah Lutz with Grandpa Lutz and little Dan, the orphaned nephew, Gus and Christine Reinmueller and their two babies.

The wagons formed a circle, with a single campfire in the center. The sun slipped down behind the rim of the world. One of the men found a spring in the creek bed and brought water. The others fed the horses and led them down to drink. The women folks got supper and washed the plates and cups at the side of the creek bed. The children were put to sleep in the wagons and the older people gathered around the fire. The stars came out, pale yellow flowers in the sky's own prairie.

A coyote howled. Another answered. It made Abbie think of a night on the journey from Illinois when she was eight, and yet this was different. Then, they had been close to the woods,—the sheltering woods. They had heard all the little night creatures at work, all the tiny rustlings of the timber. But this, paradoxically, was a silent noise. There was complete silence,—save for those distant coyotes. Silence,—save for a faint sound of shivering grass. Silence, so deep, that it roared in its vast vacuum. Silence,—grass,—stars. The group around the fire seemed suddenly too small to be alone in the still vastness, too inadequate and helpless.

What if—? Even as her fear formed itself into thought, she saw through the shadows a figure—and another—and others steal with panther-like tread between the wagons and the creek bed.

Chapter 10

Abbie could frame no words. She could only reach forth her hand and touch Will's arm, a nightmare of fear upon her. Will and the other men of the party were also looking toward the shadowy figures in the dark.

"They're friendly," Will whispered, "there's nothing to be afraid of."

Friendly? Were they friendly?

All night the Indians camped near the creek bed a little to the north. Abbie, with Mack upon her arm, did not close her eyes. Only a year and a half before, the Fort Phil Kearney massacre had occurred. Only two months before, Red Cloud had sent word that he would not sign the great Fort Laramie treaty. They were so much nearer hostile Indians here than back home. You couldn't tell from what tribe these were. You couldn't tell in the dark how many there were. All night Abbie lay in an agony of fear, her body tense, her little son at her breast.

In the morning, fears were dissipated. If there had been any evil from them it would have been during the night. They proved to be a small group of Pawnees, with their squaws and papooses. They had dozens of skinned chickens across their ponies, the flies thick upon them.

One of Henry Lutz's horses was missing from the bunch which had been staked together. After a half-concealed conference among the men folks, it was deemed wiser to accept the loss and not question the matter. One of the braves evidently had ridden away on it. The Indians ate, broke camp, came over to the settlers and examined their outfits. A brave pointed to Oscar Lutz's wife, who was not exactly dainty in size, and shrugged massive shoulders jovially, at which the other bucks showed symptoms of ingrowing mirth. They took their time to peer into all the wagons. One man picked up a little bright-colored shoulder shawl of Sarah Lutz's and coolly transferred it to the shoulders of his squaw. The others gave a few grunts of satisfaction, fell into a long straggling line and started toward the northwest, the red and black of the appropriated shawl growing fainter in the distance.

Abbie wondered if she ever again would pass through such a fearsome night.

As Henry Lutz had said, the Reinmueller place was south of the Deal acreage and his own joined it at the west. Abbie was glad to find that Sarah Lutz was the one who was to live nearer to her. She had taken a great fancy to the bride with the round rosy face, the jet black hair and the little beady black eyes that seemed always twinkling. For Christine Reinmueller she held no great liking. Christine was uncouth, not quite clean, her little tight braids wound flat from ear to ear, greasy looking.

The wagons were now each driven onto the families' respective holdings, forming little homes on wheels until the rude houses would be finished.

As far as eye could see, the land lay in long rolling swells, unlike the monotonous flatness which characterized part of the state farther to the west of which they had heard.

There was nothing to be seen in any direction but the prairie grass and the few native trees which traced the vagrant wanderings of Stove Creek. The undulating land covered with prairie grass, the straggling line of trees along the creek bed and the cloudless sky composed the entire picture,—these, and the Deal, Reinmueller and Lutz covered wagons,—little toys in the vastness of the lonely prairie.

Gus and Christine Reinmueller set about at once making a dug-out at the end of a ravine near the creek bed. They dug into the low hillside, set sturdy tree trunks a short way from the opening and covered the top with poles cut from the branches of trees, across which they packed a solid roofing of sod. Into this, with only the hard dirt floor, and the one opening, they moved their few possessions and their two baby boys. To Abbie it seemed that they were burrowing in like moles. But Gus was too anxious to get to work on the land to put much time on living quarters.

The Lutz family began a frame house at once, Henry and his brother both working on Henry's, so that when it was finished, the two families could live in it while Oscar's was being built. They took turns making the long trips to Nebraska City for material. The foundation of the house was merely rocks under the four corners, which, free for the picking up, were hauled from Weeping Water. The house itself was a two-roomed affair, with rough boards nailed up and down on the studding, and battened with narrow strips, but without plastering, so that for the first winter, Henry would nail burlap sacking all over the interior.

Will started a sod house. He did not feel that he could yet build as good a frame as he wanted, and every one said soddies were warm in winter and cool in summer. He cut strips of sod three feet long and laid them up as a mason would lay so many huge bricks, leaving places for the windows which Henry Lutz agreed to haul out from Nebraska City with whatever other lumber Will needed. The inside dimensions of the house were thirty by eighteen, so that when the partition was run through, the general living-room was eighteen by twenty and the bedroom eighteen by ten.

Abbie's physical ill-feelings and homesickness had been with her thus far through the making of the house. The sight of the prairie grass blowing and dipping in the wind under the cloudless sky still gave her a sensation of dizziness and nausea. The water from the spring at the edge of Stove Creek had a peculiar taste, so that she longed for the old well-water back home. She longed also for a sight of her mother's placid face under its white cap, and for a talk with Belle or Mary or Janet. In her low state of mind she felt uncertainty concerning their prospects, strange forebodings for the future, a torment that she was to die at childbirth and leave Will and little Mack.

But on an afternoon when Will was putting on the sod roofing, something lifted from Abbie's heart. Perhaps it was only because she was physically better that the deep depression seemed lightened, the intense homesickness for old scenes lessened. She put Mack to sleep in the wagon and walked farther up the long rolling land.

A sense of lightness, such as she had not known for weeks, was upon her. A revival of hope and courage possessed her. This was their own land. They, who had never owned a foot of ground, were now the sole owners of one hundred and sixty acres. Rich soil, too, Will said,—black and rich. A farm of their own upon which to make a home,—a home for Mack,—and one other! She wondered, as all mothers have wondered, which the new baby would be. And could not quite determine, as all mothers have been not quite able to determine, which she rather it would be. A boy would be the nicer for one reason,—he could be a chum for Mack. But a little girl,—down in her heart she hoped it would be a little girl. She remembered what she had said to her mother in the old cabin loft, back home. "Some day we may have a little girl. We will be rich then and she can wear the pearls." Well, maybe the baby would be a girl,—here was the good black soil upon which to get rich,—and over in the wagon were the pearls. She and Will were young. Life was all before them. With neighbors not far away, it was not going to be so lonely. Sarah Lutz—already she loved Sarah. And Christine Reinmueller,—even though Christine was so "Dutchy," she was kind hearted. Their own land, two babies, youth, neighbors! No, life here was not going to be so bad.

She raised her head to the cloudless September sky.

> "Oh, the Lady of the Lea,
>   Fair and young and gay was she,"

Her voice rose clear, full-throated, mature.

> "Dreamed of visions longingly,
>   The Lady of the Lea."

Yes, she and Will would soon be wealthy. Will had said so. Youth, babies, friends, wealth! She put the joy of it into melody:

> "When she held in bower or hall
>   Banquet high or festival,
>   On every side her glance would fall . . ."

A crow, flying above her, wheeled and dipped down toward her, "Caw! Caw!" it threw down at her saucily, Abbie broke off singing.

"Were you jeering at me?" she called after the vagrant wanderer.

"Caw! caw!" it threw back raucously.

Maybe it was a sign. Maybe it was a *bad* sign. Grandma Deal would have said it was. Then she threw back her head and laughed. Oh, well, she was young. Her voice wouldn't run away and leave her. In a little while she could get to a teacher somewhere,—over the prairie to Nebraska City or back to Plattsmouth, or perhaps even up to Omaha some day.

As she started back to the prairie schooner, with the song unfinished, a long, slimy, gruesome Thing slipped, belly-flat, through the grass. Abbie shuddered and scrambled into the sheltering wagon.

The rough edges of the black sod of the house were now treated to a thick coat of mud plaster and a board floor laid. The low partition, over which she could hang clothes, and the crude board door, Abbie papered with hoop-skirted feminine paragons of style out of Godey's *Ladies' Book*, from which vantage point they looked down upon the humble interior with supercilious pride.

This, then, was the house into which Abbie moved from the prairie schooner,—Abbie, the granddaughter of Isabelle Anders-Mackenzie with her town house and her two country estates, her silk shawl, her pearls and her jeweled fan, her reddish-brown hair and her long slender fingers that tapered at the ends. But with the same pride that had rearranged the sumptuous furnishings in the ancestral home across the sea, Abbie now hung curtains at the windows, tacked burlap gunny-sacking on the floor, put down the small braided rag rugs, and made up the two clean beds. Under one of these she put the calf-skin-covered chest which held the pearls and the paints, and in the deep window-seat formed by the width of the sod strips, she set the Seth Thomas clock with the little brown church painted on the glass. There was one "boughten" cupboard for the dishes and Will made another one of store boxes to hold Abbie's books,—the Shakespeare plays and the Bible, the McGuffy readers, and a few other textbooks

There was a four-holed stove whose long pipe protruded

through the sod roof, three chairs, and a table with a declivity in one corner of it in which Doc Matthews had always rolled pills. A couch, which might also serve as an extra bed, was made of the same type of sod strips which had been used in the house, and covered with a feather bed and "The Rose of Sharon," one of Grandma Deal's quilts of intricate design. The rooms were both furnished now. The little soddie was not much of a house, but it was that other thing,—that intangible thing of the spirit called home.

As soon as his work on the house was finished, Will started on a shed for the stock. And in the mild October weather before the frosts had come, he broke sod on one portion of the land, so that it would be ready for slightly easier plowing in the spring.

With November the mild weather ceased. The winds, that seemed never still, blew harder from the open country to the north and west. Dried tumbleweeds, round in shape and as large as bushel baskets, rolled over the prairie with the winds, like great platoons of charging cavalry. Abbie, standing sometimes at the little soddie window, would watch the ceaseless riding of the brown-coated swashbucklers, the unending onslaught of Nature's artillerymen. On and on they came,—mounted rifles, dragoons, hussars,—columns, companies, regiments, brigades. They swept by, to disappear in the distance, only to be followed by reserves from farther out on the prairie.

It gave her a sense of fear,—fear that the unseen force which sent the slender-stemmed, globular-shaped weeds on their endless journey, might suddenly send her, too, on the hard ride.

When Will took the long drive to Nebraska City for supplies, her desolation seemed complete. She would catch up little Mack, who was a year and a half now and toddling everywhere, and hold him to her with a prayer for safety from all the unknown terrors,—Indians, winds, prairie fires, storms, her own hour of travail.

Will brought back corn meal and one precious sack of white flour for which he had paid ten dollars. so sparing was Abbie in its use, that it was nearly spring when the last bit was baked and the sack made into an apron for herself.

It was in the middle of the first night in March that Abbie

knew her hour had come. The March winds, like so many wild March hares, were running past the little soddie. Will dressed hurriedly, replenished the fire, and with a word of encouragement, was gone into the night. Abbie, bolting the door behind him, knew the greatest fear of all for prairie women,—to be alone on the desert of grass with the pangs of childbirth upon her. "Oh, God, bring Will and the doctor safe home." The winds blew. Little Mack slept. Abbie's body was wracked. "Oh, God, send some one."

And then some one pounded on the door: "*Ein! . . . Las mich ein . . .* Christine." Abbie opened the door, and Christine Reinmueller came in, her fat face red from the cold wind, her little tight greasy braids flattened from ear to ear. She looked beautiful to Abbie.

It was hours before Will came with the doctor from Weeping Water. And then Abbie had her little girl,—the little daughter who was to wear pearls and all the lovely things that should go with them. Will brought Mack in and showed him the new sister, and Mack promptly welcomed her by poking a fat forefinger into her eye and mouth to see if she really worked.

They named her Margaret,—for both grandmothers. "It will please them both," Abbie fibbed politely. Almost she could hear Grandma Deal saying: "What did they do that fool thing for?"

Mackenzie Deal and Margaret Deal! A son and a daughter! Such a big family! She and Will laughed together in their relief and happiness.

And now, Abbie's love was divided between two babies. No, that is not true. There is no division nor subtraction in the heart-arithmetic of a good mother. There are only addition and multiplication.

March was cold, windy, snow-filled,—the land a desolate waste. Grayish-white snow over the low rolling hills,—a grayish-white sky like the pale reflection of those rolling hills in an opaque glass! And into the gray vastness of the sky, three little thin lines of smoke from the stove-pipes through the roofs of a dugout, a chink-battened frame and a soddie, —incense ascending to the God of Homes!

And then, the miracle! Spring came over the prairie,—not softly, shyly, but in great magic strides. It was in the flush of green on the elders and willows by Stove Creek. It was in the wind,—in the smell of loam and grasses, in the tantalizing odor of wild plums budding and wild violets flowering. Nature, the alchemist, took them all, the faint odors of the loam and the grasses, the willow buds and the little wild flowers, and mixing them in her mortar, threw them over the prairie on the wings of the wind.

Will could scarcely wait to begin spring plowing. Only then would it seem that the work on the place was really under way. He saw the frost ooze out of the broken sod and the heavy rolling clouds lose their frozen firmness. Twice he made an attempt to start the hand-plow and found the ground not ready. And then on a morning, with the prairie-lark calling to him, he started. Abbie took the baby in her arms and went out, with Mack toddling by her side. Gyp, the young dog of nondescript breeding which they had brought with them, ran frantically about, chasing some little flying thing. Abbie constantly darted a look near Mack, never allowing him more than a few feet from her, the fear of the deadly rattle-snake always with her.

Usually undemonstrative, Will slipped an arm around Abbie. Serious and reticent, he seldom voiced his deepest feelings. But now he spoke them:

"It'll be a pull, Abbie-girl, but some day you'll see I was right. The furrows will go everywhere up and down these rolling hills. Bigger plows than mine will roll them back. There'll maybe be a town here," he pointed to the limitless horizon, "and a village there. Omaha will be a big center. The little capital village of Lincoln will grow. It's bound to come. Not to-day,—nor to-morrow, but some other day and some other to-morrow. You'll live to see a fine capital building and schools and stores and churches and nice homes."

Prophetic words! A town lies here and a village there. Huge tractors turn a half dozen furrows in one trip across the fields. Omaha and Lincoln are great centers for commercial, industrial and educational interests. Where once the Indian pitched his tepee for a restless day, there are groupings of schools and churches and stores and homes. And Abbie Deal lived to see the beginnings of the tall majestic tower of the most beautiful capitol of them all lift its white shaft to the sky,—a capitol unashamed of its native products, into whose marble artistry have gone the buffalo and the corn and the goldenrod.

Will stood a moment, a little abashed at his emotion, so that immediately he said lightly, "Well, here goes."

The first loam turned back, clean-cut with the sharp knife of the plowshare, mellow, black as a crow's wing. A fringe of coarse grass held fast to the heavy soil, as though the two could not be parted after all these wild, free centuries together,—the grass maiden clinging to the breast of her prairie lover.

Abbie turned abruptly and went into the house with the babies. Inside she cried a little into the long roller towel, —she did not know just why. Then she pulled herself together. "This will never do. There's no time for idle tears. If I am to do my share in all that Will thinks he sees, I must get a good dinner for him." The man at the plow, the woman at the stove,—it was symbolic.

That spring the new life began in earnest. To Abbie, the future gleamed with bright prospects. New settlers were coming in every day,—already the precinct had thirteen families. In such a little while the community would be well settled. In such a short time they would all be rich. And so Abbie Deal went happily about her work, one baby in her arms and the other at her skirts, courage her lode-star and love her guide,—a song upon her lips and a lantern in her hand.

Chapter 11

That summer was a summer of hard work and high hopes. Everything was to be done. Will, in his keen desire for results, worked early and late. He broke out more raw prairie and planted it, cut and hauled wood from the creek, chopped it in stove length, cared for his stock, and did the work of two men. He dropped into bed when he could not see to do anything more and was up before the sun rose over the fringe of elms and elders and willows on Stove Creek.

And Abbie? Abbie took care of little two-year-old Mack and the new baby, Margaret, washed with little water, ironed with cumbersome flat-irons next to a cook stove that was a fiery furnace, cooked from a meager store of supplies, made soap out of doors, standing over the hot contents of a huge iron kettle, sewed and mended, tried vainly to keep the house clean, and took sole care of the chickens, which, like their owners, boasted a sod residence. The tapering Mackenzie fingers were never idle.

Will had many long trips to make, and Abbie, bundling up the two babies and taking along supplies for them, went with him. They drove the long way to Nebraska City to get cottonwood seedlings from the sand-bars there, as the little young trees growing in the pliable soil could be pulled out with one twist. They left feed and water for the chickens, but took the cow with them, tying her to the wagon. Abbie put in her churn with some cream in it, and the lurching motion of the wagon furnished them with butter, which was passable, although decidedly not as good as when cooled in the spring water. Will took his double-barreled shotgun along and killed prairie chickens on the way, which Abbie, as she sat in the back of the wagon, picked to cook for supper.

"It's a good thing we're not trying to run away from the law," she called out to Will, "for we could be traced clear across the prairie by a trail of chicken feathers."

Whenever they came to the homesteads of settlers they tried to move straight with the surveyed sections, but over railroad and school lands they drove to their destination through the trackless prairie grass as straight, if not as swiftly, as the crow flew.

Both the cottonwood and the willows would grow also from cuttings, so that on their return Will brought up a huge cottonwood branch from the creek and Abbie cut the whole thing into slips for Will to set out to the north of the sod house for a potential wind break. From their own creek bed they obtained willow whips and these were planted near the chicken house. Every one was planning for future shade.

To the north and west of them, Oliver Johnson, a young bachelor and a Dartmouth graduate, put out a timber claim. By planting and caring for ten acres of trees for eight years he would be able to obtain a good one hundred and sixty acres from the government.

In every activity on the place Will took pains to plan right. "We have to think what we're doing and lay it out just as we want it in the future," he told Abbie. "We'll be able to build a good frame house one of these days and we want the whole place planned so we'll not need to make changes."

Abbie pondered a great deal over the arrangement. "Right over there, Will, the new house ought to be . . . on that rise of ground. Then some day there'll be a road. I can kind-of see now how it will be. A nice house up there on the rise and the road running east and west past the house, then a lane road turning in from the main one. And fences. . . . Oh, I think, Will, when we get fences, I'll like it better. It seems so sort of heathenish to come across the country any way. There ought to be nice straight roads everywhere and fences to show where our land begins and ends. And a picket fence around the house yard . . . a nice fence, painted white . . . with red hollyhocks and blue larkspur along by it, against the white pickets."

Will laughed. "You're quite a dreamer, Abbie-girl."

Abbie did not laugh. She was suddenly sober. "You have to, Will." She said it a little vehemently. "You *have* to dream things out. It keeps a kind of an ideal before you. You see it first in your mind and then you set about to try to make it like the ideal. If you want a garden,—why, I guess you've got to *dream* a garden." Then she looked out at the small plot of vegetables, and laughed,—not quite joyfully, a little ruefully. They looked so wilted and so lackadaisical, so uninterested in life, those potatoes and turnips and beans.

All this time they had used the spring at the edge of the creek, and now Will was digging the well. Henry Lutz came over to operate the windlass that raised the buckets which Will filled with dirt. In return for the work, Will was to assist Henry in the same way as soon as his own well would be finished. On one of the days of the well-digging Henry brought word that the Burlington road had sent its first train across the Missouri to Plattsmouth. It made the men feel good. Things were coming along fine, they told each other.

On a later afternoon Henry could not come, and Abbie, as anxious as Will that the work should go forward, pitted her own young strength against the weight of the dirt-filled buckets. All afternoon, her face purple with heat and exertion, she worked under the sun's fire and in the wind's hot breath, only leaving her post to nurse the baby at her heated breast.

When it seemed that she could not stand it longer, that through the perspiration of her eyes she saw only a tortuous shimmering heat over the land, Will signaled to be pulled up.

Slowly, painfully, exerting every ounce of strength she possessed, Abbie wound the rope of the windlass. Suddenly, treacherously, the handle slipped from her perspiring hands and struck her head with black and blinding force. When she came slowly back from the dark spaces of some vacuous cavern, she could hear Mack's wailing cry of, "Muvver . . . Muvver," as he bent over her and pulled at her fluttering eyelids,—could hear Will's faint and frantic call, "Abbie . . . Abbie . . . where are you?"

She sat up and tried to recall just what had happened, suddenly remembering that Will must have been dropped back into the well with terrific force. He might be badly hurt. It gave her strength. She was up and calling to him. No, he was not hurt, was shaken up a little, but nothing to worry about.

And then Abbie must go for help to get Will out. Over and over she cautioned little Mack to stay away, up by the house, explained repeatedly how he must not go near the big hole. Then, bruised and bleeding at the forehead, she went across the hot prairie to get Gus, the fear of the horrible rattle-snake present with every grass-hidden step. There was no one home at the Reinmuellers'. Repeated callings brought no one from the dug-out or rude sheds. Back to the Henry Lutz place she sped, where she found Henry and Sarah, who immediately hitched the team, brought her back in the wagon, and rescued Will.

Indians came through the community every little while in their straggling, single-file way of traveling. They were said to be friendly, but the settlers could not trust them. Nothing ever filled Abbie with so much fear as the sight of two or three unidentified figures appearing upon the horizon. And in August, when news filtered into the community that a band of ten government surveyors had been massacred by a band of Sioux under Pawnee Killer out in the Republican Valley, she felt that only a word from Will would be needed to abandon everything and go back home.

Only a few days later four of the fear-inspiring creatures stopped at the house and signified they wanted eatables. They ate greedily of the pork and beans Abbie set before them and when they seemed satisfied, coolly turned the remaining food into their dirty blankets, and went on over the prairie in their straggling single-file way, the poles of their teepees dragging from the scrawny ponies' sides.

It was late that same month that Henry Lutz came tearing up to the Deal soddie on a horse.

"Something has happened to little Dan," he called without dismounting. "We don't know what. Go over and stay with Sarah, will you, while I ride for Doc Keeney?"

Will hitched the horses hurriedly and Abbie got in with Mack and the baby, Margaret. When they started away they saw Christine coming, so they drove back and waited for her.

Sarah Lutz was frantic, her round rosy face drawn with fright. They had been pulling their cabbages from the weed-bend of the creek to make kraut, she said. Dan helped a little, but about four he said his leg hurt. "We told him to rest . . . thought he was just tired. He complained more about it after we got to the house . . . and when we looked at it . . ." Sarah covered her blanched face with her hands. "It's swollen . . . twice as big . . . and it's . . . Oh, God, Abbie, it's black."

Doctor Keeney came. He went into the little bedroom and when he came out, his tired face above the grizzled beard was drawn and his eyes grief-filled.

"It's . . ." he threw out his hands in a gesture of despair, "snake-bite. I'll do what I can . . . but . . . it's too late. . . ." He had whispered it, but the words rang through the room . . . tolled through the house. Little Dan, with his sunny ways, to be a victim of the Menace!

They all waited there in the night,—waited for death to find little Dan on the wild barren prairie. Such a little boy for death to find in the vastness of the new country! But it found him. Riding over the prairie with the wind that was never still, the white horseman found him.

Will made the pine box down at the barn, and Abbie and Christine lined it with Sarah's best quilt. Sarah, grief-stricken, would let no one else wash and dress him. Henry rode to Plattsmouth for a missionary minister. Other settlers came long distances to the Lutz house in their wagons. Their sympathy was deep and sincere. And it took concrete form. They brought wild-grape jelly and corn biscuits, baked prairie chickens and a roast of pork.

They buried the little boy on a knoll of the Lutz land. The settlers with bared heads stood around the deep yawning hole in the ground. Abbie, her throat too stiff and tense to follow the melody correctly, sang an old hymn. The minister talked of a God who made all things work together for good. Abbie thought she could not stand it! Death! How she hated it and feared it!

There was not a tree near. The August sun blazed down on the rolling hill. The hot wind from the southwest blew over it. The blackbirds and crows flew and wheeled low above it. The coarse prairie grass bent before the wind. *Blow . . . wave, . . . ripple, . . . dip. . . . Blow, . . . wave, . . . ripple, . . . dip. . . .*

Chapter 12

There was very little crop that fall. The settlers learned that sod-corn never amounts to much. What few ears formed, Will fed on the stalk.

"I don't care. I'm not disappointed," he said, "I knew it would take a year to get a start."

But Abbie knew it was not so. Abbie knew that Will cared.

The stubble and roots, rotting all winter in the newly broken fields, fertilized the ground, and so it was with high hopes that Will went into the field the first spring of the 'seventies.

Abbie's summer was one of fighting sickness, in addition to her many tasks. Both children had the measles and the whooping cough later, as did the Reinmuellers' three and Sarah Lutz's new baby daughter, Emma. The mothers doctored them as well as they could with simple remedies, catnip tea and Indian herbs, hanging over their beds, watching anxiously for every change. When her children came out from under the cloud of illness, Abbie felt that it was like coming out of a dark cavern into the sunshine. Once more she sang at her tasks.

The crop of 1870 was only fair. So much hard work for so little results! Nothing but the cottonwoods seemed to thrive luxuriantly. Already after their second summer, some of those which they had brought from the sand-bars were as tall as Will. Their little shimmering, dancing leaves were a solace to Abbie. They seemed courageous and cheerful, undaunted by the hot sun, undisturbed by cold rains, unafraid of the rushing winds.

Will had set out an orchard now. Oscar and Henry Lutz had sent east to their brother for nursery stock, and the Reinmuellers and Deals ordered fruit trees, too. The spindling whips of apples and cherries with their names still tied upon them, looked a rather hopeless lot rambling row upon row over the raw prairie.

There was always so much to be done. One never could satisfy the demands of Work, that taskmaster which drove every one in the new country before the lash.

Sometimes Abbie would stand at the door of the soddie and look across the unshaded prairie where the sunflowers added their brilliant yellow to the blinding yellow of the sun, and standing so for a few moments, she would think of the lovely lady with the bronze tints in her reddish hair. She had wanted to be like her. But how could one be a lovely lady when there was not always enough water to keep immaculately clean?

Will was her strength and her courage. In one of her hours of depression she had only to confide her mood to him, to have it lifted by his optimism.

"Everything is going to be all right," he would assure her. "Think of the Burlington road reaching Lincoln last week. Think of it! Building right up,—everything is."

"Yes, but Will,—there are so many things we need. And I want, . . . Oh, Will . . . I want an organ so *bad*. I'll be twenty-four this fall . . . and my music . . ."

"My, you're getting old," he would joke her. "Most an old woman, ain't you?" And then more seriously, "Maybe you can have your organ next year, Abbie-girl. We'll have good crops next year."

But next year, 1871, the crop, like the others, was only half a crop. Will was right about the land. The soil itself was rich enough. But the rains held off. Day after day the clouds, as white and dry and puffy as milk-weed seeds, scudded high with the winds.

In that fourth fall, on a mild September day, the air was hazy and they could detect the telltale, far-off odor of smoke. Not a man left his home. Will, the Lutz brothers, Gus Reinmueller,—all were out for hours plowing wide strips around their places. They knew there were only three things that would stop a prairie fire in its mad, wild flight, and even those were ineffective at times,—wide strips of upturned loam upon which there was nothing for the fire to feed, creeks that were wide enough to prevent the flames from leaping them, or a back-fire,—the burning of a wide strip of prairie grass by the settlers themselves, so that when the flames arrived they found themselves beaten by their own kind.

It was close to three in the afternoon when they saw it roll in from the northwest, the black of the smoke, and the low running scarlet of the fire.

Stove Creek, the best friend in the world to the four families that day, lay between them and the hideous advancing Thing. The men, Will and Gus Reinmueller, Henry and Oscar Lutz, all scattered along the creek bed, ready to pounce upon any flying embers that might cross the deadline. All afternoon the women carried wet gunny-sacks back and forth. They could see the little house where Oliver Johnson "bached it," standing in the way of the angry flames. Oliver, himself, came across the creek over to the Deal side, riding one horse and leading the other, a big wash boiler in front of him. He had been away, he said, and arrived home only in time to grab a boiler, thrust his Sunday suit, some money, a tin-type of his girl into it, and leave. Even as they talked, they saw the little house catch fire and almost immediately a great bunch of geese feathers flying up into the air, like a puff of white smoke.

"There goes my mother's feather bed," was Oliver's laconic remark, as he fell into the work of wetting the gunny-sacks along with the others.

When the last of the jaws of flame ceased reaching for their prey, the land across the creek was a desolate black waste, the trees on the north bank charred and gone. One more enemy was temporarily vanquished. But it had left its mark on the land and the fear of it branded forever in the minds of the settlers.

The next spring, the State Board of Agriculture, through a resolution offered by J. Sterling Morton, a Nebraska City man, set aside the tenth of April, as a special day on which the settlers should plant trees. They called it Arbor Day. Although Will had set out a great many trees previously, he spent the day adding to his own windbreaks and hauling cottonwood saplings for Henry Lutz who was sick at the time.

When Henry was up again, he built an addition of two rooms on to his house and opened a store in one of them, the stock consisting of six brooms, ten bolts of cloth, a dozen bottles of patent medicine and a few staple groceries. His first customer was Christine Reinmueller who bought brown denim for her baby's dress. She put one corner of the goods between her teeth and pulled on it. "Everyt'ing . . . *sie reis* . . . rip." She jerked the cloth to test its strength. "You t'ink dis *sie reis* . . . rip . . . nein?"

A few rods to the east of the Lutz combination store and house, Oscar Lutz built a blacksmith shop and hired a blacksmith-preacher to do the work. For six days Sam Mowery labored at the anvil and on the seventh day the Reverend Samuel Mowery preached three miles away in the school-house known by the appropriate appellation of Sodom College. A store and a blacksmith shop! People began saying, "Over to the Stove Creek store," and then, "Over to Stove Creek."

Mail was brought now by a man on horseback, en route from Weeping Water to Ashland. Twice a week he would stop with the little packet at the Lutz store, as Henry had been made postmaster.

They began to talk about getting a doctor to come in. Will heard of a young Dr. Hornby, who had just arrived at Nebraska City after graduating from Rush. He rode on horseback to interview him, and the young fellow returned on his own horse behind Will, his mutton-chop whiskers blowing back against his pink-cheeked boyish face, his medicine-case and a valise tied on the saddle.

A store, a post office, a blacksmith shop, a preacher, a doctor,—and all in two buildings. The town had begun.

It was Sarah Lutz and Abbie Deal who began talking about the crudeness of the "Stove Creek" title. They were both setting out little cedar trees, Sarah in a clump behind the store, Abbie in a row in front of the soddie.

"Cedar City, Abbie," Sarah said suddenly.

"Or Cedartown," Abbie added.

"Yes, I believe I like that best . . . all in one word."

Cedartown! A store and a blacksmith shop! But the Deals

and the Lutzes, the Reverend Samuel Mowery and his wife and Dr. Hornby would all correct any passerby who asked innocently if this was Stove Creek.

"Cedartown," they would say impressively. And so, Minerva-like, Cedartown had sprung forth from the brow of the prairie.

The crop of that year, 1872, was as poor as that of the previous summer. In September, Abbie's third child was born. Sarah was there helping, now, and Christine was at home with her own new baby. The child was a son, healthy, loud-voiced, hungry. Abbie and Will joked a little over the size of their family and they argued some over the newcomer's name. Will wanted to call him John.

"It doesn't sound just right," Abbie protested. "John Deal. It's too short . . . like 'Tick-tack' . . . or 'Pot-luck.' "

"Oh, I don't care," Will gave in readily enough. "I just liked it. It sounds solid and substantial as though he might amount to something."

Abbie pulled the little soft sleeping form into the hollow of her arm. "I *know* he'll amount to something."

After that she could not get the thought of the "John" out of her mind. "John Deal," she said it over several times. "Will's right. It just fits him. Some day people will say, 'Go and ask John Deal. He's a smart man. He can advise you.' " She lay and smiled at the vision. If the faith of all the mothers could blossom to its full fruition, there would be no unsuccessful men in the land.

Mack was nearly six now and Margaret four, so that when Abbie was up again, and strong enough, she began to teach them their letters. Will painted a board with black paint and brought some soft chalk-like deposit from the Platte with which they could print. The oldest Reinmueller and Lutz children had started to school at Sodom College, but Abbie would not let Mack go so far. So to her other labors she now added teaching.

All winter during the deep snows when they were shut in, she gave the children lessons to do, hearing them recite in their queer little ways, while she was mending or mixing bread or ironing. It was tiresome, shut in the small soddie, and spring was a welcome guest. On Easter morning, accompanied by the faithful dog, who would kill a snake whenever he found one, Abbie took Mack and Margaret and little John down to the creek bank for flowers. Will had made a wagon in which to pull John, the wheels of round disks cut from a young cottonwood, and now at seven months, the baby lay in it and blinked solemn eyes at the April sky. It was an advanced spring and they found blue and yellow violets, Dutchmen's breeches, ferns, and the tiny red buds of the hawthorn.

"Smell!" said Abbie, "smell the springtime on the prairie." And Mack and Margaret stood and sniffed miniature olfactory organs.

"What makes it smell sweet?" they wanted to know.

"Because everything,—every little wild plum-blossom, every little tiny crocus and anemone and violet and every tree-bud and grass-blade is working to help make the prairie nice," Abbie told them. [And who is there to say this was not a beginners' class in philosophy?]

The day was hot, with a strong wind from the south, so that they did not stay long at the creek bed. On the way back to the house it clouded, and by the time they had reached it, the drops were falling. In the night the rain changed to snow and when the family awoke in the early morning, the storm was shrieking around the soddie with cyclonic fury. Great wet clumps of snow were being hurled against the small half-windows and snow had been driven through the cracks of the door. The wind and the snow, whirling together in their wild Bacchanalia, seemed laughing drunkenly at the tiny pigmy inmates of the tiny prairie house.

Will started to open the door to go to his stock and could scarcely shut it again against the storm's rage. In the brief interval of its half opening, huge chunks of soft snow, with a rush and roar of wind had been blown the length of the room. With the life of the stock dependeding upon him, he made another attempt to leave the house in the afternoon. He succeeded in getting to the barn, but came back discouraged, for the snow had blown through every crack and crevice.

By the third day of this holocaust of Nature's, the storm abated. Will found some of the chickens dead, and his horses and three cows had stamped so much snow under their feet that their backs were nearly to the top of the shed. There were dead prairie chickens everywhere, and the trees along the creek bank where the little family had so recently picked violets, were packed so solid as to make a snow wall.

The snows melted and the creek rose. The flowers bloomed again and summer was upon the land.

But if the previous years had been hard, that one seemed to reach the lowest point of the settlers' existence. The panic of 1873 was upon the state. The bottom of the market dropped out and prices were so low that it did not even pay to haul the scanty crop to market. When eggs were five cents a dozen and butter eight cents a pound, cattle and hogs two cents, wheat fifty cents a bushel, and corn eight, of what use to haul them all thirty or forty miles? Of what use to haul a load of corn a day's journey and bring back a load of coal which cost much more than the corn? So Will and Abbie, along with the neighbors, began burning the corn for fuel. It made a fire of intensity, a fire that crackled and held its heat as well as any coal. Sometimes, too, they used hard twisted hay. When winter came on, Will took Abbie's washboiler and removing the two front lids of the cook stove, turned the boiler upside down over the open holes, forming a sort of drum that seemed to heat the room a little better.

The crop of 1874 was the sixth crop and it seemed to give a little more promise than the previous ones. By the twentieth of July, Will had laid by all his corn. Most of his small grain was in the shocks, but one oat field of a few acres was still uncut. Standing there under the July sun, its ripened surface seemed to reflect back the yellow rays. In the afternoon Abbie went out to pick a mess of beans. The garden had come to be Abbie's care. Aside from the potato crop, to which Will attended, she looked after the entire garden. It was quite generally so,—the men bending all their energies to bigger things, the corn and wheat and the stock, with the chickens and the gardens falling to the lot of the wives. Some of the women went into the fields. Christine Reinmueller was out beside Gus many days. Will drew the line at that. "When you have to do that, we'll quit," he said.

Abbie, in her starched sunbonnet, began picking beans for supper. She could see Will and Henry Lutz working together, shocking the last of Henry's oats. To-morrow the two would work together on Will's last stand. It was nice for the men to be so neighborly.

It seemed hazy in the west. By the time she had finished the low rows, a big panful of the yellow pods in her arms, Will had come home from the Lutzes.' In the welcome shade of the house Abbie took off her bonnet, wiped her flushed, perspiring face and waited for Will to come up.

"My . . . it's a scorcher." She looked hot and tired.

In a moment of tenderness, more to be desired because of its rarity, Will picked up Abbie's hands. The slender nails were stubbed and broken,—the grime of the garden was on her tapering fingers. He lifted her hand suddenly and kissed the hollow of it. As his lips touched the calloused palms, his eyes filled with rare tears. He uttered a short swift oath, "I wish you didn't have to, Abbie-girl. It's tough for you. Some day . . . in a few years . . . we'll pull out. Weather conditions may change . . . the land will be high. . . . You can have better things . . . and your organ. That singing and painting of yours . . . maybe we can get to a teacher then. . . ."

It affected Abbie as it always did. In a moment like that it seemed the end and aim of everything . . . the family. All her dreams for herself were as nothing. In her own moment of emotion she returned, "We'll make it, Will . . . don't worry!"

For a moment they stood together looking out over the raw rolling acreage. Even as they looked, the sun darkened and the day took on a grayness. They looked for the storm, and heard it as soon as they saw it,—a great black cloud roar out of the west, with a million little hissing vibrations. Their eyes on the sky, neither moved. Then there was a cessation of the roaring, a soft thud of dropping things, and the cloud of a billion wings lay on the fields.

"Grasshoppers," they said simultaneously, incredulously.

The grasshoppers swarmed over the young waist-high corn and the pasture and the garden. By evening the long rows of sweet corn had been eaten to the plowed ground. The tender vines of the tomatoes were stripped down to the stalk. The buds of the fruit trees were gone. Part of the garden was a memory. The chickens had feasted themselves to the bursting point. Gus Reinmueller, driving up to the door, could hardly control his raring horses, so irritated were they by the bouncing, thumping pests. The farm was a squirming, greenish-gray mass of them.

All evening Will sat by the stove with his head in his hands. It was the first time he had visibly lost his grit. Abbie went over to him and ran her hand through his hair. She tried to think of something to console him. "Don't, Will. . . . There's one thing we can do. There's the string of pearls. We can always fall back on it. There must be jewelry stores in Omaha that would take it and pay well. You take the team and make the drive. . . . You can do it in three days, . . . and I'll look after things here. When Mother gave the pearls to me, she said, 'You'll ne'er starve with them' . . . and we won't, Will. We'll sell them for the children's sake."

Will threw her hands away from his hair roughly and stood up. "Hell . . . no!" He yelled it at her. "I've taken your music away from you and your painting and your teaching and some of your health. But, *by God*, . . . I won't take your mother's present to you."

He slammed the rough soddie door and went out to the barn.

Chapter 13

By the next night the stalks of field corn were skeletons, a few delicate veins of leaves left, like so many white bones bleaching on the desert of the fields. At the end of three days the oat field was stripped almost as bare as the day the plow had finished its work. The young orchard was a graveyard of hopes. Some of the small grain previously harvested had been saved, and luckily, one digging of early potatoes was in the hole in the ground in which Will always kept them. But everything else went through the crunching incisors of the horde. It was as though the little grayish-green fiends became a composite whole,—one colossal insect into whose grinding maw went all the green of the fields and the gardens, all the leaves and tender twigs of the young fruit trees, all the dreams and the hopes of the settlers.

The pests were everywhere, with nightmarish persistence, they appeared in everything. As tightly as Will kept the well covered, he drew them up in the bucket, so that he began going back to the old spring for water. Abbie caught them eating the curtains of the little half-windows and sent them to a fiery death. She was forced to dry the weekly wash around the cook stove, her one attempt to hang it in the sun ending speedily with a dozen perforations in the first billowing garment.

The garden was a total loss. They had tried to save some of the beans by putting gunny-sacks over them and weighting them down with stones from the creek bed. The grasshoppers, after eating the beans, had begun on the gunny-sacks.

"Will they eat the stones, too, Mother?" Mack wanted to know. And they could not laugh at him.

Abbie wrote a letter to her sister Mary, telling of this last hard piece of luck. Even letters were expensive luxuries so that one was made to do for the entire group of relatives back in eastern Iowa. She gave the letter to Will, who said that he would ride over to the little post office in the Lutz store as soon as he had finished caring for the stock. In an hour Will came in holding the letter by a corner. The edges of the envelope had been eaten all the way around with little neat flutings so that the two sides fell apart and the letter fluttered to the floor. The pocket of his old denim coat, where the letter had lain, was flapping down, cut on two sides by the same diabolical jaws.

What could you do? You could not fight them. You could not kill them. They were an army with an uncanny and unnatural power. Abbie looked out upon the devastation of the fields and the garden upon which they both had worked so hard. The hot wind blew over the ruins with Mephistophelean laughter. She looked up at the cloudless blue,—huge, cruel, sardonic.

"God, . . . *you* ought to help," she cried aloud. "We can't do it alone. *You* ought to help!"

All through August, Abbie went about in a dull, stupid way, depressed by the last hard luck that had descended upon them and the knowledge that her fourth child was coming. She was nervous,—cross to Will and to the children. Sometimes, in a temper, she jerked one of her little tots by the arm or spanked one angrily,—figuratively standing off and looking at her own actions in contempt. She seemed doing things she did not want to do, seeing a nervous, cross woman, who was not herself, allow her love for husband and babies to begin slipping. The song in Abbie's throat was stilled that summer and not even an echo of the melody lingered on. For the first time she was sorry about her condition, sorry and bitter. One more mouth to feed, she said to herself acridly,—she, who was a born mother. And then, in a sudden revulsion of feeling at her disloyalty to motherhood, she thought, "Oh, I don't want to feel that way about a child. I ought *not* to say that . . . I won't . . . I *never* will again."

In the letter which came in time from her sister Mary, was

the comforting word, "Well, Abbie, you ought to have married Dr. Ed Matthews. His wife was here visiting this summer and she had fine clothes,—a purple silk dress and a little lavender velvet bonnet with pansies on and the widest satin strings, and lavender silk mitts. She has a Paisley shawl, too, and a big cameo breast-pin."

Abbie let the letter fall into her lap and sat thinking of Ed Matthews in New York. Occasionally some one had written an item about him. "Ed Matthews and his bride came to visit. She is an eastern girl, and tremendous stylish." And later: "They say Ed is in a New York hospital where they have as many as fifty beds."

And now sitting there with the hot wind blowing over the stripped fields, Abbie's thoughts went back to the knoll near the Big Woods. "You're wonderful, Abbie! You're gorgeous! You coquette! I'll take you with me. You can study all you want . . . with the best teachers. . . ."

If she had known—if she could have foreseen—the drouth and the grasshoppers,—the blizzards and the winds that were never still—the hard work,—and the privations,—the song that might never be sung,—the four babies in eight years. "No. . . . No!" She pulled herself out of the dream. "No. . . . No! Don't let me think it. Don't let me *think* of thinking it. It's wicked. There's nobody but Will. It's just the crop failures and the terrible hard luck that made me think it. Those things have nothing to do with love." But even as she said it, Abbie knew that it was not true. Abbie knew that unless you are very strong, those things have something to do with love.

In an overwhelming return of affection for the children, she picked little John up and covered him with kisses, her tears on his cheeks. She drew Margaret to her and cuddled her, too. Margaret's little hand had a dingy rag around it to cover a cut, and in an ecstasy of mother-emotion, Abbie kissed the little hand, kissed the plump baby neck between the soft brown ringlets and the colorless calico dress. She went to the door and called, "Mack, come in."

"What do you want, Mother?"

"Nothing, Mack, . . . nothing but to kiss you, darling. Oh, little son, I love you so. Kiss Mother, Mack."

Mack, who was seven now and a little superior to the

demonstration of women folks, stood the ordeal with fortitude and then pulled quickly away. "I'm helping Father sort things, . . . all the nails for him, . . . the little ones, . . . and the horseshoe ones, . . . and . . ."

"That's it. That's a good boy. *Always* help Father, Mack. He's the *best* father in the world. You'll never forget it, will you, darling?"

She did not want Will to know what Mary had written, so she read the letter aloud to him, blithely skipping the tart reference to Ed Matthews.

During that summer the whole family went in the wagon along the creek to scour the thickets for wild grapes and wild plums. Abbie rode three miles on horseback to a Mrs. Tomlinson's to get some late pieplant which had miraculously escaped the scourge of the robber insects. And when Will came in one day with two huge beets which he had found when taking down a pile of boards, Abbie sent word to Henry Lutz's to come over and the two families feasted on potatoes, corn bread and sliced boiled beets.

Every one was in want. In the early fall people began going past the house. "Going home," they all reported. Many times parties of them stayed all night. They had their own quilts and would arrange their beds on the main-room floor. They were beaten, they said. One could stand a few disappointments and failures, but when everything turned against one, there was no use trying to fight.

"The land hasn't turned against us," Will would argue stubbornly. "It's the finest, blackest loam on the face of the earth. The folks that will just stick it out. . . . You'll see the climate change, . . . more rains and not so much wind . . . when the trees grow. We've got to keep at the trees. Some day this is going to be the richest state in the union . . . the most productive. I'll bet anything next year . . ."

Always "next year"! It was a mirage, thought Abbie, an apparition that vanished when one came to it. Six times now they had said, "Next year, the crops will be fine."

And so she could not throw off the blue mood that had descended upon her, a horde of worries that had come upon her even as the horde of grasshoppers had come upon the land. The thought that there was nothing to do with; that they could scarcely keep body and soul together; that she probably would never be able now to do anything with her voice; that another child was coming,—they all harassed and tormented her. All fall there was in her mind a tired disinterest over things. In spite of what he said, that surface courage which he pretended had returned to him. Abbie detected that Will, too, was morose. To her keen eye he seemed dull and stoical, underneath an assumption of cheerfulness.

Before cold weather, the old grasshoppers were gone, but first they had taken infinite pains to leave a reminder of themselves in the newly broken prairie everywhere,—holes the size of lead pencils in which they laid one to two dozen eggs in a sack. In a six-inch square of ground, Will testing their number, found a double handful of the next year's hatching. There seemed not even a hope for the following crop.

It was in November that the barrel and box came from the folks back home. Will drove up to the soddie with rattling announcement of their arrival. A letter from Grandpa Deal had been the forerunner of the donations and already Abbie knew that an old brass horn of Dennie's was among the things for Mack. She determined to slip it out without his knowledge and put it away for Christmas. They all gathered around the barrel while Will pried open the top, Mack and Margaret dancing about in an ecstasy of excitement. The first thing to be taken out was an envelope marked "For Abbie," in Grandpa Deal's handwriting. In it was twenty dollars. Abbie cried a little, tears of love and homesickness, happiness and relief, and put it away with secret thoughts of the desired organ. She sensed that Grandpa had slipped it in with his one hand the last thing, so Grandma would not see it.

There were flower seeds and sugar and beans, seed-corn and dried apples in the barrel. Mother Mackenzie had tied and sent two thick comforts. Regina Deal sent an old soiled white silk bonnet with a bead ornament and a cluster of three little pink feathers on it,—"tips," Abbie told the children they were,—and a pair of dirty white "stays" and some old white hoop-skirts. Abbie laughed until she cried at the sight of them.

"Maybe I could put the hoops over some stakes next summer and keep the setting hens in them," she suggested. She put them on over her work dress, the hoops and the stays both, and perched the dirty bonnet on her red-brown hair,

dancing about in them, the three noble tips nodding with
uncertain dignity as though, like their former owner, they had
no sense of humor. She pushed Will and Mack and Margaret
into position for a square dance and showed the children how
to "whirl your partner" and "alamand left." The four of
them pranced around in the impromptu dance, the children in
their patched dingy clothing, Will in his denim work things,
and Abbie in the foolish soiled castoffs which Regina had sent
with so little thought. The two older children laughed and
clapped their hands and shouted that they had never had so
much fun in their lives, and little John toddled in and out and
between them in an ecstasy of bubbling spirits.

It broke something in Abbie, some tight-bound band around
her heart and throat, which had not been loosed for months. She
hid the old brass horn of Dennie's in the bedroom. She put
away the precious dried apples and pop-corn, the seed-corn and
the big solid Greenings from the orchard behind Grandpa Deal's
house. She hugged the huge warm quilts as though they were
the fat pudding-bag body of Maggie Mackenzie. The bad luck
was temporary. They were young and well. The children
were all healthy youngsters. Why, how wicked she had
been! She was only twenty-seven. She mustn't let her voice
rust the way she had done this summer. In another year or so
she could have an organ and maybe even get to a music teacher.
She mustn't let youth slip away and her voice go with it. She
was ashamed of herself that she had not sung for months.

> "Oh! the Lady of the Lea,
>   Fair and young and gay was she."

Her voice rose full-throated, mellowed now with tribula-
tions and sympathy. The children clapped their hands that
Mother was singing.

> "Beautiful exceedingly,
>   The Lady of the Lea."

She replenished the fire of twisted hay and corn-cobs in the
stove with the four holes and the iron hearth in front. She
cooked cornmeal mush for supper and set the table. Several
times she sang the same verses over.

"Many a wooer sought her hand,
For she had gold and she had land,"

The teakettle sang and the children chattered happily at the window. She lighted the coal-oil lamp with the red flannel in the bowl and washed her hands in the tin basin. The prairie twilight came on. The winds died down.

"Everything at her command,
The Lady of the Lea."

Will came in from doing the chores.

"It's the nicest time of the day . . . isn't it, Will . . . the red fire of the corn . . . and the steaming teakettle . . . supper ready . . . and the children all alive and well . . . and you and I together?"

Will put his arm around her for a brief, rare moment.

"It's the nicest time of day, Abbie-girl."

Chapter 14

Yes, the coming of the barrel seemed to put something back into Abbie which had been gone temporarily,—laughter and hope, courage and faith. She began planning right away for Christmas. Mack was nearly eight, Margaret six and little John two. They were going to have the finest Christmas they had ever known. To Abbie's pleasure, Will entered into the preparations, too. He was as glad to see Abbie come to life as she was to see him throw off a little of his moroseness.

She told Gus and Christine Reinmueller their plans.

"*Ach!* Christine snorted. "So? *Gans närrich* . . . voolish."

"A hell of a Christmas we'll have," was Gus's equally enthusiastic response.

But Abbie found sympathy in Sarah Lutz,—Sarah, with her little black beady eyes and her cheerful, energetic way.

"You know, Sarah, I think every mother owes it to her children to give them happy times at Christmas. They'll remember them all their lives. I even think it will make better men and women of them."

"I think so, too, Abbie. We're going to have a cedar tree hauled up from the Platte. Henry can get you one, too."

All day long Abbie worked at the tasks that demanded attention, washing, ironing, patching, mending, baking, churning, caring for the chickens,—all with meager equipment or no equipment at all. Two wooden tubs, three heavy, clumsy flat-irons, a churn with wooden dasher, scissors, needles and thread, and a baking board with a few heavy dishes and utensils. But from them, clean clothes, sweet butter, neatly made-over suits and dresses and food that was palatable. The tapering Mackenzie fingers were calloused and burned and pricked. As tired as all these tasks left her, she would get the children to bed early and then bring out the Christmas things and begin working on them.

She got out the precious paints Mrs. Whitman had given her and worked on a picture for Will when he was away. It was a scene of the prairie with a clump of cottonwoods in the foreground. She tried to get the afterglow of the sunset but even though she worked faithfully, she could not get it. "If I only had some one to help a little," she would say. "Some day I want to take some painting lessons again. If I could just make a picture as I want to,—it would satisfy something in me."

From the barn she got clean husks and made a family of dolls for Margaret. She made the bodies, heads and limbs from the husks and braided the corn-silk for hair. A man, a lady and a baby, she made, and dressed them in corn-husk clothes. Will built a small bedstead for them. Out of one of the coats in the barrel she made Mack a new suit and con-cocted a bonnet for Margaret out of the old one Regina had sent, trimming it with a little wisp of the pink tips. With her paints, she marked off a checkerboard for Mack, and Will whittled checkers from the circumference of some small cot-tonwood branches. She cut a pattern and made a calico dog for little John, stuffing it with corn-husks, and covering it with knotted ends of carpet rags to give it a woolly appearance. She ironed out brown wrapping paper, tied the pieces with yarn and drew waggish-looking cows and horses on it for him, too.

Margaret laboriously hemmed a handkerchief for her father and Mack made him a box for his newspapers. There was a State Journal now, and as scarce as money was, Will had subscribed. "We can't drop out of touch with other parts of the country," he had said. "And we must know what the rest of the settlers are doing."

The children could talk of nothing but the approach of the wonderful day. The word "he" had only one meaning in their vocabulary,—a portly gentleman with a white beard and a sack on his back.

"Are you sure he'll come this year, Mother? Heinie Reinmueller said he wouldn't. He said his mother said so."

"Of *course* he'll come," Abbie assured the three. "Because Father and I are making things, too, to help him when he comes."

With Scotch-Irish cleverness, she could think of a dozen things to do with her meager supplies to add to the festivities. She ran tallow in tiny molds for the candles. She made a little batch of molasses candy and baked cookies in star and diamond shapes. She boiled eggs and painted faces on them and made little calico bonnets for them.

Christine was contemptuous toward the unnecessary festivities.

"For dot . . . no time I haf. You learn 'em vork . . . cows milk 'n' pigs svill . . . 'n' dey for foolishness no time haf."

"Oh, don't let us ever get like Reinmuellers," Abbie said. "We're poor. If we were any poorer we might as well lie down and give up. But we can fight to keep civilized . . . can fight to keep something before us besides the work."

On the day before Christmas the snow lay deep on the prairie and the children's greatest anxiety was whether "he" would find the little house which was half buried. Margaret, with the characteristic ingenuity of the female of the species, suggested tying a piece of bright cloth where "he" would notice it. And Mack, with the characteristic daring of the less deadly of the same, got on top of the low house via a crusty snow bank and tied one of little John's red flannel shirts to the stove-pipe.

At lamp-lighting, they all hung up their stockings, even Will and Abbie. The children were beside themselves with excitement. By their parents' stockings they put the little presents they had made for them. They danced and skipped and sang. They cupped their eyes with their hands, pressing their faces to the little half-window and looking out into the night. The gleam of the stars was reflected in the snow, and the silence of the sky was the silence of the prairie.

"I see the Star."

"So do I. Right up there."

"It looks like it was over a stable."

"Yes, sir. It looks like it was over a manger-stable."

"Now it looks like it's stopping over us."

"Yes, sir, it looks like it's stopping right over *our* house."

Wide-eyed they went to bed. The three faces in a row on the pillows, with the patchwork quilts tucked under the chins, were flushed with anticipation.

"Always keep the Christmas spirit going," Abbie told them. "Promise me, that when you get big and have homes of your own, you'll keep the Christmas spirit in your homes."

"We will," they promised in glib and solemn accord.

When at last they slept, Will brought in the little cedar tree. The morning found it trimmed with popcorn and tallow candles. And a marvelous flock of butterflies had settled upon it. Their bodies were of dried apples dipped in sugar and their antennae were pink and feathery, looking surprisingly as though they had once adorned Regina Deal's bonnet. Will had made and painted Abbie a corner what-not with four shelves, secreting it in the stable behind some straw bedding. And he had constructed a monstrous hobby-horse for the children, the body and head of cottonwood chunks, real horse's hair for mane and tail, reins and a bit in the steed's cut-out mouth. The wooden horse of Troy never looked so huge. And then the old brass horn was unwrapped.

"I'm so excited," Mack said, in solemn ecstasy. "I'm so excited . . . my legs itch."

Historians say, "The winter of 'seventy-four to 'seventy-five was a time of deep depression." But historians do not take little children into consideration. Deep depression? To three children on the prairie it was a time of glamour. There was not much to eat in the cupboard. There was little or no money in the father's flat old pocketbook. The presents were pitifully homely and meager. And all in a tiny house,—a mere shell of a house, on a new raw acreage of the wild, bleak prairie. How could a little rude cabin hold so much white magic? How could a little sod house know such enchantment? And how could a little hut like that eventually give to the midwest so many influential men and women? How, indeed? Unless, . . . unless, perchance, the star *did* stop over the house?

Chapter 15

There was a great deal of suffering among the settlers. It was extremely cold. The government issued flour and beans and some army clothes left over from war days. A supply came to the Lutz store and Will took advantage of the offer of the flour, but only after some protest of pride.

"I don't want to, Abbie,—like beggars."

"Will Deal,—from your government, after you fought to keep it going!"

In the Lutz store, one day later, Abbie met Mrs. Tomlinson from Poor Man's Hollow. She had on one of the blue army coats and a pair of men's coarse army shoes.

Word came from back home that Grandpa Deal was very sick,—the disease which had caused his arm's amputation, had broken out again.

A few weeks later in the winter, Grandpa Lutz, Henry's and Oscar's old father, died. Homesick for the neat Michigan farm and a sight of lake water, uncomplaining, gently, he died. And once more the settlers stood around an irregular hole in the ground on the Lutz knoll of land where little Dan lay.

With scarcely a fortnight's passing, a letter came from Louise Deal telling of Grandpa Deal's death, too. In a winter of intense cold, little to eat, a dubious outlook for the future, and the worry of Abbie's pregnancy, the news of kind Grandpa Deal's death seemed too much to bear.

"I sat by his bed and Ma was mending stockings over by the window where the light was," Louise wrote. Yes, Grandma

Deal would not want to be wasting any of the daylight, thought Abbie, as she read with tear-dimmed eyes. "He said, 'Sis!' . . . you know he sometimes called me that . . . 'Sis, how do you reckon it'll be, all gold and wings and harps and pearly gates? No meadows and lane roads and maple sap running and honey-locusts and young corn growing . . . and no jokes?' I told him I didn't know, and then in a little while he nodded his head over to where Ma was sitting and said, 'Sis, it'll be mighty lonesome sittin' around waitin' for her.' And when I looked at him again he was dead."

Abbie could not see the rest of the letter for the tears. She had loved Will's old father.

The winter seemed nothing but snow and cold, trouble and misery. Only the children were happy. Too young to sense the desperate straits of the family, they played joyfully through the winter and worked cheerfully at the little tasks assigned them.

It was cold and rainy through March and part of April. And then spring came. Spring on the prairie, with the teal flying out of the coarse grass, with the willow and the cottonwood and the elders over by Stove Creek bursting into green joyousness, with sweet-William and blue phlox, mousetail and wild indigo nosing up through the sod, with the odor of loam and sub-soil coming over the low rolling hills on the wings of every breeze, with the white clouds scudding low with the wind, and with hope, which springs eternal.

To Abbie the winter had seemed one nightmare of trouble and one endless toot on an old cornet. Out of the hoarse and heterogeneous collection of sounds, Mack had evolved the faint semblance of two tunes. But the noisy affair had its advantage, for when he began herding hogs on the prairie, its guttural sounds assured her that he was all right.

It was hard for Abbie to put in the garden. Nature did not mean to have a woman bend to severe tasks at such a time. Mack and Margaret did a great deal of it under her supervision. Mack, with his eight years, could hoe the rows, and Margaret, with her six, could drop and cover the seeds. Even little John, who was nearly three, wanted to "d'op 'em in," but as he had a wild and superior disregard for keeping various seeds separate, he was persuaded to make mud pies at the edge of the patch.

The Lutz store distributed government seeds and Will went hopefully to his spring planting. But first he tried hard to get rid of the young grasshoppers on his wheat acreage by laying long rows of straw across the fields into which the infant grasshoppers crawled for warmth. He then set fire to the straw and destroyed a portion in that way. With the other men of the neighborhood, he disposed of a countless number of the pests to the government for two dollars a bushel. Never was money more thankfully received.

The small grain came up with much promise. More grasshoppers hatched, small as little gray-green flies, and promptly ate it up.

In spite of the desperately hard times, Henry Lutz seemed able to buy another eighty. He paid one thousand dollars for the eighth-section, a nice acreage lying south of the young Cedartown. Incidentally, his heirs sold it many years later for twenty thousand dollars.

All the neighbors now joined the Grange, a union of farmers, which some fondly thought would better conditions. It met in the schoolhouse, where there was a great deal of talk without much result, and where the women formed an auxiliary. Because of her condition, Abbie did not join, but she helped Sarah Lutz sew the regalia,—red calico robes, a cross between a cardinal's vestments and a Mother-Hubbard, which were to be tied with white sashes. Sarah told Abbie confidentially that she was *Pomona*, and young Mrs. Oliver Johnson was *Minerva* and that Christine had been *Scylla*, but when they assigned her the name she thought they said "Silly," and had straightaway announced that even if she couldn't understand English very well, she knew when she was called names, and departed in high dudgeon.

In May, two young men stopped at the house just before dusk. They were driving six hundred sheep from the Ozark Mountains through to Cozad, which lay beyond the hundredth meridian on the edge of the country known as the Great American desert.

They were fine, upstanding fellows in their early twenties, the nephew of the editor of the Boston *Transcript*, and a chum. The uncle had just died the previous December and left the nephew five hundred dollars. With an equal amount of money the friend had joined him and formed a partnership.

Besides the sheep, their chattels seemed to consist of a wagon, three small horses, a coffee-pot and a skillet.

They made camp for the night a little to the north and east of the Deal place, taking from the wagon a collapsible corral consisting of yards and yards of muslin, one end of which they tied to the wagon wheel and then used stakes driven into the ground for temporary fence-posts around which to wrap the muslin.

After the children were in bed, the young fellows came to the house and talked with Will, but Abbie stayed in the bedroom. The next morning they went on to add their fine young courage and energy to the building of the state.

Only a few mornings later, Abbie sent Margaret out with the old dog to call Will in from the field, and told Mack to take John up to Reinmuellers. When Will came hurriedly in, he unhitched, threw a saddle on old Bird and rode over after Dr. Hornby. Sarah Lutz came riding out with the doctor in his cart and Christine came down, too. The baby was born in the afternoon.

Abbie, relaxing, was filled with that age-old gratitude that her ordeal was over. Peace enveloped her,—peace and relative ease. Her fourth child! How queer! Well, she would love it and care for it tenderly. Looking out in the other room she could see Will and the doctor, Christine and Sarah all close together. They were whispering. It seemed silent out there, —too silent,—a whispering silence. A great fright seized her, so that she raised herself up and called sharply, "Will!"

Will turned and came quickly into the bedroom.

"What's the matter, Will? I can tell there's something the matter."

Will took Abbie's hand. "It was a little son, Abbie."

" 'Was,' Will? Not . . . not . . .?"

"He didn't live, Abbie-girl."

"Oh . . . no . . . no!" She broke into wild sobbing. "Oh, God, not that. He's all right, Will. Go see if he isn't all right. My babies are always all right."

But when Will did not go and only tried to quiet her, she had to believe it. She was inconsolable. "Will, it was because I didn't want him at first."

And when he tried to reason with her, she would not listen. "I know better than any one. I'm punished. I didn't tell anybody. But I was bitter. And now I've lost my baby.'' In her whole life Abbie Deal never cried so wildly.

Sarah Lutz dressed him,—Sarah, with her black beady eyes softened with tears. And then she brought him in,—a beautifully formed child with a face like a tiny white rose. Abbie wanted him beside her, wanted to hold him.

"My baby . . . he's so cold, Will. I never had a cold baby. I want him to be warm." She did not talk rationally. "I hate death and I'm afraid of it. But I *did* want him, Will. After a while I wanted him. It was just at first." Rachel, who lives again in every grieving mother, was crying for her child and would not be comforted. And when she had worn out her hysteria and quieted, she said she wanted him to have a name. "Basil, Will,—after my father." Sarah came in and smoothed her hair, talked to her gently, and said they were going to take him over and put him by Dennie and Grandpa Lutz.

"*Ach!*" Christine came in and clucked her sympathy. "A boy, too! With the land he should help."

Abbie turned her face to the wall. Christine had no finer feelings. She lay and thought of her sister Janet and her dead baby. She could hear the faint pound, pound, of a hammer out at the barn. Every hammer stroke hit her heart. They were going to take the baby over to the Lutz burial knoll. There was no one there but Dannie and Grandpa Lutz. Dannie . . . Grandpa Lutz . . . and now little Basil Deal . . . three to make a cemetery. In a new country you had to make homes and roads and wells and schools . . . and you had to make a cemetery. You couldn't get around it . . . you had to make a cemetery, too.

She lay there and thought of the knoll and the prairie grass and the low picket fence against which the tumble-weeds piled . . . where the blackbirds wheeled and the sun beat down and the wind blew. She hated the barrenness of it. If she could put him in a shady place it wouldn't be quite so hard. But to put him in the sun and the coarse grass and the wind! She and Sarah would go over and plant some trees some day. She heard the rattle of the lumber-wagon and raised herself up to look through the little half-window set in the sod. She could see Will and Sarah in the wagon. Will was driving, and Sarah had a little wooden box across her lap. When the big lumber-wagon rattled away from the house, Abbie lay back on her pillow. For a long time she could hear the sound of the lumber-wagon rattling over the prairie.

Chapter 16

It was several weeks before Abbie could get around again to do all her work. Christine or Sarah came over and helped a little each day. Service finds its greatest opportunity and its least begrudged hours of labor among neighbors in a new community through which lines have not been drawn and into which class has not yet come.

Abbie could not get over the loss of her little son. Always she saw him in shadowy outline among the others. All her life she was to say, "Now he would be seven," "To-day he would be twelve," "He could have voted to-day for the first time." Yes, Abbie Deal was a born mother,—one of those women who love the touch of baby flesh, who cuddle little children to them, who, when their own babies have grown, catch up some other woman's child to fondle.

On the day in June in which Abbie did her first full day's work, the grasshoppers lifted their wings and flew to other fields,—as complete and unified a departure as their coming had been.

There was no small grain that summer, but a half-hearted corn crop seemed on the way. Settlers by the score were returning east. Scarcely a day passed which did not see some forlorn group go by the house. Many of the covered wagons carried statements painted on their wagons, which would have been humorous if they had not been so tragic. "Going back to Pa and Ma," was one. Another held a huge caricature of a grasshopper strangling a man with its forelegs and antennae, and the laconic words, "He wins."

Abbie, standing at the door and watching one of these bedraggled-looking outfits pass, said bitterly to Will, "When do you think our time is coming? Look at the clouds, Will. Even the clouds seem always going east."

Will did not answer. He turned on his heel and went down to the straw-covered dug-out which served as a barn. Watching him go, in his faded blue shirt and overalls with their many patchings, and his dingy old hat, Abbie called to her mind the fine figure he had made in his wedding suit,—fine enough to draw the attention of any exacting young woman. Ten years ago! And the minister at home had said you could do anything with your life. But that was not so. Life did things to you. Ten years! Small wonder that love would break under circumstances like these. Standing there in the soddie door, she seemed two personalities. One argued bitterly that it was impossible for love to keep going when there was no hope for the future, suggested that there was no use trying to keep it going. The other said sternly that marriage was not the fulfillment of a passion,—marriage was the fulfillment of love. And love was sometimes pleasure and sometimes duty.

"You traitor," she said suddenly to herself. "You Judas! As though hard luck could kill my love for Will! Will's not to blame. It's a fine love that a little bad luck can smother! It can't touch it . . . it can't. Love is the light that you see by. It's all in the world we've got to light our way, and it takes both of us to keep it bright. And I'm not doing my share . . . I'm not. I'm glum and sad and discouraged. And I'm not going to be any more. There are only two things that can help us,—and that's our courage and our love. From this very minute on I'm going to try to cheer Will up more. I'm through being downhearted."

She turned to the children. They were all around the table looking at a little picture Margaret had drawn. Margaret was always drawing. Abbie ran to them, closed warm maternal arms around all three, and bumped them together in a return of girlish spirits, so that they laughed at her unusual playfulness, their faces sparkling because Mother was full of fun. How readily they responded to all her moods. And how careful she must be with those childish impressions.

"You shall wear them, Margaret," she kissed her little daughter, "you shall wear them yet."

"Wear what, Mother?"

"The pearls."

"What are pearls, Mother?"

"Wait . . . I'll show you."

She got it from under the bed,—the old calf-skin box, and the children gathered close with excited anticipation. She took the pearls out and ran them through her fingers.

"Oh, Mother . . . the pretty beads!" Margaret's gray eyes glowed.

"Shucks, I'd rather have a watch," from the masculine Mack. Little John was not even interested.

Abbie laughed and held them up, their creamy luster inappropriate against her work-worn hand. She put them around Margaret's little sunburned neck, and they hung down over the dingy gray calico dress with incongruous comparison.

"You shall wear them, darling. Some day you shall. We're going to make it come true. We've *got* to make it come true." She caught Margaret to her. "It takes faith and courage and love and prayer and work and a little singing to keep up your spirits, but we're going to do it."

In September, Mack and Margaret started to school to a little new one-roomed frame building which some one already had christened the Woodpecker School. Little Emma Lutz started, too, and two more of the Reinmueller boys,—Christine's ideal being that it would be a good thing for them to know how to write their names, at least, and figure up bushels. On good days the children trudged the long grassy way, and on bad days, Will stopped his work long enough to take them in the wagon. Abbie shed copious tears the first morning they started, and then laughed at her own inconsistency.

"I wanted them to have a school closer than Sodom to go to, and then I cry when they do have," she said to Will. But Will said he knew how she felt. Will was always so understanding, Abbie thought gratefully.

That winter of '76 and '77 was another one of great hardship, but like many things in life, it had its pleasant side. A reading circle was formed and met at Woodpecker School every Friday night. Its members wore ribbon badges upon which Sarah Lutz and Abbie had printed the mysterious letters "S.C.L.R.C.," which, when the mystery was eliminated, were discovered to stand for the title of Stove Creek Precinct Literary Reading Circle. The membership was divided, like all Gaul, into three parts, and if there were not Belgians, Helvetians and Germans who fought and bled, at least, the "Reds," the "Blues," and the "Yellows" met in forensic frays. On one Friday night the "Reds" performed, the next two Fridays the "Blues" and "Yellows" respectively, and on the fourth Friday night a big contest was staged, in which the star members of the various colors mingled in one grand rainbow spectrum, with people imported from outside the precinct sitting in judgment upon the efforts. That winter the schooner *Hesperus* was wrecked, little Paul Dombey died, Hamlet met his father's ghost and the Raven quothed more times than there were meetings,—new "pieces" being at a premium, as they were.

Whole families came, ensconced on straw in the bottom of wagon-boxes which had been put upon bob-sleds. Every one brought heated soap-stones or hot flat-irons, as more than one load came from twenty miles away. The Henry Lutzes brought their reed-organ in the sleigh each time, so there was always music. Abbie was put on for a group of songs whenever the "Blues" performed, and always led the chorus singing. "Three Blind Mice" and "Scotland's Burning" were the favorite rounds. As for the favorite choruses, while great partiality was shown toward "Juanita," "Annie Laurie" and "Revive Us Again," for sheer volume there was nothing like "Pull For the Shore" to open the throttle. Young blades who could not carry a tune were filled with an irresistible impulse to sing whenever the life-line was brought out, and when the sailors began to make more rapid progress toward the lighthouse, they would grab oars, as it were, open their mouths and bellow like young steers.

In September of 1877, Abbie gave birth to a girl. The high bleating cries of the child were music to the mother who could never erase from her mind the misery of that whispering silence of two years before. They named the little girl Isabelle. "Maybe *she'll* be the lovely lady," Abbie thought as she ran her fingers through the tiny moist ringlets of reddish-brown hair.

The first Sunday Abbie could get out, Will hitched up the horses to the lumber-wagon, and they drove to the dedication of the new frame church near the Lutz store. Henry Lutz had donated the land, and a dollar collected here and another one there, had bought the lumber which was hauled from Nebraska City. All the men of the community for miles around had given their time for the labor, and now a little unpainted church stood at the four corners.

It had been nine years now since the Deal and Lutz and Reinmueller wagons had first crawled across the prairie. A few fences had appeared, and the old buffalo trail had begun to take upon itself the semblance of a roadway. Tracks were plainly visible, worn by the feet of a thousand oxen and horses and the wide iron rims of the dingy prairie schooners. Between the trails the grass still flaunted, and the graceful goldenrod nodded its plumed head, as a queen bows when her subjects pass by. Sweet William and blue phlox, mouse-tail and wild indigo crowded the grass of the roadway, and when the tiny primrose was gone, yellow and white mustard elbowed their way in to take the place.

The cottonwoods had shot up with unbelievable growth. The leaves, with their peculiar double motion, seemed always twinkling, always dancing. The silhouettes of the grayish-green clumps against the prairie sky were Abbie's poetry and her paintings, her sermons and her songs.

Cedartown now had its church and its school, its store and blacksmith shop, and six houses assembled in the same vicinity. And it had its cemetery, for Henry Lutz had given the community the knoll where Dannie lay. There were seven mounds inside the picket fence where herding stock could not trample. Yes, in a new country you have to make a cemetery.

Crops were no better. They were put in each year with hope, and they came up with promise. But the dry, fluffy clouds scudded high across the blue sky without moisture, or the hot winds blew, and the settlers would harvest a scant half-crop. In some way, Will and Abbie held body and soul together. In some way, the children seemed to get enough to eat and to thrive and grow.

In the fall of '79 a man with a violin case stopped at the house and asked if he could have supper. He had been drinking, and Will, contrary to his usual hospitable manner, talked with him for some time before he decided to invite him to stay.

After the meal the guest took out the violin and played for the family. The music seemed to steady him, for when he drew the bow across the strings all the wild sweet bird songs of the forest came from them. To Abbie, with her deep-worn love of music, it was enchantment.

"Can you, ..." she asked, when he had finished, "can you play a song called 'The Lady of the Lea' . . .?"

For answer, he drew the bow again and the melody came lightly, delicately, hauntingly. Abbie had not sung it for four or five years, but now she threw back her head and took the air to the violin's accompaniment.

> *"Oh, the Lady of the Lea,*
> *Fair and young and gay was she,*
> *Beautiful exceedingly,*
> *The Lady of the Lea."*

In the sod house with its cook-stove and the turned-over boiler and the burning twisted hay, with its crude what-not and its sod bed, its store-box book-shelves and its burlap floor covering, she put into her voice all the longing of her heart, all the vague hopes for the best that life could give her children.

> *"For she had gold and she had land,*
> *Everything at her command,*
> *The Lady of the Lea."*

It was as though, through sheer force of will, she was trying to make all the desire for her children's future come true,—all her dreams for them turn to realities.

> *"Dreaming visions longingly,*
> *The Lady of the Lea."*

"You have a good voice," the stranger said soberly. "You ought to do something with it."

"There are lots of things one *ought* to do," Abbie replied, —and looked over at Will to see whether he had detected the bitterness which she had not been able to keep out of her reply.

The man put his violin carefully, tenderly, into the case. "It's a Stradivarius," he said. "A man in Omaha offered me six hundred dollars for it."

Will looked up in surprise. "Offered you six hundred dollars . . . for a fiddle?" It seemed a fortune. "And you mean you wouldn't sell it?"

"No," the man said simply. "I couldn't. Thank you very much for the supper." And he went, a little unsteadily, out of the door.

Abbie walked over to the small-paned half-windows set in the sod, and looked out at the gray twilight coming across the prairie. The winds that were never still blew past the house in their unending flight.

How queer people were. All the folks in the new country were hoarding things, hanging on to old heirlooms. They became their symbols of refinement and culture. Sarah Lutz had a painting that drew your eyes to it the minute you opened the door. Oscar Lutz's wife had a pink quilted bedspread that she kept rolled up in newspapers. Even Christine Reinmueller had a bright blue vase with magenta-colored roses on it, standing up on top of the cupboard. They stood for something besides the land and the corn and the cattle. They must hang onto them, never lose them out of their lives, for if lost, everything was lost. She must hang onto the pearls and everything they stood for; Sarah must keep her painting; Martha Lutz, her bedspread; Christine, her blue vase. Else what was there in the future for the children?

"No," Abbie said aloud at the soddie window. "No, he couldn't sell it."

For some time she stood there, watching the half-intoxicated man go east across the prairie.

Chapter 17

The snow began in October that year and did not leave until the last of March. Wherever there were fences, the drifts piled high and obliterated them, so that one would not have known any had been built,—Nature's little joke, as though she were laughing at the settlers for their pains.

The children's attendance at school was broken constantly by severe snowstorms, so that Abbie again did much of the teaching herself. She often searched her mind for new ideas, trying to think what more she could do for the children. Time was slipping away and conditions were not better. Even if she must face the hard fact that she could never do anything more for herself, the children must have some of the best things of life. Will was working day and night, making an old man of himself before his time. *She* must do more for the children some way. She must not let them grow up without a taste for good things. They ought to know more about music and have more reading material and because they were not getting them, in some way she must instill in them a *desire* to have them. They must never be satisfied with things as they were. Even if she and Will were to live in a soddie all their lives, cut off from those things, the children must want to have them. If the desire were deep enough, they would find a way to seek them out as they grew older.

She began getting down the Shakespeare plays for a while each evening, and requiring Mack and Margaret to learn a passage or two. Over and over she made them repeat:

> *"The quality of mercy is not strained*
> *It droppeth as the gentle rain from heaven*
> *Upon the place beneath."*

Or, perhaps:

> *"There's a divinity that shapes our ends,*
> *Rough-hew them how we will."*

Mack protested. "Aw, shucks, I don't see any sense to them."

"It's for your own good, Mack," she would say. "Some day when you're older, the meaning will all come to you. And you'll be glad you've learned so much of them."

But Mack was more interested in his old brass horn. There was a six-piece band over at Cedartown now, and that spring one often heard the far-away blare of the three brass instruments, the toot of the fife and the rumble of the two snare drums. The organization was preparing for the first Fourth of July celebration in the community and patriotic airs were as much in evidence as the spring winds. Mack, herding hogs, would sit at the western border of his father's land and windily blow out the same tune which the band was practicing. As he was usually two notes behind the others, his part in the proceedings sounded like an echo. It began to bother the legitimate performers, so that, more from sheer self-defense than enthusiastic desire, they invited him to join them. Mack's round freckled face beamed at the invitation as one receiving a congressional medal.

All masculine hands donated work that spring toward the building of a small frame G. A. R. hall. It was completed in time for the Fourth of July celebration and dedicated with much oratory and a baked bean supper. Sarah and Martha Lutz and Abbie had sewed yards and yards of unbleached muslin together to form the top of a bowery, over which were placed branches cut from the trees at the creek-bend and under which all the residenters within a twenty-mile radius danced.

By 1880 the Deal land was all fenced. The fence was a symbol,—man's challenge to the raw west. Every fence post was a sign post. More plainly than flaunting boards, they said, "We have enclosed a portion of the old prairie. We hold between our wooden bodies the emblem of the progressive pioneer,—barbed wire. We are the dividing line. We keep the wild out and the domesticated within." The road, too, which followed the old buffalo trail had been surveyed and straightened. Man's system had improved upon the sinuously winding vagaries of the old buffalo, and the road, although still grass-grown, ran straight west past the house. The development of the road is the evolution of the various stages of civilization.

But though man could fence the prairie and direct the way of the road, he could not control the storm. "This far shalt thou go and no farther," the God of the settlers seemed to say. Snows, droughts, blizzards, dust storms, rains, hot winds and the little pigmy people,—He held them all in the hollow of His hand.

On the seventeenth of April, the Deal family drove in the lumber wagon across the prairie to attend the funeral service for a distant neighbor. The day was warm and windy and disagreeable. Little miniature whirlwinds of dust spiraled themselves ahead of the team and the dry particles of dirt blew back in their faces. As they rode, the wind grew in volume and the dust clouds thickened with the rising of the wind. Before the fury of its force great sheets of top-soil from the newly plowed fields were lifted into the air and thrown with violence over the land. When the family reached the schoolhouse, they found their neighbors sitting there with dirt-blackened faces, almost unrecognizable. The room was dense with dust-clouds, the little building shivering in the onslaught of dirt. At one blast of wind more severe than others, the minister paused in the midst of the funeral eulogy and said, "There are times when it is wiser to think of the living than to honor our loved dead. I think it wiser that we disperse at once and drive to the cemetery."

Will and Abbie thought they could not get home through the terrific storm. It was like swimming the waves of a dirty sea. Abbie held Isabelle closely, and Mack and Margaret kept John's hands in their own. In fear of colliding with some one, Will did not drive the horses off a walk. Slowly they crawled over the prairie, through the dense dust clouds, with only occasional moments of the lifting of the dirt, in which Will, watching for the road, would guide the blinded team back into the trail. The storm was like a blizzard in its fury,—a black blizzard, with grit and dust for snow, and with field dirt for the drifts through which they drove. Eyes and ears were full of the gritty earth particles, and at times it seemed that they would suffocate. Then Will would stop the team for a rest, before plunging again into the black whirlpool of dust.

At home again, Abbie thought she could not endure the sight that met her eyes. Over the burlap floor-covering lay a soft inch-thick carpet of dirt. Over the curtains and the beds lay the same grimy substance. It floated on the waterpail and in the milk in the cupboard. There was nothing in the house in condition to eat and nothing that could be worn without washing. And so, once more, the young pioneer mother bent to the task of fighting the elements, to help make a home on the prairie.

Surprisingly, that year, crops were good. There was an indication of better times to come. Prices went up. Will and Abbie began talking and planning about the new house. No, that is not quite true,—*Abbie* began talking and planning about the new house. It is the woman's prerogative. Mack was thirteen now, Margaret eleven, John eight, and Isabelle three. They were getting too old to be packed in like little chickens in a coop, Abbie said. Every moment that was free from the ever-present hard work, she sat with pencil and paper and drew plans for a house.

"Even if it's just a few rooms at first," she would say to Will, "they'll be nice, and we'll plan it so they can be added to as time goes on. Can you think of anything grander, Will, than a sitting-room, all with clean, new, white plaster, and a kitchen that's built to be *handy*, and two upstairs bedrooms for the older children?"

"I'd like to do it for you, Abbie-girl. Maybe we can, if I do a lot of the work myself."

That summer they stopped at the J. Sterling Morton's as they had often done, on their way to Nebraska City, and the visit inspired them both to greater activity in making a better home. The Morton house seemed the last word in grandeur with its bay windows and real shingled roof, its fancy wallpaper and figured carpet, its tidies on the backs of all the chairs and splashers behind the wash-bowl and pitchers.

That fall and early winter, remarkable weather prevailed. It was unusually warm. Migrating songsters stayed on,—the robins and the bluebirds, the phœbes and the red birds. Even an occasional meadow-lark gave its June call in that wonderful Indian summer. There was in the air that haze which is found nowhere but in the midwest, and at no time but late fall when winter loiters on its way,—that glamorous haze which is not air, nor sunshine, nor smoke, but a little of all three, —air from over the wild, free prairies, smoke from a thousand burning weed-bends and brush fires, and sunshine filtered through the sifting, shifting smoke and air. There was bronze on the clumps of oaks along Stove Creek, red on the maples, yellow on the cottonwoods, green in the late pastures, white clouds dipping low, and over all, that haze, which is not smoke, nor air, nor sunshine, but a little of all three.

In the last half of December the spell broke. The winds blew over the prairie. Tumble-weeds from far out on the open, rushing headlong before their terrific onslaught, piled up against the fences and the little buildings. The leaves on the clumps of trees by the creek blew into nowhere. The pickets around the little cemetery caught and held a brown drift of leaves and tumble-weeds. The birds scurried before the wind. The snows came.

By Christmas the snow was fifteen inches deep on the level, and crusted over,—a delicate shimmering steel, which held up men and the lighter animals on its surface. Will could not get to town with his team, but would walk over to the store with a sack on his back. Snow-drifts were ten and fifteen feet deep. Days were bright, sunshiny and zero at noontime. Nights were clear, white-lighted, and twenty-two below.

All winter the deep snows held. On ranches farther west thousands of cattle died. The spring found many of the ranchers ruined. The snows melted and the streams ran high. Stove Creek came half way up the pasture, and departing, left behind the slag of the creek-bed.

When the weather settled, the Deals started the new house. And Abbie Deal thought heaven could not hold more joy than the planning of those five rooms. Will hauled stone from Louisville and pine and cottonwood lumber from Nebraska City. And one day when there was a sick cow and he could not leave, Abbie went alone for the lumber. Old Asy Drumm came with his hammer and his saw and his plug of tobacco, and watching him labor, one would have thought there was some invisible mechanical connection between his jaws and the other tools, so harmoniously did they work.

"We'll have the sitting-room there and the kitchen here," Abbie told Asy. And old Asy, with few comments but much tobacco chewing, placed the sitting-room there and the kitchen here. The result was weatherproof and sturdy, but only in the light of later years was it proven artless. Only to other than the eyes of Abbie Deal did it ever appear devoid of artistry. To Abbie it was always a thing of architectural beauty, for it was conceived from love and desire in the days of her youth.

There were three rooms downstairs,—a sitting-room, a kitchen, and a bedroom for Will, Abbie and little Isabelle. Up the uncarpeted pine stairs was a room for Margaret, and one for Mack and John.

"I've planned it so we can build on a room later right to the front," Abbie would say. "Then, some day we can cut double doors from the sitting-room into a new parlor."

The cedar trees, which Abbie had set out years before, had not lived through the droughts. So now, they put out a new group, nine on each side of a potential path leading up to the front of the house. Lombardy poplars in a long row were set at right angles to the main road, following the track to the barn which Will's wagon had worn in the thirteen years. "It'll make a nice shady lane road," Abbie would plan, "and some day we'll have the white picket-fence." Yes, the real home was beginning to shape itself.

In the middle of the summer they moved into the half-finished house. They scarcely knew what to do with all the space. They could not quite get used to the fact that the family of six could spread itself out all over five rooms. After the old two-roomed soddie, the simple, plain house seemed a palace. It represented a big move forward. They were about to see daylight. After thirteen years they were actually beginning to witness results. Trees were commencing to give shade. Orchards were beginning to bear. Better crops were being harvested and high prices given. To Abbie it seemed that for the first time they were really going to live.

The Deal family was representative of other families, its condition indicative of state conditions. The western half of the state began to be settled. The old range cattle ranches were practically finished. The "grain farmer" was moving in. Wagons again passed the Deal home, going west this time. Prairie schooners once more crawled over the old buffalo trail, pushing on now to the grassy valleys which lay between the sand hills or to the fertile plains beyond.

Chapter 18

There were good crops again the next year. No longer did the dry, fluffy clouds scud high across the blue. They gathered and fell in a benediction of rains. And there were no hot winds. It put courage and high hopes into every one. A great relief was in Abbie's mind. There seemed something to live for, something ahead for the family, at last.

Abbie had her house-yard fence now, so that the chickens could not molest her flowers. Sea-blue larkspur and blood-red hollyhocks flaunted their colors against the dazzling white of the pickets. Flowers in the yard! No one but a rancher's wife, who had lived in a soddie and up to whose door had come the pigs and the calves and the chickens, could realize what it meant to have a fenced house-yard with flowers.

Life was crowded with hard work for Abbie, but it was also full of compensations. There were the children, well, capable, bright.

Mack at fifteen was big, overgrown, with a round, freckled face that reminded Abbie somehow of her mother's fat, placid one. Mack made friends everywhere. He seemed to have that knack of fitting in with every one. "It may stand him in good stead some time," Abbie would say to Will. He lived the life of the typical farm boy who had to work by the side of his father. With two old coats, a cap, a muffler and overalls tucked into knee boots, he froze in the winter hauling wood or caring for the stock. With a hickory shirt, home-made pants, galluses and a flappy straw hat, he roasted in the summer at the plowing or haying.

Margaret, thirteen, was always drawing. Her sleek dark braids and gray eyes were bent above paper and pencil whenever she had leisure time. The cottonwoods and the cedars, a bit of path between the elderberry bushes, a spray of graceful goldenrod,—she was always trying to get these down on paper.

John, ten now, gave evidence of being a replica of his father, quiet, serious, uncomplaining, reminding Abbie of Will when he was a boy. Isabelle gave promise of becoming the family beauty, for although only seven, she was attractive with her reddish-brown curls, her brown eyes and her fair skin,—and always singing at her play in a clear childish voice. "My little 'lovely lady,'" Abbie used to say to herself. "How glad I am I named her Isabelle."

It had been thirteen years since Abbie and Will had followed the trail behind old Red and Baldy, and Abbie had not been back home.

"You can come back to visit whenever you want to, I promise you that, Abbie," Will had said. And she had not gone back once. But she did not blame Will. He had been helpless to keep that promise. And now this summer he said that she must go. All the plans were made, with a new brown cashmere dress in the process of construction. Abbie sang at her work, that after all these years she was to go back home and see her mother and Belle, Janet and Mary and the boys.

And then, Mack did not feel well. Dr. Hornby came and after some time decided it was to be a run of fever,—typhoid. Abbie put away the unfinished dress and hung over Mack's bed for weeks. He pulled through, but by the time he was strong enough to be up, the fall had come and the rains, so that the roads to Lincoln and Nebraska City were impassable, and Abbie's plan for a trip back home had gone into nothing.

It was only a few weeks later that Will came in from putting up the team after a trip to Weeping Water and said: "Abbie, you can get out your old paints. There's a woman in Weeping Water just come from some place back east and they say she's a real artist. They say she'll take some pupils and I told 'em my wife was always wanting to try her hand . . ."

Abbie was already on her way to the calf-skin box under the bed, with Margaret close behind her. When she had come out with the chest and opened it, Margaret was still at her elbow, her gray eyes wide with anticipation.

"Oh, Mother,—I didn't know you had any paints now. You just said you *used* to . . . Oh, Mother, *why* did you never tell me?"

"Why did you want to know?"

The young girl's eyes were bright gray lights. "Oh, Mother . . . I want to use them . . . I want to go and see that woman . . . Oh, Mother . . . *something* in me . . ."

Will was cross. "That'll do, Margaret. You don't understand. Before you were born, when your mother came out here, she wanted to . . ."

"Will," said Abbie sternly, "hush! Of *course* you may try them, Margaret. And we'll take you over to Weeping Water some time to see the artist."

When Abbie left the room, Margaret did not even look up. She was sorting the tubes in the little box, touching them lovingly as one would touch jewels.

When Mack was seventeen, he went to Omaha with his father and came back changed. He was through with farm life and he didn't care who knew it. Will said he'd better settle down and get to work and Mack said no, he wanted to get a job in Omaha. Will said it was a boy's fool notion and Mack said it was nothing of the kind, that he was almost eighteen and he knew what he wanted. Never did Abbie feel so helpless to handle a situation, so uncertain what to say or do.

"He doesn't want to sweat," Will told her with sarcasm. "He wants to wear a white collar."

"What do you want to do up there?" Abbie was trying to keep the conversation peaceful.

"Oh, I don't know just *what*. Get in somewhere and work up."

"Get in *somewhere* . . . but *where* . . . and what?" Will had no patience with the wild scheme.

"Anything that's where there's business and a big town . . . anything but the farm."

And Will had said that the Deals had always been for the land.

Abbie stood between them for days. "Oh, Will, don't you see? The farm is distasteful to Mack."

"A farm has been good enough for smarter men than Mack."

"We don't all want to do the same thing, and Will, you said you couldn't do anything just working for your father. You've always been so understanding. Then try to understand Mack."

Abbie talked and prayed. "Oh, God, it's such little things we need help in,—such every day affairs." She saw Will's disappointment and she saw Mack's ambitions. Torn between the two, she could only smooth matters over for both.

"Let him go, then," Will said suddenly, as one who could no longer hold to his point. "But I wish to God, Margaret and Isabelle had been boys. Maybe we could get something done around here then." He slammed the kitchen door and went down to the barn. Abbie, fighting back the tears, told herself that he didn't mean it.

By fall Mack had a job in an Omaha bank. Henry Lutz knew one of the officers well, and it was through him that Mack landed the work which consisted in part of sweeping and dusting, but which "beat plowing corn all to pieces," according to the wielder of the broom and duster.

Abbie had thought she could not stand it to see Mack leave home. All day long she had sewed shirts and mended socks for him,—and all night she had stared into the dark with the worry of her boy going to the city. But with the arrival of his letters, some of her anxiety vanished. When at Christmas time he came home to spend the day, he was full of "bank talk." One would have gathered from his conversation that he was at least on the board of directors.

In the spring of '85, the day which had been set aside by the various governors for planting trees was legalized as a holiday,—and J. Sterling Morton had given Arbor Day to Nebraska, which, in turn, was eventually to give it to the other states. That summer Abbie again planned the delayed trip back home. Before she was ready word was noised about that an academy was to open in Weeping Water in the fall. It was to have a full three-year academic course preparing students for college, with special attention to the languages.

"For what anybody two vays vant to talk . . .?" Christine asked.

"I felt like telling her no one could object if *she* would

stick to one way," Abbie told Will. Christine's language was
no better than when she had first arrived in the prairie schooner.
Quite often she used both the German and the English words
in the same sentence.

Emma Lutz, Margaret's chum, and a year younger, was
going to the academy. Henry and Sarah drove over to Weeping Water in their high-topped buggy with the natural-colored
maple wheels and a red tassel on the whip, to get a place for
Emma to board.

Abbie could think of nothing else when she heard it. An
academy! Margaret ought to go,—Margaret, at sixteen, with
her braids of soft dark hair, her big gray eyes, her gentle
manner, and her love of painting. She ought to have more
schooling, to meet more young people. Several times that
summer Emil Reinmueller had come over to take her to
neighborhood socials. It worried Abbie a little. Emil was
nineteen, a blond young giant, stolid, crude, virile. What
if . . .? "Thou art mated to a clown and the grossness of his
nature will have weight to drag thee down," Abbie had read
from Tennyson's *Locksley Hall*. Emil was no mate for Margaret with her love of the niceties of life. What could a mother
do? What had *her* mother done? Nothing. "I married the man
I wanted," Abbie thought. What if Margaret, with her high
ideals and her painting talent—what if she should suddenly
turn and say, "Mother, I'm going to marry Emil." What
could one do? The worry of it was constantly with Abbie.

She began trying to plan how she could send Margaret to
the academy with little expense. The money for the trip back
home would pay the first tuition. Will did not like the idea.
"You've planned this trip for years. You ought not to give it
up for her. And she's just where she can really help you,
now, at home." He argued, "You've got yourself to think
about."

"Oh, no, I haven't," Abbie said quickly, "I've got the
children to think about."

He gave in, a little grudgingly. If Abbie thought she could
manage— And Abbie knew she *must* manage.

She took the team and drove the ten miles to Weeping
Water. When she came back, she had a place in the minister's
family for Margaret to work for her board, and a dress pattern
of red and gray plaid for best. It was all they could afford

now, but on the way home Abbie mentally made over Margaret's old dress and one of her own, trimmed a hat, and relined a winter coat.

In the last half of the summer they tied two quilts, as Margaret had to furnish her own bedding. They made over the clothes in accordance with Abbie's previous brain convolutions, mended cotton stockings, ironed out hair ribbons, made a work-apron out of flour-sacking, and packed and repacked the small trunk. Abbie could not think how the home would be without Margaret. Quiet, gentle, fun-loving, ready to help, Margaret had always been at her right hand.

Will was to take Margaret and Emma in the lumber-wagon, so the trunks could go with them. Emma had several new dresses and a dolman,—the latest thing in wraps. It was made of black watered silk, waist length in the back and to the bottom of the skirt in front, with cape-like appendages for sleeves, and rows of braid, cord, beads and buttons rambling nonchalantly all over the whole structure. Added to this grandeur was a new gold watch on a long chain which went twice around her neck and eventually came to rest in a pocket sewed on her bosom, the pocket constructed of lace so that the gold of the watch would shine through. Henry Lutz was very proud of his purchase. "There's a whole horse around Emma's neck," he would announce with complacence. It sounded rather startling at first hearing, until one realized he meant no acrobatic feat, but that the price of a horse had gone into the chain.

Will went over to town after Emma and her trunk first, and then the two came back to the farm for Margaret, who had been ready for an hour.

"You're sure you'll get along, Mother?"

"Why, of course I'll get along." Abbie was outwardly calm and confident, while all the time there was that queer sensation of a wind rushing by,—a wind she could not stop,— Time going by which she could not stay. Oh, stop the clock hands! Stop Time for a minute until she could think whether it was right for Margaret to go away and leave her.

"Good-by, dear!" Oh, stop the clock hands!

Will was calling. "Trunk's in. All ready in there?" Stop Time for a while,—until she could think—!

"Oh, Mother, do you think I *ought* to go?"

"Of *course* you ought to go." Head up, Abbie was smiling. "Good-by, then . . .!"

They were down the lane road now, past the Lombardy poplars. Now they had turned east onto the main road. Margaret was dividing her handkerchief between her eyes and waving. Abbie waved and smiled,—waved and smiled,—as long as they were in sight. Then she turned and ran blindly into her bedroom and shut the door. And, whether she has driven away in a lumber-wagon or a limousine, the mother whose daughter has left her for the first time, will understand why Abbie Deal ran blindly into her bedroom and shut the door.

Chapter 19

That fall, Dr. Hornby, Henry Lutz and Will Deal went up to Omaha to interview the powers that were, in regard to the railroad coming through Cedartown instead of farther to the north as the plans seemed to be. Later the Superintendent came down and was driven through the farming section by Henry Lutz. In consequence, Cedartown drew the branch line, and with many an expression of glee, figuratively made faces at the Weeping Water delegation which had worked against the southern route.

Margaret's school year was a wonderful experience. There were thirty tuition pupils, about half from the town of Weeping Water and half from farm homes. The minister, in whose family Margaret stayed, had a nephew who was studying to be a doctor, and who had come to visit his uncle. "His name is Fred Baker and I wish you could know him, Mother," Margaret reported. "You never in your *life* saw such a fine young man."

Abbie wondered.

In July of '86, the railroad was finished through to Lincoln. And now, Cedartown would no longer sit out on the prairie by herself. No longer would twenty-three miles of snow drifts or deep ruts of mud lie between her and the capital city. Cedartown residents held their heads a little higher, spoke largely of "train-time" and "making connections for Omaha." Already the stones were in place for the foundation of the station. A train each way every day, mail in a sack being thrown carelessly out of a baggage-car instead of from a pony's back, a telegraph machine clicking noisily in a three-roomed station. What more metropolitan atmosphere could one desire?

The day that the first train came through was a gala one. Word had been wafted about by some occult means that any one who wanted to do so could ride to the end of the line free of charge. The entire Cedartown population, including two puppies and a cat, was on hand to pile hilariously into the box-cars and ride to the end of the road. Old Asy Drumm took his hammer and his saw and his tobacco, and drove over to the track with the Deals, as he had just finished building another room to the rear of the house. Upon their return from the free railroad trip, Abbie and Margaret began painting the pine woodwork in the new kitchen. Margaret, since her year in the academy, was a little fussy about the way things looked.

Abbie's plans for going back home that summer had gone into nothing on account of the new kitchen and the fact that she realized more and more that, because Isabelle was the musical one of the family, she must have an organ.

The Lutzes were getting Emma a fine new piano, so Will bought their second-hand reed-organ. On Isabelle's ninth birthday he brought it home in the lumber-wagon. Isabelle was beside herself with excitement. Her little legs pumped furiously up and down to get air into the creature's cloth lungs and her little, slender, tapering fingers ran nimbly over the keys.

Abbie, herself, sat down and tried to pick out a few chords of an old song, but her fingers were stiff and clumsy.

"By George, you're the one that ought to take lessons," Will said suddenly, "the way you always wanted . . ."

"No . . ." Abbie got up from the whirling carpet-covered stool. "No." Her lips trembled a little so that she did not look up. "At forty it's too late."

In the spring of '87 the community was presented with the first issue of the Cedartown *Headlight*, a small sheet with growing pains. It contained a great many items pertaining to "the growth of our fair city." It said that Mr. William Deal arrived in front of the editorial office in a fine new green lumber-wagon with red wheels, that on April fools' day a cow of Mr. Oscar Lutz's presented him with twin calves, that a box social was held in the G. A. R. hall, at which a good time was had by all. One gathered from an editorial that subscriptions could be paid with cobs, butchered beef, and money, but that the greatest of these was money.

Crops continued to be good. Abbie thought that this coming summer of '87 would prove to be the one in which she could go back home. And then, before she was ready, she knew she was to be a mother. With Isabelle, her youngest child, nearly ten, Abbie thought she could not face motherhood again,—not at forty-one.

"That means I won't go back to the academy, Mother." Margaret told her. But Abbie said she would manage, that she *had* to manage somehow, for Margaret must finish.

In the fall, with Will protesting a little, Margaret and John both went to Weeping Water to school. And in November, Maggie O'Conner Mackenzie died, without having seen Abbie in twenty years. Bitterness came over Abbie with her grief. Why should life on the prairie have demanded so much of her? Why should twenty years have been so hard, so barren? By her condition, both her grief and her bitterness were accentuated.

At Christmas time, which was cold with deep snow, Margaret and John came home,—Margaret with her gray eyes luminous, her cheeks flushed with prairie-rose tints. She could not wait to tell her mother shyly that the young Fred Baker, who was a nephew of the minister, had been there again. He had only two more years in medical school and then he would be *Doctor* Fred Baker. He wanted her to write to him. And she liked him,—oh, *how* she liked him.

And Abbie wondered.

John, serious, quiet, "liked his work all right." Of all the children, John was the hardest to understand. One almost had to read his mind to get anything out of him. Mack, too, was home for the day. He had graduated from the broom-and-dust-cloth and was on the books all the time. His round face, from which the freckles had miraculously disappeared, had taken on a more alert look, his round china-blue eyes a keener expression.

Isabelle played and sang for them, "Way Down Upon the Swanee River," and "Bonny Charlie's Now Awa'," her

childish voice soaring forth lustily, her slim little legs pumping vigorously.

Abbie was thankful the children were all doing so well.

Christmas over, Mack left for Omaha, and after New Year,
Margaret and John went back to the academy. Elsa Reinmueller
came over three mornings in the week to help.

On the afternoon of the twelfth of January, Abbie put her
shawl over her shoulders and walked down the road to
Reinmuellers'. The day was like a spring one,—a soft, mild,
spring day.

"It's probably the last time I can go to any of the
neighbor's," she had said to Will, "and it will do Christine
good to think I made the effort to come over once more to see
her."

The sun was warm. There was moisture on the sides of the
cedars and cottonwoods. Hens scratched in the damp, steaming ground on the south side of the straw stacks, their liege
lords crowing ecstatically over their activities.

Abbie walked cumbersomely, heavy with child. It was
hard for her at forty-one to get about. The old buffalo trail of
twenty years before, with its faintly outlined tracks, was a
well-defined road now, running on to the big town of Lincoln,
as straight as the crow, except for one short deviation, where
it formed a letter S over the new Missouri Pacific railroad.

As she neared the Reinmueller house, Gus drove out of the
yard with two of the younger boys on their way to town.

Abbie drew her shawl closer around her and called pleasantly,
"Spring is here."

"Ya," shouted Gus. "She's come, all right. Weather-
breeder, that's what she is. Ya . . . look at that." Pigeons
had settled down before his horses' hoofs, to rise with a whirr
of wings and settle again. What did Gus mean? Was it a bad
sign? Grandma Deal would have said it was.

How queer that Gus used so much better English than
Christine, Abbie was thinking. It seemed that Christine didn't
even try to talk right.

She found Christine alone in the square, box-like house
which had replaced the dug-out. The girls had gone over to
Lutz's store, Christine said. Rosie was going to work at Dr.
Hornby's.

The two women talked for some time about trivial neighborhood things, beyond which they had little in common. Neighborliness, caused by the proximity of their houses and the fact that they had come into the new country at the same time, held them together. Christine was paradoxically rough and kind, penurious and unselfish. After a time, Abbie rose laboriously and said she must go. At the door she and Christine stood for a few minutes in parting. The northern sky was the color of dark gray ashes. It was very quiet,—the hushed quiet of a waiting storm god who gloats a little over the peace of Nature before he assaults. Suddenly Abbie felt half frightened and did not know why.

The great gray clouds were now coming in from the northwest, rolling low over the land like billows of thick smoke from a thousand factories of the storm gods located somewhere beyond on the prairie. A single snarling blast came out of the clouds and needles of snow struck Abbie in the face.

Even while she hurried out of the yard, the wind was whipping her shawl about her and a great smother of snow was engulfing her.

"Come back, you," Christine was at Abbie's side.

"No, Christine, I must get home." She had to say it close to Christine's ear in the roaring of the storm.

Christine ran her arm through Abbie's. "With you I go." Abbie made a single feeble protest and then clung to Christine.

In the welter of snow they reached the far side of the road opposite the Reinmuellers', and Christine with her left arm hooked through Abbie's, ran her right hand along the top of the wire fence for guidance. The wind lashed them until they cowered from it. The snow, in great swirling masses, drove its stinging clods into their eyes and nostrils. Irregular drifts formed at their feet in a moment's time. When there came one terrific blast of wind more infuriated than others, Christine clung harder to the wire, the ugly barbs digging the flesh until the blood came. And then the composition of the snow seemed to change. It was no longer even slightly pliable, but a cruel, hard, dry substance which cut at them like bullets and nails and knives.

Abbie's strength in her present physical condition was going. She stopped and moaned at the necessity of pushing her cumbersome self into the jaws of the storm. Christine, with her more wiry robustness, half dragged the lagging body.

Suddenly, the barbedwire gave place to picket and Christine knew that the Deals' yard-fence was reached.

"Now, not so far," she shouted into Abbie's ear. They wallowed, slackened, stopped altogether, crouched before the fury, and then gathered themselves together and plunged on again. Abbie, with her waning strength, had ceased to think, except to obey Christine.

And then the pickets ended abruptly in a post, with space beyond, and Christine realized that it was the open lane-gate and that she had unknowingly passed the small front gate.

"Vait," she shouted. But she had no reason to encourage Abbie in waiting. For Abbie had sunk into the icy bed of a huge drift with the pangs of childbirth upon her.

Chapter 20

And now Christine had to pull Abbie out of the drift and put forth all her effort to get the suffering woman to retrace her steps to the little front gate. She did not dare turn into the wide open gateway and run the risk of losing her bearings in the uncharted wilderness of the lane road.

In the added fear of her childbirth warnings, Abbie clung to Christine with all her strength. "Oh, . . . Christine . . . I can't go any farther . . ." The storm god took the words and threw them back into her face.

"Come . . . you!" Christine hurled savagely into Abbie's ear. "Of your man t'ink. Of your *kinder* t'ink. You're *verrückt* . . . crazy!"

Christine kept her freezing right arm through Abbie's, and plunging slowly ahead, grasped every picket with her left. Pausing, cowering, plunging, pulling Abbie's half-prostrate body, she came to the welcome cross-pieces of the small gate. "By de cedars ve tell," she called in Abbie's ear. They turned blindly, for all directions seemed lost in the mad whirl of snow, crawled through the gateway, and grasped the first cedar. "How many?" Christine was calling.

"Nine," Abbie moaned. She held onto the last far-reaching branch of the first cedar while Christine felt for the second.

"*Zwei!*"

Pushing on, cowering before the white smother, they crawled. The storm tore Abbie's shawl from her and the frozen icicles of her wet hair beat her face like tiny razor blades.

"*Drei.*"

As she felt Christine pulling her forward, the hideous agonizing childbirth pains shook her freezing body again and she sank in a wildly whirling drift.

"*Du narr!*" Christine snarled at her ear. "Come . . . *du narr* . . . fool!"

She set her teeth and plunged ahead while the icy needles drew something moist and trickling from her face.

"*Vier.*"

And now her breath was going. One could not struggle on when there was no air to breathe. Christine was pulling her. Because she had no breath, Christine was pulling her.

"*Fünf.*"

Abbie sank to her knees in pain. Christine jerked at her fiercely. "Get you up." In her ear Christine was yelling. "You die . . . you like dat dying' maybe . . . nein? Your baby . . . you keel heem . . . you like dat keelin' your baby maybe?" No, she must not kill her baby, so she must do as Christine said. But it was so painful——

"*Sechs.*"

Abbie began to be too numb to feel the cold. What was the use of obeying Christine? Christine had no right to boss so.

"*Sieben.*"

The white suffocating smother was turning dark. There seemed no use fighting the hideous black thing that was closing her breath.

"*Acht!*"

Christine was pushing and dragging her. She ought to help Christine push and drag . . .

"*Nein!*"

Together they plunged to the wall of the house. By the loyal cedars they had found their way. In a war of snow, when the whole world was fighting it in mortal combat, only the cedars seemed not to have lost their heads. Only Abbie's cedars and Christine seemed faithful to her. Abbie knew that Christine was dragging her now into the warm shelter of the house. She heard Christine say something about: "Heis vater, qvick!" and then she tumbled into a sea of suffering to which there seemed no shore and in which time was not measured. It was hard to breathe. Sometimes she saw faces dimly which came and went. Sometimes she vaguely heard whisperings. Sometimes she smelled steamy woolens and moist hot flannels.

Most of the time she was sinking under cold smothering water. Only one thing brought her back,—a light,—a lantern shining down into the icy waters. It shone to light the way back up for her. Each time she sank, she kept her eyes on the light and said, "Will . . . Mack . . . Margaret . . . John . . . Isabelle . . ." And the saying of the names bore her back to the surface and the light.

And then, in some queer intuitive way, she knew her life was going out with the tide. The light grew fainter and farther away.

She did not care especially, except for one thing. The light! She ought not lose sight of its faint gleam. Some tiny spark of memory kept reminding her that she must never take her eyes away from the far-off glow of the lantern. So that, sinking, she kept pulling herself feebly back toward its faint gleam with "Will . . . Mack . . . Margaret . . . John . . . Isabelle." She told the words over as a nun touches her beads.

Her mind was not lucid enough to understand that through constant utterance, she was trying to pray that she might come back to her responsibility,—that she had so much to do yet for the family,—that they could not get along without her. Over and over, she said them, "Will . . . Mack . . . Margaret . . . John . . . Isabelle." Each name a bead—each bead a prayer. And when her mind cleared a little, and she heard a strange new wail, she remembered a new responsibility and said them over again. "Will . . . Mack . . . Margaret . . . John . . . Isabelle . . . *the baby*." Each name a bead,— each bead a prayer. Fighting the icy waters feebly, with only the thought of the light to keep them from closing over her, she came back at times to the consciousness of the homely red face of Christine by her bed, nodding, jerking up, nodding——

And when the light grew clearer and more steady and the cold water seemed gone, Will told her that the baby was a girl.

"We'll name her Grace," Abbie said feebly, "Grace of God. She'll be a comfort. She'll stay with us longer . . . maybe . . . than a boy. Where's Christine, Will?"

Christine Reinmueller came in to stand by the bed, her short shapeless body in a blue calico dress, her greasy little tight braids of hair wound flat from ear to ear, her fat red face scarred with scratches.

Abbie reached up and pulled her down. Arms close around her, she kissed her rough cheek. "Christine . . . my friend . . . my friend for all my life."

Christine writhed in embarrassment, "*Ach! Du sans garrich* . . . voolish." She pulled away. "*Es ist nix* . . . nossing."

It seemed odd to Abbie to have a baby again after ten years. Sometimes she said she was afraid she had forgotten how to care for one. But when she grew strong, it all came back to her. The Abbie Deals do not forget.

Margaret graduated from the academy in the spring of that year. Fred Baker, the minister's nephew, who was to be a full-fledged doctor in one more year, arrived in time for the graduating exercises, and brought her a stereoscope with views of "Niagara Falls," "Hudson Bay by Moonlight," "The Wedding Party," and several others with subtle suggestions of a romantic nature. Margaret rode home in the lumber-wagon with the stereoscopic views in her lap and her head somewhere beyond the prairie clouds.

John went back to the academy in the fall, but Margaret was at home with Abbie for the year. And that year was to seem very short to Abbie, for Margaret was getting ready to marry the embryonic doctor. And as all the estate, real or personal, which the two owned, consisted of the stereoscope and the twelve picturesquely romantic views, the year was crowded with the making of quilts, the hemming of sheets, and the sewing of carpet-rags.

The next spring, Abbie's dream of a parlor came into the world of reality. They built it on the south side of the old part, protruding toward the road. They wanted it done before Margaret's wedding, and the wedding was already set for June. Old Asy Drumm, a little more stooped and silent and tobacco-stained, finished the last door-latch and the last piece of mop-board several weeks before the momentous occasion. John and Will painted the pine exterior and Abbie and Margaret varnished the pine interior. There were two modish details about that parlor of which Abbie was inordinately proud, —the fan-shaped colored-glass window toward the road and the double doors that slipped mysteriously into the wall when pushed backward. To be sure, in looking through the fan-shaped glass one saw a bilious green sky, sickly yellow cedars, a wavering blue picket fence and a nightmarish red lawn, but this was a mere bagatelle beside the touch of distinction it gave. Also the doors, after mysteriously disappearing into the walls, could not always be coaxed readily out of their hiding places, so that the women folk would have to call "John . . ." or "Father . . . come help us, will you?" Abbie was proud of them, though, and all her life made loyal excuses for "the doors sticking just a little to-day."

Abbie and Margaret rode up to Lincoln on the branch line, with its small engine, its one coach and baggage car, and bought a red and green sale carpet for the new parlor, Nottingham curtains, an oak patent-swinging rocker, and a marble-topped stand with a blue plush album. It seemed too much grandeur at one time for a single family to acquire. Abbie's rather critical conscience reminded her constantly that Rome was at the height of its glory just before the fall. She sewed the strips of carpet together and then the united family put it down over a layer of newspapers and fresh oat straw. Will, Abbie and John crawled along one side of the room on their hands and knees, pulling and stretching and tacking, while Margaret kept the straw pushed down as level as she could, so the result would not be Rocky-Mountain-like, and Isabelle kept little Grace, a year and a half old now, from putting the tacks into her mouth. When these two stupendous tasks were accomplished, and the carpet was taut and springy over its oat field, they put up the curtains, moved in the organ and the what-not, Abbie's old painting of the prairie, the new chair and the stand, the blue plush album and the stereopticon views, which, luckily, were to remain in the parlor through the wedding. Surveying the finished product, Abbie wondered if any of the Astors or Vanderbilts about whom she had read, ever had anything quite so stylish.

And then Margaret's dress was to be made and all the wedding to be planned. Margaret said she had her heart set on a navy blue silk with white ruching and—

Her mother stopped her. "Don't you . . ." Abbie was wistful. "Don't you wish we could afford a white satin dress and white slippers and a veil?"

"No, Mother . . . the navy blue silk is just what I want.

As long as Fred and I are going right to the rooms over the drug store, I want my clothes to be suitable and I might never have use for a white satin again. Besides, now that I'm going to live in Lincoln, I want to save every penny toward painting supplies. I'm never happier than when I'm opening up the paint-box and getting at the oil and brushes. You know, Mother, my housework won't be much . . . just think . . . those few tiny rooms to keep and not any of the work there is here on the farm . . . and I'm going into my painting for all it's worth. I can't explain it to you, Mother, but there's something in me . . . that if I could just get down on canvas the way the cottonwoods look against the sky, or the way the prairie looks at sunset with the pink light . . ." she broke off. "Oh, I suppose you think I'm daffy . . . you wouldn't understand."

Abbie, at the east kitchen window, looked over the low rolling hills where the last of the May sunshine lay in yellow-pink pools on the prairie. Her lips trembled a little. "Yes, I would," she said simply. "I'd understand."

And then, quite suddenly, it was the night of the wedding. The moon slipped up from a fleecy cloud-bed and with silvery congratulations swung low over the farmhouse behind the cedars. The whole countryside was there. In a community where there have been few lines drawn, one does not begin to draw them at wedding times. The lane road held all manner of vehicles,—lumber-wagons, buggies, phaetons, carts, surreys, hayracks. The Lutzes were all there and all of the Reinmuellers but Emil, who sat on a milk stool in the barn at home all evening and sulked. Sarah Lutz looked stylish in her tight-fitting black dress of stiff silk, with jet earrings against her rosy cheeks. Christine had a new blue calico gathered on full at the waistline.

Mack surprised them all by driving up the lane road in a shining black buggy with canary yellow wheels, yellow lines over the horse's black back, and a yellow whip. He drove over to the Lutz's and came back with Emma Lutz, who was trying her best not to look important.

The presents were all in the sitting-room, the small things on tables. There were two red plush chairs, a stylish castor, a green glass pitcher with frosted glasses, three lamps with snow scenes on the globes, several hand-made splashers and tidies, and enough cold meat and pickle forks to supply a garrison of soldiers with fighting equipment. Gus and Christine, out of deference to the literary tastes of the family, had bought a huge volume, their decision over the purchase having been based upon weight rather than content, and which now, upon inspection, proved to be *Twenty Lessons in Etiquette.*

Some time before the ceremony Abbie climbed the uncarpeted pine stairs with the little calf-skin-covered chest under her arm. Just as her mother had climbed the sapling ladder in the old log cabin, she was thinking. Wasn't life queer? Such a little while ago, it seemed. Where had the time gone? Blown away by the winds you could not stop,—ticked off by the clock hands you could not stay.

Margaret was nearly dressed. Her blue silk, with its fifteen yards of goods, was looped back modishly over a bustle, the train dragging behind her with stylish abandon. Abbie sat down on the edge of her daughter's bed, the chest in her lap. "You know, Margaret, it was always a kind-of dream of mine that by the time you were married, we'd be well enough off to do a lot of things for you. I always saw you in my mind dressed in white with a veil and slippers,—not just that I wanted you dressed that one way,—but I mean as a sort of symbol,—that we'd be able to do all the things for you that should rightfully go with the pearls. But," Abbie's voice broke a little and she stopped to steady it, "things don't always turn out just as we dream,—and we're not able to do much for you. But anyway, you shall wear the pearls to-night if you want to."

Margaret, holding up her long dress, crossed the rag-carpeted floor in little swift happy steps, and threw young arms around her mother.

"*I* know all you've done for me, Mother." She took Abbie's rough hands in her own firm ones and held them to her lips. "And it's *everything*,—just *everything* that you could do. Never as long as I live can I ever repay it." There were tears in the young girl's eyes and to keep them back, she said lightly, "No, thanks, Mother, dear. I'm all right with my lovely blue silk and the white silk ruching at my neck. Keep them for Isabelle or baby Grace. You and father will be well-fixed in a few years. The land will be higher. You're having good crops now and by the time Isabelle is married, your dream can come true. And besides, Mother, dear," she put her young cheek against Abbie's, "*you know that when you marry the man you love, you don't need jewels to make you happy.*"

Yes, yes,—how the words came back, borne on the breeze of memories! How swiftly the clock hands had gone around! Abbie could not speak. She must shed no tears on her little girl's wedding day. So, she only patted her and kissed her, smiling at her through a thousand unshed tears. And you, who have seen your mother smile when you left her,—or have smiled at your daughter's leaving,—know it is the most courageous smile of all.

And then it was time to go downstairs. Margaret and young Doctor Fred Baker came down the enclosed pine stairway and across the parlor, Margaret's silk dress dragging stylishly over the red and green spirals of the sale carpet. Isabelle pedaled and played the wedding march, lustily, the sound of the wind pumping into the reeds rather prominent above the melody.

A solemn hush fell on the friends gathered from all the farms and the little village. Abbie stood by Will, who was holding Grace in his arms. John was at her other side. Mack sauntered over and stood by Emma Lutz. Isabelle stopped playing and the voice of the preacher came hurtling against the silence:

"Inasmuch as we are gathered together—"

Abbie thought she could not stand it. She must call out in one great scream that she could not let her little girl go away from her.

"For better or for worse." *Oh, God, don't let Margaret have to go through all the hardships I did.*

"Until death do you part." There, they were speaking of death again. Why did they always talk about death when there was only life before them?

"Do you take this man . . ."

And now Abbie was going to break down and cry. She threw up her head. No, not a tear, not a single tear! If she started, she would turn into a Niobe to weep herself to death.

And then, quite suddenly, Margaret Deal was Mrs. Fred Baker.

After that, with Isabelle pumping away faithfully, if windily, on the "Blue Danube Waltz," and "By the Blue Alsatian

Mountains,'' some of the young folks danced on the new sale carpet, with the straw underneath working itself up into little hummocks.

There were biscuits and pressed chickens, cakes and lemonade out on the side porch. Christine Reinmueller and Sarah Lutz took turns in shaking the fly-brush with its long paper streamers over the tables, so that no unusual number of flies woud light on the food. Every one had a grand and glorious time. There was only one queer thing about the whole affair,—a new dish among the refreshments which no one in the community had served before. Men folks going home, asked their wives why in Sam Hill the potatoes were all cold, and their wives said to hush and not show their ignorance, that it was something new called ''potato salad'' and it was *supposed* to be cold. At which, most of the men laughed long and raucously and said by golly, for their part, they'd take theirs hot-fried or baked in the skins.

And back on the porch of the farmhouse behind the cedars, Abbie Deal stood and watched her married daughter drive away under the starlit summer sky. Then she turned and went into the kitchen and wound the old Seth Thomas clock with the little brown church painted on the glass.

Chapter 21

After Margaret's marriage, life seemed to move along in a monotonous regularity that summer. Letters came from her twice a week and they were full of enthusiasm and plans. It was nice to have her so happily married, Abbie thought. Mack did not write so often. When he did, the letter was brief and businesslike. He had received a raise in wages. The president, himself, commended him about something. Omaha was growing. You would be surprised to see how large it was getting. One gathered the impression from Mack that he was joint-owner in all the enterprises. Well, it was a good trait, Abbie thought. Loyalty! It was nice for a boy to feel so much a part of a town.

John was helping his father with the farm work,—a silent boy. Abbie, looking at him curiously at times, wondered if she would ever understand him. Isabelle, at twelve, was practicing several hours a day, with no coaxing, "General Grant's Grand March" and "Dance of the Flowers." Sometimes, in her interest over it, she would forget time altogether, and Abbie would scold, "Come, Isabelle, too much of that at once isn't good for you." Little Grace at eighteen months was toddling everywhere and into everything. It seemed to Abbie that she pulled her out of one thing, only to turn and see her getting into something else. She loved her deeply. "Whatever would we have done without her?" she would say to Will.

There had been days of ordinary happenings in the summer

of '89 until the heat of August hung over the land like a blanket.

Abbie had learned to know the prairie in all its moods, —and the mood of August was a lazy, somnolent one. There was a noticeable decrease in the songs of birds, for molting time had begun, although one could hear the cardinal's "what cheer" and the pee-wee calling his own name with plaintive patience all through the day and even after sunset and twilight. Elderberry bushes massed along Stove Creek, had exchanged their lacy headgear for black bonnets of ripe fruit. Along the grassy roadway, one's skirts touched Queen Anne's lace, field mustard and yarrow. Wild morning-glories tangled through the grass, and metallic beetles of iridescent red and green climbed the sticky stems of milkweeds. The yellow of sunflowers, the white of boneset and the azure blue of chicory stood in friendly groups on all sides, and everywhere there were plumes of goldenrod, like plumes from the hats of lovely ladies. Spiders, the highwaymen of all the insects, spread their webs in the pastures to hold up their victims. A covey of baby quail, nearly full-grown, could be flushed almost any time a horse and rider crossed a field, and down by the creek bed the mink and muskrat families had begun breaking home ties, with the brown sons and daughters hunting for themselves.

On one of these August afternoons, with the sun hot, and the hollyhocks blood-red against Abbie's white pickets, with the sound of crooning hens outside the windows and a settled air of languor over the whole farm, Abbie heard a sound of snorting horses, and looked out of the east kitchen window to see John's team charging down the field, the knives of the mower close upon their heels, and John not in sight.

With a horrible sensation of fright, so nightmarish that she seemed not able to pull her wooden limbs along, she ran out. John was lying against the barbed wire of the fence, white as the pickets of the garden gate, a sickening stream of scarlet trickling from his foot. Ill at the sight, Abbie ran to a small new plum tree and broke off its top. She pulled up the lower barbed wire of the fence and crawled through, snatching off her apron, and binding it above the ankle, with the plum stick knotted in between. John's eyes opened, and clung in fright to his mother.

"Mother, do something for me," he moaned in the old little-boy way.

Abbie heard some one, who seemed not herself, saying, in a steady cool voice, "Yes, John, trust Mother."

The horses, frothing, now, at the bits and flanks, were standing against the fence at the far side of the field, trying to reach green corn-ears over the wire. Across the haystubble Abbie ran to them. On the way she kept saying, "Oh, God . . . one more thing . . . help me through this *one* more thing." With frantic movements, she unhitched and led the team back into the yard and hitched them to the lumber-wagon. She seemed to have acquired Amazonian strength. Isabelle, who had run out, was crying in silent fright. "Bring pillows from the beds," Abbie called. Back into the field she drove in the wagon. Fearful to leave the horses, which had not yet settled down to their usual docility, she tied them to the fence post.

"Mother . . . do something."

"Yes, John,—trust Mother."

Together, Abbie and Isabelle, pulling and lifting, got the suffering boy into the wagon with his head on a pillow. Already the apron was scarlet. Abbie jerked off the wagon-seat, piling the other pillows on it, and propped up the mangled foot. She jumped out, untied the team, and climbed back over the wheel into the wagon-box.

"Look after the baby," she called to Isabelle, and started the horses out of the field on a gallop. Against the dashboard she stood and clung to the lines which almost cut her as they sawed through her hands. The wagon bounced and careened and rocked. The pins came from Abbie's hair, and the red-brown mass, faded now, and with a few graying streaks, fell over her shoulders.

In Cedartown, people ran out of their houses and looked after her. As she reached Dr. Hornby's, she had to use all her strength to get the team stopped. Men, running out from the little stores, came to help, catching the horses by the bits and tying them to one of the long row of hitching posts. Dr. Hornby and Henry Lutz and Asy Drumm carried the boy into the one-story office.

"Stay by me, Mother."

"Yes, John, I won't leave you."

Abbie held the boy's hand, her thick hair still tumbled over her shoulders while Dr. Hornby cut and cleansed and tied. When the last neat bandage was fastened, Abbie Deal slipped to the floor in a crumpled heap.

John's life was saved only by a few moments,—only by the time gained through Abbie's wild drive into town. For weeks, his foot propped in its one position, he suffered all the agonies of a cut and tortured tendon of Achilles. And always he was to carry a horny scar.

It was the nearest that death had come to the family since Abbie's long illness. Will and Abbie, sitting on the side porch, on a warm August evening, talked of it in low tones.

"Death . . . Will," Abbie said. "How the fear of it always hangs over me. If John had died . . ."

"Death," Will repeated it. "Death . . ." He looked beyond the Lombardy poplars, stared for a moment up into the deepening prairie twilight. "I wonder why we fear it?" He spoke as though to himself. "The naturalness of it! Wild geese flying over . . . cattle coming home . . . birds to their nests . . . leaves to the winter mold . . . the fast sleep. How natural they all are, and yet of them all, we fear only the sleep. When my time comes I wish my family and friends could think of it that way . . . without tears."

"Oh, Will, don't talk so. If you should be taken away from me, I couldn't stand it."

"Oh, yes, you could, Abbie-girl. You could stand it. It's the people who have loved and then lost their love . . . who have failed each other in some way, who couldn't stand it. With you and me . . . all we've been through together and all we've meant to each other . . . with us, it couldn't be so terrible. Nothing could take away the past from us. You are so much a part of me, that if you were taken away, I think it would seem that you just went on with me. And I'm sure if I were the one taken I would go on with you, remembering all you had been to me."

So seldom did Will speak that which was in his heart. And now he had spoken. Abbie sat and looked out into the star-filled sky. There were the summer night odors,—clover hay and ripening apples and sweet alyssum. There were the summer night sounds,—cicada and frogs and a crooning bird. There were the summer night movements,—the trembling of the leaves on the poplars, a night hawk dipping low, a bit of lacy cloud slipping across the moon. For a moment, Abbie Deal seemed greater than herself, larger than humanity. For a brief time, a sense of deep wisdom was within her, a flood of infinite strength and peace enveloped her.

I would go on with you . . . remembering . . .

All fall and early winter John, suffering, blue, discouraged, was kept in with his bad foot. It had been a terrible cut, but it was healing; and he was not going to be crippled, thanks to the ministrations of a country doctor with few instruments and meager equipment, but with a sound surgical knowledge. Young Dr. Frederick Baker commended the older doctor's care of the case with the cheerful condescension of the recent graduate.

By studying at home and taking his tests, John was able to graduate with his class at the academy. Still favoring his foot a little, he went into the field with his father.

That summer of '90 was the summer of the great drought. Day after day, Will came into the kitchen with the pails of morning milk to say, "Another scorcher. Not a cloud in the sky."

The hot belching winds blew in from the southwest. The grass in the pastures knotted and scorched on its roots. The brittle leaves of weeds rattled, like so many tiny castanets, whenever the chickens walked through them. Blackberries hardened on the bushes and fell to the ground. Raspberries were purple warts. Peaches dried in the forming.

The small grain amounted to very little. The corn began to curl and brown and bake on its roots. Crops were stillborn in the womb of Nature.

Reports from other parts of the country were the same. The state seemed to have slipped backward into its beginnings, to be going through the same hard period experienced in the 'seventies. Rumor came from the northern border that the Indians were dancing the ghost dance. Abbie commenced to wish the family had not been so extravagant,—buying the organ and the carpet, and building on the room. That joke of hers about the fall of Rome was beginning to seem ill-timed.

But the bad summer seemed not to bother the children. Grace was two and a half now, "a smart little tike," every one said. Margaret came home sometimes, but her young doctor husband was too fearful of missing a case in the growing town of Lincoln to leave often. Margaret was as happy as Abbie had ever wished her to be. She was busy, too, with her painting, reveling in the time and opportunity to work with it. She brought sketches out to show Abbie and the two spent long moments talking them over.

Mack had good reports to make. Whenever he came for an occasional Sunday in his friendly, breezy way, Abbie always felt a renewal of pride in his virile young manhood, a feeling of elation over his unceasing energy.

"People like Mack," she would say to Will, "but what's better, they have confidence in him."

John was Will's standby in the farm work. Quiet, serious, seldom speaking his mind, he seemed to Abbie more and more like Will.

Isabelle was talking and thinking "music" all day. She was taking lessons now from a woman in Cedartown. Abbie always drove with her over to town on Saturday afternoons. While Isabelle took her lesson, Abbie traded out the butter and eggs she had brought to the Lutz store.

On one late Saturday afternoon in October, as Abbie was taking Isabelle over to town for her music lesson, she met Dr. Fred and Margaret riding out home with Oscar Lutz. They had come on the late afternoon train to surprise the home folks.

A warm feeling of happiness was with Abbie when she drove the old white mare back toward the lane road by the Lombardy poplars. Mack was coming the next day, too. Never did life seem so complete as when the children were all at home. Home was the hub of the wheel. Always she and Will would live there, and always, no matter where the children's activities led them, they would come home to father and mother in the white farmhouse behind the cedars. She was thinking this in a general way, and that she would have chicken and hot biscuits for Sunday dinner, when she turned into the lane road by the poplars.

Every one was out by the windmill,—John, Margaret, Dr. Fred Baker, Grace, Oscar Lutz, Gus Reinmueller. They were standing in a group,—a quiet, silent group,—only standing and doing nothing. Something smote Abbie like a chilling hand, clutching at her heart and throat. There was complete silence in the crowd,—a whispering silence,—the same hushed silence of the time when the baby was born dead. They all turned when she came up the lane road,—turned toward her, but did not move,—looked at her,—and were silent. Abbie got out of the buggy with wooden movements and went over to the group. Dr. Fred Baker was kneeling on the grass. By his side Will lay at the foot of the windmill, staring beyond the Lombardy poplars.

Abbie knelt down by him, too. But he did not look at her. He only lay and looked beyond the Lombardy poplars,—stared up into the deepening prairie twilight.

Oscar Lutz's voice, hoarse and far away, said: "Is he . . . ?"

Dr. Fred's, low and far away, also, said: "Yes . . . gone." He turned his head away and slipped a hand gently over Will's eyelids.

Gus Reinmueller gave a sob. Oscar Lutz said, "There was a *man* . . ." The children,—John, Margaret, Isabelle, little Grace,—all began to cry wildly.

Abbie Deal dragged her eyes away from Will and looked across the prairie as towards Golgotha. No one moved. There was no sound but the children crying.

The cows were coming up to the pasture gate. The leaves of the Lombardys floated onto the lane road. A bird flew into the cedars. A long wedge-shaped line of wild geese flew low. Will lay sleeping.

Suddenly, Abbie Deal seemed greater than herself, larger than humanity. A sense of deep wisdom was within her, a flood of infinite strength enveloped her. She rose and threw up her head. "Hush!" she said quietly to the children. Almost sternly she said it: "Hush! Not a child of Will Deal's is to shed a tear."

Chapter 22

It is the prerogative of the dramatist to lower the curtain upon a scene and raise it upon a later one,—of the story-teller to close one chapter and begin another when time has passed. Real life is not so. There is no kind interval of time as the settings of the various experiences shift,—no heart-easing period of days between the chapters of life.

Life is Time's galley-slave, forever shackled to its relentless master. If its hardest blow be dealt at three o'clock, then four o'clock must be met and five and six,—the first dark, agonizing night and the first pale, torturing dawn.

And so it is unreal, even cowardly, to leave Abbie Deal wrestling with her deepest emotions,—living two lives; one within herself, wracked and tortured,—the other, an outward one which met all the old duties and trivial obligations with composure,—leave her in the garden of her Gethsemane, to meet her many months later. Only the children had kept her going. Only her motherhood, whose first characteristic was love and whose second was duty, had kept her hands busy and her head unbowed. These,—and one other thing which she could not explain: the unseen presence of Will himself. She told no one,—made no attempt to discuss the experience with any other. But much of the time Will did not seem to be away. Whether the phenomenon were of the spirit world with the metaphysical involved, a touch of the supernatural which no man understands, or only a comforting memory, she did not know. She accepted the solace in blind faith and with soul-filled gratitude.

Through what agency came the consolation she could not say, but she felt able to keep in touch with him. There was nothing of the weird about it,—no foolish incantations to the dead. He just seemed with her. It grew in time to give her a slight sense of peace. It took from the separation the raw, tearing hurt. They had been so close, so companionable, that she seemed always to know what he would have said or done under any conditions. She grew to imagine she was talking to him,—telling him the small inconsequential affairs of the household, just as she had always done. And he seemed to answer.

"We had the Lutzes out for supper, Will."

That was pleasant, Abbie.

She knew that she made her own answers, but paradoxically, they seemed not to be. She had known Will's opinions so thoroughly that, almost without her volition, the answers sprang to her mind.

"The Reinmuellers were quarreling to-day, Will. You know, Will, sometimes I think you and I are nearer even now than Gus and Christine."

That's true, Abbie.

"I shall never tell any one," she said to herself. "I know just how they would feel. They would look at me queerly and think I was 'touched.' You do talk to me, Will, don't you?"

Why, of course, Abbie-girl.

And, so, like an unseen presence, it came to give her a sense of comfort, until the day on which there would come a reaction, and she would plunge into a dark state of depression during which she would turn upon herself with accusations of a childish belief in her own fragile imagination. And then, in time,—something would quiet her again. Something,—she did not know what,—the wind in the Lombardy poplars,—the spirit of the deepening prairie twilight,—the stillness of the star-filled summer night,—or the memory of a voice saying, "I would go on with you . . . remembering . . ."

The greatest antidote in the world for grief is work, and the necessity of work. And Abbie had more to do than she had ever done in her busy life.

John was the one upon whom she most depended. All the winter, after his father's death, he had looked after the stock and all spring he had worked faithfully putting in the new crop. Many times one of the Reinmuellers had helped out, but John had shouldered the greater share of the field work. His presence was the only solution now to the problem of making a living on the place. He was only eighteen, but in the years to come, if he wanted to marry, Abbie told herself that he could have a small house built near by,—or perhaps it would be better the other way around,—she and Isabelle and Grace could live in the small cottage and let John have the bigger house. John was so much like his father, quiet, faithful, uncomplaining. He had none of Mack's friendliness toward every one, but a reserve which was close to dignity. Every night, all winter, after the chores were done, he had cleaned up and with no explanation, mounted the enclosed stairs to his own room. What did he do there, Abbie wondered, as she built up the fire, so that the room above, heated by a "drum" on the stovepipe, would be warm enough.

It was when she was cleaning the room in the spring that she found the Blackstone tucked away between a homemade book-shelf and the wall.

"John," Abbie said to him, "something is on your mind. What is it? Won't you tell Mother?"

She had to work to get it out of him. And then, like one whose resistance had snapped, he turned on her, "It's working on this darned farm all my life. I hate it, I tell you." He had the fury of a reserved person who stores up his grievances until one exploding moment. It reminded Abbie of the few outbursts of Will during their years together.

Abbie put her hand on the back of a chair to steady herself. "What do you want to do?"

"Study law." And Will had said that the Deals were always for the land. "I think of it all day and—then dream it. And I'm going to, some day."

That was like Will, too, Abbie thought,—to think a thing over for a long time and then come to an irrevocable decision.

"But I know what you'll say to that." He spoke almost sullenly.

It hurt Abbie so, to have him turn on her that way.

"I'm not unsympathetic, John. We'll have to plan some way it can be done if you feel that way."

"Yes, and have you mad and disappointed about it." Why, oh why, did children say things to hurt one?

"No, I'll not be mad," she controlled her trembling lips, "and I'm not disappointed. I'm proud of your desire, John. For just a few minutes I was . . . was confused."

"Then promise me you'll sell the place and take the two girls and move into town."

"No, John," Abbie said with dignity. "I'll not sell. Land is low, . . . and last year's crops so poor . . . No, it's my place and I'm going to stay on it. We'll manage, somehow."

"Then that settles it. I'll stay too."

For long weeks Abbie labored with him. He was such a good boy, so clean and energetic, and so stubborn. Then, when Abbie had argued over and over again how she could manage by renting part of the acreage to Oscar Lutz on shares, and hiring Pete Reinmueller for the part of the work she could not do herself, John went away to the University in the fall, with his one suit, a few dollars in his pocket, and the promise of two jobs,—caring for a professor's fires and a doctor's horses.

Isabelle entered Weeping Water Academy that fall, doing part-time work in the minister's family for her board. And not once did either she or John ever realize how many times their mother put on an old coat and felt hat of their father's and went out to some of the heavy work herself. Isabelle began immediately to make splendid progress in music under a good teacher from the East. "It's her voice, though, that's going to count," the instructor said. "We must watch it and guard it."

In the summer, almost the first minute that John came home, he put on his old clothes and went out to the field to work. But his course was to be long and Isabelle's must contain all the music she could get, so Abbie began figuring in what ways she could help the two more. After several weeks of thinking it over and consulting the boys, she took Oscar Lutz's offer for eighty acres or half the farm. Oscar paid her one thousand dollars in cash and gave his note for the other three thousand.

"It's not good business to sell for that," Abbie said. "I think land's going to be higher some day, but it's now that the children need a little help. I can get along. With the chickens and eggs and butter and my pension money, I can keep things going."

The crops were poor again, the drought of the year before almost repeated. In spite of the general depression Henry and Sarah Lutz went away on a trip back to the World's Fair at Chicago. Henry had many irons in the fire, a blacksmith shop, his store, the farms. He and Oscar seemed to get along. They always "came out of the big end of the horn," people said. Sarah looked dressy when she started away. She had a flaring black skirt and white shirt-waist and a stiff black hat which she told Abbie was a genuine Knox sailor.

"So's mine," said Abbie, good-naturedly. She took off her own shabby old hat and twirled it on her hand. *"Hard knocks."*

When Sarah came back, she had some little garnet earrings and a half-dozen spoons with the Fair buildings engraved on them and pictures of the Infanta Eulalie from Spain and Mrs. Potter Palmer.

In September, Abbie left Grace, nearly five now, with Sarah and went up to Lincoln to be with Margaret. She drove the team and took along the feed for it to save the two-dollar train fare that would pay for four music lessons for Isabelle.

She got up at three and had started at four. Hours later, at Stevens Creek bridge, she rested the team under some cottonwoods and ate breakfast out of a shoe box. It showered during the last three miles and the wheels threw mud and the buggy almost mired.

The Bakers had moved into a house with a yard and a stable. Dr. Baker's practice was picking up, although fees were hard to collect. The hard times permeated into all businesses.

Abbie walked the floor in an agony of sympathy for Margaret. "I went through this six times," she thought, "but this is harder than any of them." Sometimes she slipped into the bedroom. "Mother's here, Margaret," she said, cheerfully, "keep up your courage."

And then the Bakers had a son,—Fred, Jr., they called him.

At home again, Abbie found everything all right. Christine had milked the two cows and had taken care of the pigs and chickens. The farm activities, thanks to the Reinmuellers, had gone right on. Only the clock had stopped.

Abbie wound the works behind the door with the little

brown church painted on the glass. She stood for a few
minutes and looked at the homely painted face of the old Seth
Thomas time-piece and listened to its sturdy faithful ticking.
"A grandmother!" she said to it. "I'm a grandmother. And
it's not quite believable."

"You — can't — stop — time — you — can't — stop —
time — you — can't—"

"Yes, you're right," Abbie admitted. "We won't argue
it." She put the key behind the little brown church painted on
the glass and shut the door.

"Well, Will," she said to that comrade who was only
spirit and memory, "you have a grandson."

I'm pretty proud of that, Abbie.

And then, the next spring, the whole community knew that
Mack was going to marry Emma Lutz,—Emma, with her
mother's beady black eyes and her rosy cheeks and a merry
come-hither in her eyes. And apparently the whole community was pleased, for good-natured Emma Lutz was the village belle.

Mack was twenty-five, and having been promoted to a
window in the Omaha bank with the mystic word, "Teller"
on it, he was by way of being something of a capitalist in the
eyes of his old neighbors.

They were married at the Lutz house over in Cedartown on
an October evening of 1893. The Lutzes had a new house
with a squatty cupola on the southwest corner that looked like
a shingled bee-hive. The ceilings were high and there were
wooden rosettes over all the doors and windows and some
new-fashioned spindles on the stairway, through which little
Grace fed wedding-cake to the monkeys, actively imperson-
ated by the Oscar Lutz grandchildren. Mack and Emma left
for Omaha at once, where Mack had rented a little cottage on
Dodge Street.

Abbie was forty-six now. The gray streaks in the red-
brown hair were prominent. There was a noticeable slumping
of the lithe shoulders, a thickening of hips. The peasant body
of the O'Conners was coming into its own. In all these years
Abbie Deal had not done anything with her voice, and she
had not painted. But as every good mother lives again in her
children, her personal disappointments were assuaged by Isabelle giving great promise in her music, and Margaret improv-

ing in every canvas she did. So Abbie felt that the children were doing the things she had so deeply wanted to do. She realized that the time was long past for her to build any more hopes on developing either of those two talents for herself, but she still cherished a secret ambition to write something.

"If I could just get down life as I have seen it," she would think, ". . . and people as I have known them. . . . Old Grandpa Deal with his shaggy head and the twinkle in his eyes, and his wit and his patience with Grandma . . . the story of my mother with her head-shawl and her Irish eyes, pulling a rose for my father . . . Isabelle Anders-Mackenzie, trying to make a lady of her little Irish peasant daughter-in-law . . . the journey out from Illinois with the stolid old oxen and the smell of the burning maple boughs in one's nostrils . . . the first lonely nights of camping in Nebraska with the silence of the stars and the sky and the shivering of the prairie grass." It was something she could do. She vaguely sensed her power to construct the scenes in writing, knew that she possessed the emotions which one must feel before he can transfer those feelings to another.

It gave her a delightful sense of anticipation on this October day. With the half-crop husked and in the crib, she could begin to write down some of the things she desired. It gave her a feeling of buoyancy that all her hard work could not down,—a renewal of youthful desires. By careful management she could plan her time, so that there would be moments each day in which she could forget everything else and carry out this dream that was as old as herself. If the results seemed clever—the thought gave her a warm sensation of pleasure—she would show them to the children. And then,—if they were good enough,—there were several ladies' magazines now, which printed such things. How proud the older children would be of her,—Mack, and Margaret, John and Isabelle.

"Do you think I could, Will?"

I'm sure you could, Abbie-girl. Yes, that was the answer Will would have made. Always kind, always encouraging, he would have said just that.

In the sheer pleasure which the vision gave her, she pulled little Grace up to her and hugged her. "Maybe Mother can find time now to do something she's always wanted to, darling.''

Grace, looking over her mother's shoulder, pulled away.

"Look, Mother,—who's that coming?''

Gus Reinmueller was driving away from the front gate, and a tiny little figure in black, with huge old-fashioned bonnet, was hobbling up the path between the cedars, half-carrying and half-dragging an old black valise.

Amazed, and uncertain who her visitor might be, Abbie went out to meet her. It was Grandma,—Grandma Deal, —eighty years old, with a thousand wrinkles in her little shriveled brown face.

"Why, Grandma Deal!''

"Well, Abbie, I've come to live with you. I'd rather live with you than any of my own blood. It won't be long, though. I shan't last long. Why didn't I die when Pa did? What makes old folks hang on when they ain't no good any more to their relatives? What makes my daughters so hard to get along with?''

Abbie could scarcely believe it,—that Grandma Deal had packed up and come alone out to her. What could she do with her? How could she take care of her? In kaleidoscopic fashion her thoughts tumbled about. Why, it was all she could do to help Isabelle at the Academy, to give John assistance sometimes, look after the house and farmwork, and take care of little Grace. And this last plan,—this new thing of writing she was just planning to do. Why, it would take time to do it! How could she add Grandma Deal to her burdens?

Grandma stood in the pathway, the old valise by her side.

"Maybe you don't want me?'' her voice rose thin and querulous. "Maybe you're like all the rest of 'em. Maybe I'd better go back. I won't go back to Regina's though, that's sure.''

"Oh, Will, how can I ever take care of her, too?''

She's my mother, Abbie-girl.

Abbie put warm, tender arms around the little old black figure.

"Why, Grandma, how can you think it? You're Will's own mother. Of course I'll take care of you.''

Grandma Deal pulled away and looked around her. "Whatever did you set out them cottonwoods for? I can't bear that white fuzz blowin' around. What did you face the house south for?'' A thousand wrinkles in her little thin, brown face, a thousand worries under the old, rusty, black bonnet.

One arm around the bent, wiry figure, the black valise in the other hand, Abbie piloted the arrival into the sitting-room, where Grace was crying silently for fear of the queer little old woman.

''Why, Grace, this is your own Grandma,—Father's mother, and she's come to live with us. We'll give you our bedroom, Grandma, and Grace and I'll go upstairs to sleep.''

''What you goin' to put me in a bedroom on the east side for? Sun's hot there in summer and east winds blow on it in the winter.''

''Well, you try it a while, Grandma, and we'll change the bed if you're not comfortable. Now, you rest and I'll go out and get supper.'' Oh, where would she get the strength to be patient with Grandma?

Out in the kitchen, she stepped to the side porch and looked up at the sky beyond the Lombardy poplars. How could she do any more than she was doing now? Where did a person get help for all the trials of life? Why must she always be doing something for some one else? Why had Will been taken away? How could she assume this added burden without him?

Whether it was of the spirit world, a touch of the supernatural, the wind in the Lombardys, or only a memory,—she did not know. But quite distinctly she heard it:

I would go on with you . . . remembering. . . .

Chapter 23

Grandma Deal lived with Abbie for two years, the last thirteen months of which she was bedridden, and during which she was consistent in only one thing,—regularly spending a portion of each day in wishing she had not come. Abbie washed for her and ironed for her and cooked as well as she could with a frugal larder, to satisfy her childish cravings. Sometimes she picked up the frail little body and carried her to a couch near the window. And in the two years, she did not leave Grandma with any one else a half-dozen times. Margaret and Mack and John all scolded about it. "It seems as though Mother *always* has some big extra job on her hands," they would tell each other. Regina, fat and easygoing, came out once to help with the care, but the arrangement was not a particularly happy one, inasmuch as Abbie had two to wait on then, rather than one.

Strangely enough, of the whole family, Grandma took the greatest liking to the one who did the least for her,—Isabelle. Dreamy-eyed, thinking of nothing but music, Isabelle seldom did anything for Grandma but sing for her. Home from the academy that summer, the girl was expressing her desire constantly for a piano instead of the old reed organ.

"What you alwa's wishin' for a pianny for when you know you can't have it?" Grandma wanted to know.

"I might just as well have some fun wishing for it," she announced pleasantly,—Isabelle was always pleasant,—"when I know it's as far away as the moon." And she sat down at the old reed organ and played a windy accompaniment to her thrush-like singing of "Home to Our Mountains."

Grandma lifted her little wizened face from the clean white pillow. "Come here," she said suddenly. "Bring me the black bag out o' my valise, and mind you, don't look in it, either."

When Isabelle had brought the bag, Grandma took out a smaller pouch, and with Isabelle's eyes almost starting from her head, counted out fifteen great gold double-eagles.

"There's your pianny," Grandma said tartly. "Gold . . . all of 'em . . . and minted in the 'fifties. I'm savin' ten of 'em to bury me. You tell your Ma. Tell her when I die . . . I want her to take the money out o' this bag and buy herself a railroad ticket and go along home with me. I ain't goin' to have no mistake made. Like's not if she wa'n't along they'd send me on to Chillicothe or Kalamazoo."

"Oh, Grandma . . ." Isabelle could not yet comprehend the gift of gold that had come from the Aladdin lamp of the little black bag. "How can I *thank* . . . oh, Grandma . . . I *never* can thank . . ."

Quite suddenly, Grandma broke into a dry old sobbing. "Don't thank *me* . . ." Her voice cracked weirdly. "Thank your dead father. 'Twas his draft money. I'd never touch it." Her quavering old voice was torn into hoarse shreds, "Thirty years I kep' it . . . come in the house 'n' put it in my lap . . . said, 'Mother, there's your money' . . . blood money . . . I alwa's said 'twas. . . ."

Isabelle was frightened and ran out for her mother.

When Fritz Reinmueller and John, Oscar and Henry Lutz unloaded the wonderful shining affair at the parlor door, Isabelle would not have exchanged places with the first lady of the land. Grandma greeted the purchase with "What'd you get that color for? Why didn't you get a plush stool? What're you settin' it in *that* corner for?"

On a morning in July, Grandma's restless spirit took its grumbling flight, sputtering a little at the Lord for the time spent upon her demise. Abbie took a piece of Will's gold draft money, and with Grace, accompanied all that was mortal of Grandma back to the old home. "Poor Grandma," thought Abbie on the train, "I wonder if she's finding fault with the way the angels' wings are put on and the direction the River of Life flows."

It had been twenty-eight years since Abbie had traveled the miles toward the setting sun behind old Red and Baldy. After the services for Grandma, she stayed a week, finding a thousand changes. But the greatest change of all she found in herself. She did not like the old places as well as she had always dreamed. Houses were too thick. Trees were too close and shady. The air was too humid. She felt hemmed in. "I would want to see out more," she thought to herself, ". . . to far horizons. I belong to the prairie. That's home now."

She visited her mother's grave and Grandpa Deal's and the tiny one of Janet's baby with the wild honeysuckle tangled over it. Her mother lay under a tall pine on which the dried cones rustled all the afternoon in the summer breezes. Abbie sat and thought about her,—the little peasant girl whose life had changed because a young hunter rode by. She thought of the trail of graves across the country. Her father was buried in New York State, a little brother in Illinois, her mother in Iowa, her husband in Nebraska. A trail of graves marked the westward trek of her family.

When she got back to town they asked her to guess whoever she supposed could be there. "Dr. Ed Matthews' wife from New York City," they told her.

Abbie could not think that it would be so hard to meet any one. Surely, at forty-seven one did not care about things like that.

The woman was slender, wasp-waisted, beautifully dressed, her huge leg-o'-mutton sleeves the height of style. She had on a whole garnet set, a pin, earbobs and bracelet.

"They tell me you are one of Doctor's old sweethearts." She smiled at Abbie with her graying hair and her sunburned skin and her work-worn hands. Abbie's heart was pounding ridiculously. Certainly at forty-seven one ought to have more poise than that. She leaned over Grace and fixed her sash. When she raised her face it was composed. She smiled back, "Oh, he used to come past the schoolhouse sometimes where I taught . . . and stop to talk."

When Abbie came back, she stopped in Lincoln a day to visit Margaret. Fred, Jr. was two years old now, and sitting up to the table on Gus's and Christine's wedding gift of *Twenty Lessons in Etiquette*, but as far as Abbie could see, the association was a lost cause, for Fred, Jr.,'s table activities were of such an adventurous type that an onlooker might gather he was sitting on *The Life and Voyages of Columbus*.

Abbie arrived at the farm to face the utter ruin of her corn crop. During that week of July in which she had been back to the old home, the hot winds had blown out of the southwest with their scorching, blighting breath, and the young, shoulder-high stalks were so many blistered pieces of pulp.

She had been home two days when Henry Lutz drove out to tell her that Sarah was not well enough to go to Omaha to be with Emma during confinement and to ask her to go in Sarah's place. The hot winds had wearied Sarah, Henry said,—just tired her out.

For a few brief moments Abbie felt a fierce resentment that Sarah was always so well taken care of. Wasn't it hot for her too? Just back from burying Grandma, after caring for her two years, with the chickens and the house and everything to see to,—wasn't *she* weary, too? Oh, why could she never live any life of her own? For a few minutes resentful thoughts tumbled about in her mind, and then she said cheerfully, "Why, yes, tell Sarah I'll go."

Mack and Emma had a sturdy little son, now, too, Stanley, they called him.

"Another grandson, Will," Abbie said at home again.

We're both pleased, Abbie.

That fall Abbie put in her first small sowing of winter wheat, the new experiment about which some of the farmers were talking. In November, with a light dash of snow on it, the small rectangle of vivid green stood out on the landscape like a bit of spring which had lost its reckoning of time. The crop in its experimental stage did well enough so that she added to her list a small sowing of the other new one, alfalfa, the tiny bluish-purple flowers later sending out a haunting fragrance that vied with the sweet fresh odor of the red clover.

But in general, it was a hard row that Abbie was having to hoe. Under the best of circumstances, with plenty of man-power on the farm, the owners were having a series of hard years. For a woman to face the problems seemed next to impossible. She rented parts of the eighty to Oscar Lutz and Gus Reinmueller for a share in the grain. But one year of drought followed another, so that a share in a poor crop was sometimes next to nothing. Pete and Heinie Reinmueller worked for her at times on shares. If they butchered they took their pay in meat, if they cut down trees they took it in wood. The chickens, the horses and the two cows she cared for herself, and except at farrowing time, the pigs. She made butter and sold it to town customers, and she traded eggs and chickens for staples at the Lutz store. Aside from a cloak which Mack gave her one Christmas and a dress from Margaret, Abbie Deal had nothing new in the way of clothes for years. Every stitch, every penny, every thought was for the schooling of the children. "If you can help any one, help John and Isabelle get through school," she would say to Mack and Margaret. And those who think she was not cheerful through it all, do not know the Abbie Deals of the old pioneer stock.

She made light of her hard times. "I've worn the same black hat for so many years," she would say, "it's like an old friend. The jet ornament on it has gone the whole rounds. It's been sewed on the front and on both sides and on the back. And now next year, I'm going to try it sort of northeast between the front and the side."

The Lutz families and the Reinmuellers had gone away beyond their original ownership of land. Henry and Oscar Lutz had bought several eighties from families who had given up and returned East. Gus Reinmueller owned six eighties now, instead of the two of the earlier days. He and Christine seemed to have a perfect obsession for adding acres to their possession. Everything went into more land,—nothing into the house or for the children. The Henry Lutz family was now the "best fixed" one in Cedartown. Henry had done well in the store, had bought and sold land by that sharp businesslike bargaining which brought him always the better of the trade. Unlike the Reinmuellers, the Lutz family was the first to get new things and conveniences. Sarah Lutz, with her little black beady eyes and her still rosy cheeks, was always well dressed, always merry, always hospitable in the new house with the fancy wooden rosettes and the stylish cupola.

The year that John finished his law course found an opportunity presenting itself to locate in Iowa with a friend. He took the Iowa bar examination and was in the firm by mid-summer. It seemed queer to Abbie that John should go back to her old state to live.

That same June, Isabelle finished the Academy, the star pupil in piano and voice. Abbie in her turned and made-over dress, sitting in the audience of the church where the exercises were held, cried a little behind her program, and there are those who will understand the nature of her tears.

That was the same summer too, that Mack and Emma turned into the lane on a tandem bicycle one afternoon. Abbie could not believe her eyes,—that Emma, the mother of a year-old boy, would pedal from Omaha on one of the mannish-looking things. Emma was gay and unconcerned about little Stanley. She had left him with "the girl." He was as "fine as a fiddle" and the girl knew "just what to do with him." Yes, Emma was going to be as carefree and irresponsible a person as Sarah, her mother. Dressy, too, like her mother. She had on a dark green wool skirt, tight-fitting over the hips and bell-shaped at the bottom. Her white waist had sleeves the size of smoked hams. She wore a green necktie, and on top of her huge head of black hair was perched a little creased felt hat with a green quill at one side,—an "Alpine hat," she told Abbie. How could a young mother take her duties so lightly, thought Abbie.

In the fall, Isabelle, dreamy-eyed with musical plans, went up to Lincoln to live with Margaret and attend the University. Abbie sometimes opened the sliding double doors and went into the parlor where the piano stood, silent now, and ran her long slender fingers, stiff and knotted with outdoor work, over the keyboard. Sometimes she sighed a little for a lost dream, but more often she thought only of her pride in Isabelle.

Grace, at eight was in the Cedartown school, quick, keen-eyed,—"smart as a whip," people said. For two years, Abbie had hitched up on bad days and taken her in to school, but now a second building had gone up in the north end of town, and Grace was no farther away from it than many of the town children. It lightened Abbie's work materially when Grace could skip off to school by herself down the lane road under the poplars.

It was not until early winter again, with its half-crop of husking out of the way, that Abbie turned to that old desire of hers, that girlish ambition to write some of the things she had heard and seen and lived.

In that saving, frugal way, born of necessity, she ironed out dark brown wrapping paper, which she had saved for years, and cut it into sheets. At forty-nine Abbie was finding her first opportunity to take time from duties which had always confronted her, to carry out this old ambition. For several afternoons she wrote of the things she had been wanting forever to get down on paper. The things she had wanted to say did not come as readily as she had always anticipated. The task was a little more labored than she had thought. When she had finished several of the brown papers, she put them away carefully in her bureau drawer.

Duties descended upon her again before she had a chance to read over what she had written—those urgent duties which seemed always to confront her. Isabelle came home for vacation, burning incense before Euterpe's shrine. Even as a freshman, she had been chosen one of the new members in a musical organization, and what was of more practical benefit, had been asked to sing in one of the church choirs. Isabelle's fresh mellow voice was the open sesame to meeting many new friends and experiences.

Christmas came and went with every one, but John, home. On one of the short January days with the snow thick on the Lombardy poplars, Abbie, with almost a girlish enthusiasm, took out of the drawer the story she had written in the fall. She read it through and then, amazed and chagrined, she read it a second time. It was flat, insipid. None of the things which she had been thinking as she wrote, was there. The statements were dull and lifeless. Grace, at nine, might almost have written them. What was the matter? She, who had so loved life, and so deeply lived it, could she not of all people get down on paper that which she had lived and loved? Apparently not.

How did they do it, she wondered? How did those writers you loved make you live in their stories? How did their people move across the pages like flesh and blood friends? How could they bring tears to your eyes and laughter to your lips? How could the winds sweep through their books so that you heard its endless rushing? How could the prairie grass blow for them so that you saw it wave and ripple? How could the Mayflowers and the honey-locusts drip their fragrance for them, so that you smelled it across the years. She did not know.

For some time she sat in stunned disappointment and looked at the snow thick on the cedars, and the gray bowl of a sky turned over the world. All her life she had dreamed of constructing something. She had told herself that if only she could find time, she would write of life as it was. And she had found time. But she could not write of life as it was. She had tried to tell of the journey over the uncharted sea of grass, of the nights under the star-filled sky, and the winds that were never still. But the words she had set down had not told it. Only the memory of it remained in her heart, like a song that would never be sung. She thought of her younger days, —the gleam which seemed always ahead,—of the vague allure which accomplishing something in the arts had always held for her. And now she was nearly fifty and she was not to know the fruition of any of those hopes.

"Oh, Will, I am so disappointed," she said to that invisible comrade who was only spirit and memory. "I can only *feel* those things,—not do them."

Isn't motherhood, itself, an accomplishment?

She knew that she made her own answer, and yet it gave her a sense of satisfaction and peace. Will might have said it. It sounded like him.

"But I've made so many mistakes. . . . Will. . . . even in that."

You are a good mother, Abbie-girl.

Yes, it gave her a sense of peace and comfort.

Chapter 24

It seemed to Abbie that the years began to move more quickly now. The leaves of the almanac over the wooden kitchen sink were turned with almost unbelievable rapidity. Abbie never tore them out and never destroyed one of these outlived chronicles of time.

"Don't you ever burn up any of the old things that have accumulated?" Isabelle asked when she was home from the University.

"Oh, no," Abbie said hastily.

"Why not?"

"Oh . . . I don't know. Some one might need them sometime. I've always found a use for everything." And so every button, every string, every paper sack was carefully hoarded.

Isabelle was in the second semester of her sophomore year. She had only two dresses,—her brown school dress and her tan Sunday one, but she had a knack of wearing them well. It was the Era of Throttled Throats. Isabelle would pin a long ribbon at the front of her neck, wrap it tightly several times around that maltreated part of her anatomy and tie it in a huge bow under her ear.

"It's a wonder it doesn't shut off your epiglottis or whatever it is you sing with," Abbie said in disgust.

Isabelle was attractive with her reddish-brown hair and eyes and her mellow voice,—attractive apparently to Harrison Rhodes, a young man who sang in the same choir with her. When he had been out to the farm and sung "Whispering

Hope," with Isabelle, looking down at her while she played the accompaniment, Abbie thought that all who ran could read, and the language of the message was in that Esperanto, the universal language of romance.

"But then I'm sort of romantic, Will, and maybe I just imagine it."

I thought so, too, Abbie.

In June of that year a national political convention named a Nebraska man for its presidential candidate. He was defeated in November, but Abbie said, "At least they know now there are some states west of the Mississippi."

Letters came from John regularly and Abbie thought to herself, with no small amount of glee, that John was far more communicative through the medium of pen and paper than when he was with her. His firm was "getting along pretty well," although he himself was not doing much more than the collections and looking up references. He would be glad when he had a real case. Later he had joined the local unit of National Guards. They met and drilled right along. Rather foolish, maybe, when there was no likelihood of war, but it was good for them, as they were mostly fellows in offices. His foot bothered him yet sometimes,—a little stiff after he had drilled.

Peace had been over the land for thirty years,—and then suddenly there was no peace. Spanish-American controversies, which had been piling up like so many logs on a pyre, were touched off by a match of news which flashed across the land. The *Maine* had been sunk in Havana's harbor. And in the wing-and-ell farmhouse behind the cedars, Abbie Deal was reading a letter from John:

"And so we arrived here in camp Des Moines, Tuesday. It was the most impressive and magnificent sight I ever saw yesterday morning when we left. The G.A.R. and band and drum corps escorted us to the depot, and thousands of people on every side waved flags and cheered and cried as we marched along. At the station friends were bidding good-bys, and mothers, sisters and sweethearts were weeping and saying their farewells. . . . We arrived in Des Moines and our regiment was quartered in the speed stables. . . . We have ten box stalls to each company. . . . I didn't come home first for I didn't want to say good-by to you. I know how you will feel, Mother. But if you saw a bully licking a little youngster, you would think I was cowardly, if I didn't jump in and . . ."

Yes, yes, how the words came back! A boy she knew long ago had said that same thing.

War! War again! How terrible! O God, stop war!

"Our John's going to war, Will!" Abbie's stiff lips could hardly frame the words.

I would have wanted him to do his duty.

And then Abbie could think of almost nothing but her boy; could do almost nothing but fix things to send him,—cookies, a cake, a needle-book, a Testament. Always the Abbie Deals must be doing something for their children.

The letters came frequently. John was willing enough now to pour out his thoughts to his mother.

"Our regiments commence where the numbers of the regiments of the Civil War ceased,—that is, the First National Guard (the regiment our company belongs to) is now the Forty-Ninth."

Why, how terrible! Abbie looked up from her letter. How terrible that the numbers should go right on. Would they always go on? Mack's little boy, Stanley,—little Fred Baker, jr.—four and six now,— In twenty or thirty years— The idea was unthinkable. O God, don't let the numbers of the regiments go right on!

"We found that we all had to submit to another physical examination by a regular army physician. This was bad news for me and I feared it on account of the scar on my ankle. A number were rejected and I was one. . . ." Abbie's heart gave a bound of relief. John's near-tragedy, then, had been a blessing in disguise . . . "but another examination before a board of regimental surgeons passed me. . . ."

And so there was no relief and no blessing,—nothing but war.

There were other boys of the neighborhood going, too. Fritz Reinmueller for one. "*Ach!* Wid plantin' time come," Christine said in her half-English. "Such a *schlechte zeit* . . . bad time."

How queer Christine was,—to think always of the land and the crops and the money.

It had been in April that John's first letter had come from the box-stall in the Des Moines speed stable.

On a warm night in May, Isabelle came walking up the lane road under the poplars. Abbie had not expected her home and she ran to the sitting-room with cheery words of greeting. On the porch steps Isabelle stood and looked at her mother with wide tragic eyes. Did nothing,—said nothing, —but stood and looked with wide tragic eyes.

"Isabelle!" Abbie's heart was pounding tumultuously. "What is it?"

"I'm married." The girl's voice was dull, without expression.

"Married?" Abbie repeated in a voice equally as dull, and with equal lack of expression.

Isabelle put out her hand. There was a wide gold band on her slender finger.

"Last night. And he's gone."

"You mean you're married to . . . to . . ."

"He's gone," she repeated dully. There was only one man in the world, so why name him?

"You married Harrison Rhodes . . . before he left?"

"For San Francisco."

Abbie pulled Isabelle into the house and with shaking hands took off the girl's hat.

"They'll be sent to the Philippines," Isabelle said in that same expressionless way. Abbie was trembling in every limb. She had read about such things happening to other mothers. And now it was happening to her. She could not think it,—that her own little Isabelle Deal had married in that hasty manner. Why, she wasn't even Isabelle Deal,—she was Isabelle Rhodes. Everything seemed tumbling about Abbie's head,—all her plans for her musical girl. Why, Isabelle was only finishing her sophomore year. And then, suddenly, Abbie thought of the pearls lying in their velvet box in the old calf-skin-covered chest, waiting for Isabelle to be a bride. For a-moment, a great disappointment overtopped all her other emotions. Oh, why had Isabelle done this hasty thing?

"Oh, Isabelle . . . without a wedding! I've always wanted every one of my girls to have a wedding at home."

"Oh, what difference is a *wedding*?" And Isabelle began to cry, great wrenching sobs that shook her.

Abbie put comforting arms around her. "There . . .

there . . . dearie. That's right . . . after all . . . what difference
is a wedding?''

"He cared for nothing in the world but me and music,"
Isabelle said in her bitterness, "but he went to war."

Abbie held her close, rocked her as if she were a child.

"Yes, yes, Isabelle. They care for nothing in the world but
women and their work . . . and they go to war."

Isabelle would not go back to school for the remaining few
weeks of the year. She would only sit at home and wait dully.
And now Abbie had the new experience of attempting to keep
another person courageous. It was more trying than to keep
up her own spirits. Why must she always be strong for other
people? How Isabelle sapped at her strength! She seemed to
have no stamina. Sometimes Abbie thought the girl was
selfish in it, and then she would say. "But I'm her *mother*.
I'm the *one* for her to take her troubles to." Abbie had John
to think about also. She felt a little jealous that Isabelle was
thinking of Harrison all the time, when John was in the same
danger.

By the middle of June, John, the lawyer, was sweltering at
drill in Camp Libre in Florida; and Harrison, who cared for
nothing in the world but Isabelle and music, was sweltering
before Fort Malati, doing outpost duty.

They came home in the summer of '99. Harrison, who had
been in much action, came home fairly well; John, who had
done only camp and guard duty, came pale, emaciated and
weak from typhoid contracted in Cuba. Harrison and Isabelle
made plans to move immediately to Chicago. Abbie thought
she could not stand it,—to have Isabelle live so far away.
Why did children do that! It made her envy Christine, whose
children were all settling down on the various eighties that
Gus had bought,—Heinie here, Emil there, even Fritz, just
home from the Philippines, had married and started into the
field.

Isabelle took the piano. "I hate to, Mother, with Grace
eleven now. It seems selfish."

"No, you take it," Abbie told her. "Grace can't bear to
practice. She just reads and reads. My,—how different you
children all are."

And then it came about that Chicago seemed not far,
almost neighborly, in comparison with John's new location.

After recuperating at home that summer, John left for Seattle and Nome. Abbie was stunned. Nome,—in Alaska,—from which there could be no return in the fall after the ice had frozen, from which there could come no word until late spring when the ice had gone out. In his characteristic way, John had told his plan casually only a few days before he left. There was a future in Alaska. It was the place for young fellows. Fortunes awaited their picking up. He would open a law office in Nome and keep his eyes open for anything presenting itself on the side. He was using his army money for the purpose. How queer, thought Abbie,—just as Will had taken his army money for the long-ago trip into Nebraska. Soldiers of fortune, both.

Calm and dry-eyed, Abbie told her son good-by. But all winter, day and night, her thoughts were with him. Every night when she was ready for bed she would look over the snow-covered prairie to the northwest, toward the land to which no word could go,—toward the land from which no word could come.

It was June before the first of the winter letters came. There were many. John had written her often. Many nights, then, as she had stood looking across the snow-wrapped prairie, John had been writing to her. After all, no distance could sever the tie that bound them,—nothing come between her and her silent boy. The letters were of an intense interest to home-keeping Abbie,—descriptive of the gold rush. Most important of all, John had been appointed U.S. Commissioner and was going up above the Arctic Circle.

In the late fall of that year, when Mack's and Emma's boy, Stanley, was six, a second son was born to them. They named him Donald. And he immediately upset Abbie's plans for Christmas by acquiring colic to such a noisy degree that the Mackenzie Deal family decided to stay in Omaha behind closed doors with their vociferous offspring.

The annual Deal reunion did not prove so complete a success as usual with John and Mack's family all absent. Abbie went through all the preparations for the event, as she always did,—the pop-corn balls and the taffy candy, the tree and the little hidden packages, but it was never the same for her when one child was missing. This was the fourth Christmas John had been away from them. More than ever, Abbie's thoughts were with John in that far-off land of the midnight sun, now that he was so much farther away than Nome.

What was there about John that seemed always to bring her thoughts of anxiety, Abbie wondered? From the time he was small, it seemed that she had always thought and prayed more about John than any of the others. His silence, his independence, his way of doing things without telling her, worried her. And now in Alaska, above the Arctic Circle, with no means of communication until the ice floe should go out, —what was he doing? What were his experiences? His pastimes? His temptations? What sort of women was he meeting? Abbie would stop in her work and utter a prayer for him,—and, sent as it were from the bow of a mother's watchful care, bound by the cord of a mother's love, the little winged arrow on its flight must have reached Some one,— Somewhere.

The Dr. Fred Bakers were out at Christmas. Grace, twelve, and Fred, Jr., eight, were the only children at the Christmas reunion that year.

Isabelle and Harrison, though, came from Chicago, enthusiastic over their music. They were both studying and practicing hours every day, and singing in a suburban church choir. They each had a few music pupils. Isabelle looked stylish in her brown silk shirtwaist and wide brown serge skirt with fifteen gores, stiffened with buckram.

The two stayed a day after the Fred Bakers had gone.

"Don't you get tired of all the extra noise and work, Mother?" Isabelle wanted to know when they were alone.

"Oh, my! No, dear," Abbie returned. "When you have children, Isabelle, you'll understand what I mean."

"I might as well tell you now, Mother,—we're not having children."

"Not . . . *what*, Isabelle?"

"I'd really rather be honest with you than hear you talk that way. We're not having a family."

"Why, Isabelle, you talk as though . . . as though . . ."

"But I mean it. We're really not well enough off. You know, yourself, Mother, that Harrison and I will never be rich and what's more, neither one of us really cares. Mack has a good business head on him and is well on the way now to being well-to-do. Doctor and Margaret seem to have the ability to lay up treasures where moth can corrupt. No telling what John will do. He may be a big attorney some day. We don't know Grace's future when she's only twelve. But all Harrison and I care for is our art. Music is our very life. Knowing that we're going to be so devoted to it and perhaps never be well enough off, we're just not having children.''

"But, Isabelle, if people waited to be rich to have children. If *we!* . . . Oh, Isabelle! . . . You'd make me laugh if I didn't feel so like crying. 'Can't afford it?' How can you afford to *miss* it . . . little children . . . their soft warm bodies and their little clinging hands . . . their cunning ways . . . miss *motherhood?*''

"Of course, I might have known you wouldn't like it . . . but I want to devote all of my time to my voice. To have children you ought to have plenty of time and money for their development.''

Abbie Deal looked out of the window, down through the long row of cedars. "To have plenty of time and money for their development.'' Instead of the cedars, heavy with snow, she was looking into a sod-house where a little painted black-board stood against the mud-plastered walls, seeing one shelf of books and a slate and some ironed pieces of brown wrapping-paper. The mother there was hearing reading lessons while she kneaded bread, was teaching songs while she scrubbed, was giving out spelling words while she mended, was instilling into childish minds, ideals of honesty and clean living with every humble task.

For a long time Abbie Deal sat and looked out at the cedars bending under the snow, like so many mothers bending under their burdens. But she did not answer Isabelle. Maybe there was no answer. Perhaps there was no argument. She did not know.

Chapter 25

John's letters came again in the late spring, in them an echo of the breeze that blows over the Kotzebue Sound. "For Christmas dinner we had fish balls and egg sauce, baked white-fish, ptarmigan pot-roast, mashed potatoes, baked dressing, ice cream from condensed milk, and coffee. After the white people ate, the Eskimos took turn and made a thorough clean-up. When one of them found something that struck his palate, he proceeded to devour the entire contents of the dish. Eighty white people ate and twenty-five Eskimos. The miners came dressed in their parkas and mukluks. . . .

"Thermometer has been down to 38 degrees all day, 46 below in the night. This morning about eleven the ice began moving on the Keewalik and kept coming all day. There is an ice jam at the bluffs below town, and a number of cabins are in danger of being carried away. . . .

"Strike on Kugruh has been confirmed,—the whole river and benches have been staked."

Abbie, with the letters in her lap, would look out over the familiar fields, green in their spring wheat and their parallel rows of young corn, and wonder how a child of the prairie could have gone so far away.

And now Nature began to seem less parsimonious with her rains. No longer was the sky a dry blue bowl turned over the dry brown earth. Heavy with moisture, the clouds gathered and fell in a blessing of light showers or heavy, soaking rains. Out of Nature's benediction grew fine crops, better times, high land prices.

A union of farmers to market their own crops was being formed in many localities. Abbie took two shares of stock in the Cedartown Elevator. "It's the beginning of something pretty big, I believe," she told Mack.

In the fall, Henry Lutz died. And over in the house with the cupola and the wooden rosettes and the fancy grill-work, Sarah Lutz clung to Abbie constantly, so there was one more duty at hand for her. After her father's death, Emma came into the possession of a large amount of land. Selling here, buying there with good business judgment, and aided by the upward swing of prices, Mack, who was now assistant cashier of the bank, placed the Mackenzie Deal family on the best of financial footing.

One more year went by with John proving his ownership of the title "Judge Deal" in the land of the dog-team, and then he came back. In that characteristic way of suddenly doing something with no preliminary talk, he opened a law office in Cedartown. To Abbie, it seemed unbelievable and far too good to be true, that the wanderer of the family should settle down closer to her than any of the others.

Margaret was painting many canvases every year now. Pencil and drawing-book with her, she often came out home to wander for hours in the vicinity, sketching the cotton-woods or the maples or a rolling bit of pasture land. "When the day comes, Mother," she would say, "that I can get the light that lies over the prairie at evening, to suit me, I believe I'll be satisfied."

Isabelle, in Chicago for three years, was forging ahead in her career, singing at some of the select musical affairs. Abbie's natural garment of modesty showed large perforations in it, when it came to anything concerning her children's accomplishments. More than once she hitched up the old white mare and drove into the *Headlight* office to proffer some item about one of her offspring's achievements.

"The Deals all seem to do things," Abbie heard a visitor to the community say to Oscar Lutz once. The two men were sitting on a bench under her kitchen window, before one of the many neighborhood suppers. Abbie, paring potatoes, could hear every word of Oscar's reply.

"The children do. Will, himself, was a good man but not much of a manager. Was always planning some wild scheme for the whole community. You can't get anywhere if you spread your plans all out over the whole country. At all the school meetings he talked about the day when the country school would be graded like the town. Talked about the day when the roads would be fixed. Had some fool plan about hauling little stones from the quarry at Louisville . . . loads of little stones and gravel and running a roller over 'em. Heard him say once right after a long drought that Nebraska was the best state in the Union . . . had the best soil . . . that the day would come that the climate conditions would change and it would be the most productive of them all. Talked about trees . . . trees . . . trees. Was as loony as old J. Sterling Morton himself about setting out timber. Would go after saplings and cuttings and help haul 'em in for the careless ones if they'd set 'em out. No, he wasn't lazy . . . lord, no. . . . Just plannin' fer the whole kit 'n' bilin 'of 'em instead of himself. Carried the whole precinct on his shoulders. Didn't leave Abbie anything very much besides this one half-section, but the five children and the good name o' Deal.''

Abbie, bending over the potatoes, with the neighbor women bustling around her, said softly to one they could not see, "Will, I'm glad,—glad that you left me the children and the good name of Deal.''

John was not much more than settled in his new Cedartown office when his thirtieth birthday arrived, via the 1902 calendar. Thirty having been the meridian between youth and old bachelorhood in Abbie's young day, she concluded quite definitely that he was never going to marry. And as has happened since the time Naomi's sons appeared before her with Ruth and Orpha, Abbie was suddenly astounded by John writing her, while on a business trip, that he was bringing home a bride. She was Eloise Wentworth, a teacher he had met in Iowa, and they would arrive on the four o'clock, Saturday.

Abbie sat with the letter in her lap, the world tumbling grotesquely about her. This bolt from the blue, so characteristic of John, was hard to realize. A peculiar form of jealousy tore at her. "I'll bet she did the courting herself," Abbie said grimly, and was too wrought up to laugh at herself. Why hadn't he picked out some one she knew? Emma Lutz, Dr. Fred Baker, Harrison Rhodes,—she had met and known them all before they came into the family. Why had he done this, anyway? Did he know the girl well? What was she like? Of all the children, John was the one who had to be handled with gloves. Would she know how to get along with him? Why hadn't he married one of the home girls? Why hadn't he ever mentioned the girl? All at once Abbie began to laugh aloud, almost hysterically. "I'm talking for all the world like Grandma," she said. "Oh, I mustn't let myself get like Grandma Deal."

She never dreaded anything so much in her life as the prospects of that meeting on Saturday. It took all of her will-power to get herself in hand to welcome them. She was glad that Grace was home with her. Grace was fourteen now and in the Cedartown High School. No longer did children of the community have to go from home and board at the old Weeping Water Academy, for the Cedartown High School was now accredited to the University. Grace was a nice girl and a good student,—efficient, neat, a little prim. Looking at her sometimes, critically, Abbie wondered why a keen sense of humor had been omitted from Grace's makeup. She laughed at a joke when it was in a column duly labeled as one, and warranted to tickle the risibilities. But humor, that vague, elusive thing which had pulled Abbie through many a monotonous day and over many a harsh experience, seemed a missing ingredient.

The two, Abbie and Grace, met the newly-married couple with the surrey. Abbie was fifty-five now, her once glorious reddish-brown hair colorless where it was not gray, her shoulders drooping, her body rather shapeless.

Eloise was pleasant,—a nice looking young woman with firm lips. She had on an Alice-blue skirt made the new way with all the gathers in the back, and dragging a little on the station platform. A tight silk waist of the same shade with a cream-colored lace fichu, and a blue hat fitting firmly to her coils of light hair in the back but protruding fashionably to the front far over the large roll of a high pompadour, completed her most up-to-date costume. She met Abbie half-way with cordiality. She fitted herself into the family, firmly, as though she had arrived with the preconceived idea that she was going to make the most of John's mother. Grace took a liking to her immediately. The two discussed school affairs earnestly, with Grace hanging on her new sister's every firm word. Abbie, cleaning up the table and listening to them, said to herself, "For all the world, I believe she and Grace are two of a kind."

"Mother," Eloise said firmly, after supper when John had gone over to the office, "I'm going to call you 'Mother' right on the start and then it won't be hard."

"I hope," said Abbie gently, "it won't be hard to call me 'Mother.' "

"Oh, no," Eloise said firmly. "I'm not going to *let* it be hard. That's why I'm beginning at once. Mother, John's and my marriage is to be different from other marriages."

"How, Eloise?"

"Because I'm going at it in a businesslike, systematic way."

"Yes," said Abbie, "that's a good way."

"I'm going to make our home a well-organized place of rest and peace for John."

"That will be nice."

"You see mistakes on all sides and *I'm* not going to make any."

"No," said Abbie, "of course you won't."

"I've been reading everything on the subject and I *know* that I'm well prepared."

"Yes," said Abbie meekly, "I think you are."

"She has everything, Will," Abbie said to the spirit who was comrade and confidante, "education, looks, high ideals, efficiency,—everything but a sense of humor. And oh, Will, *how* John will miss it."

He admires her, Abbie.

"And loves her, Will, and love covers many things."

The next year Abbie sold the rest of the acreage to Gus Reinmueller, retaining the five acres which contained the house and out-buildings, the orchard and one pasture. Gus paid twelve thousand dollars for it, giving four thousand in cash and an interest-bearing note. "Now we can plan for Grace to go to the University," Abbie said. "Grace wants to be a teacher and now I can help her."

Now that the land was sold, Abbie did not have to think of the responsibility of the crops, but her hands were still busy with chickens, and pigs and the cow. She drove a sorrel mare now back and forth, attending everything that went on in Cedartown, which she felt would benefit her mentally, and she did not miss a church service or Ladies' Aid. One of the attractions that summer, which she and Grace patronized, was an entertainment in the opera house, purporting to be a sort of magic-lantern show in which the people in the picture would move about as they were thrown on the sheet.

"It may be true," Abbie admitted, but added with frank suspicion that there was probably a catch in it somewhere.

The program opened with a piece by the Cedartown orchestra. Probably the Boston Symphony could have done as well, but old Charlie Beadle, who was leader and drummer, would not have admitted it. A male quartet next sang, "Out on the Deep When the Sun Is Low." One gathered the rather disquieting impression from their forlorn and hopeless tones that there was small prospect of ever seeing the center of the solar system again. Miss Happy Joy Hansen then spoke "The Raggedy Man, He Works for Paw," with so much childish lisping and so much coy twisting of an imaginary apron, that one never in the world could have guessed her age, unless he had known, as all Cedartown did, that, neither happily nor joyously, would she ever, ever again see thirty-two.

And then, the picture. The male quartet, having apparently recovered from the sad effects of the setting sun, launched forth into a spirited presentation of: "When Kate and I Were Coming Through the Rye." A field of grain was plainly visible on the cloth, and, incredulous as it seemed, it waved and jerked and twitched. Kate came into sight, and, unbelievable as it was, Kate also waved and jerked and twitched. A young man close behind her, with every indication of St. Vitus' Dance, also waved and jerked and twitched. But they moved. The advertisement had not lied. Across the sheet the people moved. "Dear, dear," Abbie said on the way home. "What next can they do? There's just nothing now left to be invented, Grace."

Late that fall, Abbie helped organize a Woman's Club. "I don't know that we will do a great deal of good, but we won't do any harm, and much of life is an experiment, anyway."

Christine was disgusted when Abbie told her. "A club! *Ach!* for what? To hit mit?"

On the very day in which Abbie drove home with the office of second vice president of the Cedartown Woman's Club upon her shoulders, a touch of the old raw prairie days presented itself like a bit of the past. She met Oscar Lutz with a wild deer which he had shot and killed in the timber a mile east of Stove Creek,—a young buck that, quivering and at bay, seemed the last survivor of his comrades that had once roamed the east-Nebraska country.

Grace graduated from High School when Abbie was fifty-eight. She gave the valedictory for her class, an earnest if youthful dissertation on "Heaven Is Not Reached by a Single Bound."

The Sunday after the exercises, all of the children, but Isabelle, were home for dinner. At the table Mack said: "Mother, you ought to offer the place for sale right away to get a buyer by fall. It will make some farmer who wants to retire, a mighty good place,—a nice little five-acre tract with the orchard and a pasture and all."

"I would have before this," Abbie admitted, "but I haven't been real sure in my mind that I'd leave at all."

They all voiced the same sentiment, "Oh, yes, Mother, you ought to move to Lincoln with Grace."

"There's no real use for your staying."

"With Grace gone, just think how lonesome you'll be."

Dr. Baker and Margaret were willing to have Grace and her mother live with them just as Isabelle had done for those two years. The Bakers had been married fifteen years now. Dr. Baker's firm was a leading one, Dr. Baker himself prominent in his profession. They had a nice comfortable home. Lincoln was a city.

"Oh, no, I wouldn't want to do that," Abbie said. "Not *both* of us. That would be one too many, anyway. If I go, Grace and I will have a little place of our own."

That set them off on another tangent. There were nice cottages going up everywhere, several attractive ones of the new type called bungalows.

Before they left, they went over all the arguments for selling. "The place is too big for you, Mother. What do you need of a yard this size? Or a house with this many rooms? Or a barn?" Their talk was sensible. All the arguments seemed on their side. "And above all the reasons, is the one that it's going to be lonesome for you here." They were unanimous in that opinion of their mother's coming loneliness.

Abbie thought about it a great deal that summer before it was time for Grace to go. At times she decided that she was foolish to stay in the old place. The children were right. It was only old-fashioned, narrow people who never made a change. She believed she would go up to Lincoln and look at cottages. In the city there would be a larger life for her, new contacts, opportunities to see and hear better things. Just as she had half reconciled herself to the plan, she would walk down the path between the cedars, which she and Will had set out, look at her hollyhocks and delphinium, blood-red and sea-blue against the white pickets, stand for a time and gaze over toward the heavy fringe of willows and oaks and elms along Stove Creek. Everything looked familiar,—friendly. There would never be another real home for her. Home was something besides so much lumber and plaster. You built your thoughts into the frame work. You planted a little of your heart with the trees and the shrubbery.

It was the only old home the children had ever known. There ought to be a home for children to come to,—and *their* children,—a central place, to which they could always bring their joys and sorrows,—an old familiar place for them to return to on Sundays and Christmases. An old home ought always to stand like a mother with open arms. It ought to be here waiting for the children to come to it,—like homing pigeons.

On the next Sunday Abbie was ready with her decision. "No, I've decided. I'm going to stay here. This is my home."

They went over all the arguments again. "The place is too big for you, Mother. What do you need of a house this size? Or a barn? And above all, with Grace gone, it will be too lonely for you here. . . ."

Abbie looked beyond the poplars, stared for a moment beyond the Lombardy poplars into the deepening prairie twilight.

"No," she said quietly, "you wouldn't understand. It won't be lonely here."

Chapter 26

That fall after Grace went away to school, John's and Eloise's first child was born.

"You'll want me to come, won't you?" Abbie had asked Eloise with her usual desire to be helpful.

"Oh, no," Eloise had said hastily,—a little too hastily. "John wants me to have a *trained* nurse,—the very best."

Little hurts! Little pleasures! How they made up the whole of Abbie Deal's life.

Eloise named the boy Wentworth, and proceeded to bring him up by the ritual of a red volume in which she held implicit and humorless faith.

"It would make a dog laugh, Will," Abbie said at home to that invisible comrade who was only spirit and memory. "He was crying and she ran and got the little red book and looked up something in the index. I went over and picked him up and it was nothing but a safety-pin sticking him."

That was the fall, too, in which Cedartown was astonished and entertained by the spectacle of Mack Deal and Emma with the two boys coming to town in one of the new automobiles. The noisy approach was borne in upon the ears of the residenters some time before the machine's actual appearance, so that a welcoming committee, in the form of a large delegation of the citizens, was on hand to greet the proud owners.

Mack and the ten-year-old Stanley were on the front seat. Mack at the wheel, eyes bulging and elbows out at right angles, looked neither to the right nor the left as he piloted the popping, sputtering land craft through the choppy seas of a rough road. Emma, in the back seat with the four-year-old Donald, was in a state of perpetual motion, caused by dividing her frantic clutches between her youthful offspring and her large flapping hat, wound round with many yards of veiling. Through town and to his mother's house, Mack and his new possession were followed by a cavalcade of interested, not to say envious spectators. The crowd surrounded him when he pulled up in front of the small gate, Mack having decided that he would not try to navigate the lane road, with the eventual possibility of his inability to turn around or back out.

The machine, as red as Oscar Lutz's thrasher, was almost immodest in the exposure of its many complicated internal workings. There were wicker baskets along the side, which Mack explained to inquirers were for picnic lunches. There were a hundred other questions he was required to answer. Yes, he had bought the windshield and the lights extra. Thought he might just as well get everything while he was about it. Only thing he hadn't bought was a top. They cost a lot more and anyway it was so much harder to run the things with one on. You could get them put on later any time you wanted to. Yes, he had come the forty-six miles in three and one-half hours. At which almost incredible statement, there was a shaking of heads and murmured, "Gosh, . . . almost fifteen miles an hour."

All of the boys and most of the men in Cedartown visited the exhibit during the day, and a large aggregation was on hand to see the departure at four in the afternoon, the time Mack had set for leaving, so that they could get back to Omaha before they would have to light the carbon lamps in front.

The next year Abbie had five grandchildren, instead of four, for Mack and Emma were the parents of a girl, whom they called Katherine. There was considerable rejoicing in all branches of the family, for this was the first girl among the five small cousins.

Emma was back at her social activities soon after the baby's advent, much to Abbie's uneasiness. "Emma certainly takes her duties lightly," Abbie would say to Margaret, who was her confidant in all the daughter-in-law gossip. "She and

Eloise ought to be shaken up in a hat. Emma is too easy about it all for any use, and Eloise makes such hard work of it, that it's painful to see her."

Near the close of her University course, Grace came home one Friday evening, ate supper with her mother and wiped the dishes for her, remarking quite casually, "Mother, Wilber Johnson, the engineering student I told you about, asked me to marry him."

Abbie, who was cutting bacon in readiness for breakfast, nearly cut a finger in her surprise and excitement.

"Why, Grace . . . and you've kept it from Mother two hours . . . you rascal! Well, he's a nice boy, I'm sure. I knew his father and mother years ago and better people never lived. She came as a bride to the half-section across the creek from us . . . where Fritz Reinmueller lives now. She could hardly help but have a fine son. Well . . . well . . . *my baby!* I can't *think,* Grace, that you're twenty and old enough to know your own mind. How soon the years go by. . . . It's the right way, though, and the natural one. . . . I'll be glad to see you. . . ."

"Goodness, Mother, stop and listen. . . . I'm not going to marry him."

"You're not?"

"Why, of course not. I didn't say so. I just said he asked me to. I wouldn't *think* of it."

"Then you don't love him?"

"Of course not."

"That *is* a joke on me . . going on that way. He's such a nice boy and his folks are so nice and well fixed. I guess I never gave it a thought but that you meant you wanted to marry him."

"Well, I don't. I don't feel a bit like it."

"That's all right, dearie. I know just how you feel. He isn't the one, is he? But you just wait. There will be some one,—and then you can wear the pearls I've been keeping all this time for one of my girls to wear. I'm glad you know your own mind. Lots of girls don't. They just marry the first man that asks them. But you're a strong character, Grace, and I'm glad of it. One of these days the right one will come along. I've got a little poem in my scrap book that says:

> *"Asleep, awake, by night or day,*
> *The friends I seek are seeking me;*
> *No wind can drive my bark astray,*
> *Nor change the tide of destiny.*
> *The stars come nightly to the skies.*
> *The tidal wave unto the sea,*
> *Nor time, nor space, nor deep nor high*
> *Can keep my own away from me.*

You just think of it that way and one of these days you'll meet the right man."

Grace seemed a little impatient. "Oh, Mother, I don't know that I want to."

"Want to what, Grace?"

"*Ever* marry."

"Oh, yes, you do. Just now after this little affair you don't think so. But you will, Grace, you just wait."

In 1909 Grace graduated from the University with Phi Beta Kappa honors, secured a good high school position farther out in the state, and was not home until the annual Christmas reunion. When she came home she seemed to have developed a maternal attitude toward her mother which was paradoxically pleasing and irritating to Abbie. She was pleased that Grace was thoughtful and considerate of her, irritated that she began to think of her as old.

"Mother, you ought to take a nap every afternoon," Grace would say didactically. To which Abbie would retort, "I'm not exactly feeble yet, Grace." Or, "Mother, there's a splendid new book on avoiding old age. You ought to read it."

"I'm only sixty-two, Grace, and I don't see any signs of senility. You can't avoid old age, but you don't need to think about it."

A week after she came home at the close of her spring term, Grace went away to summer school. There was not a lazy bone in Grace's body, Abbie often said. She was energetic, efficient. Sometimes, watching her or thinking about her in the way Abbie was always watching or thinking about the children, she wondered if Grace was not just a bit hard, just a trifle unsympathetic. She seemed to have no patience with inefficiency, no time for any one who was not succeeding.

Abbie was ashamed of herself that she did not get more

comfort and companionship out of Grace. She loved her with her whole being, but they seemed to antagonize each other at times. She sometimes admitted reluctantly to herself that Grace was not the daughter which she had dreamed she would be,—a daughter to sit and talk, a companion with whom to hold long discussions. She was too energetic to sit quietly anywhere, and whenever the two held any discussions they usually ended in Abbie having her feelings hurt.

Grace was always impatient with the old order of things, always so sure of herself, so certain that one could accomplish in this world whatever task he set himself to do. Her conversation was always dotted with the words "progress," "efficiency," "ideals." She spoke of everything in generalities: Citizenship, economics, causes, rights. Abbie was all for the individual. "Yes, but old Mrs. Newsome, Grace. How about *her?*" She could not think of people in masses. A great sympathy would surge up in her heart for the one whom life had used harshly. But when she would express herself, she would be met with a flood of information from Grace, a flat statement of statistics, before which she would be compelled to retire ignominiously.

"Why, I'm glad she's that way," Abbie would say to herself. "She's smart, Grace is. And she's only twenty-two. When you get older, you get more sympathetic with the underdog. When you grow out of your youthful years you have more charity for folks who haven't succeeded." It was so characteristic of Abbie,—charity,—charity that vaunteth not itself and is kind,—that she could not see how others could ever leave it out of their make-up.

In the last of the summer Grace was home again, having made several credits toward her master's degree. She was energetic even in the heat, ready to help with the work, full of plans for improving the house. "Dear, dear," Abbie said to herself, "Grace is so energetic, she is like the wind,—so active that she's tiresome."

It was during these weeks of activity that Grace decided to have an afternoon party for her mother,—some friends out from Cedartown and two or three from Lincoln,—women whom Abbie had met and enjoyed at Margaret's and at Sarah Lutz's. Abbie was pleased with the idea. It was kind of Grace to do this for her. "I suppose I would never get around to do it,'' Abbie admitted to herself. "That's one thing about Grace, she does get things accomplished.''

Abbie made out her list, and Grace looked it over preparatory to inviting the guests.

"Mother, you're not going to have Christine Reinmueller?"

"Oh, yes, I am, Grace.'' Abbie was sure of herself.

"Not with those Lincoln women. I wouldn't care if it were just the Cedartown people. But not with those Lincoln women and especially not with Mrs. Wentworth. Whatever would *she* think of Christine?''

"I'm sure, Grace, I can't help *what* Eloise's mother would think of her!''

"I don't see how you can be so friendly with Christine, anyway. She's so Dutchy and so narrow and so ignorant.''

Abbie Deal set her mouth to keep it from trembling. Loyalty . . . it was the very fiber of her. In that swift flight of memory with which the human mind can make a non-stop journey across the years, she heard: "Hold-tight. Get the ground up. You die already yet. *Du narr!* Ya . . . you like dat dyin' . . . maybe.'' She opened her eyes to the odor of steam, onions, hot water, flannels, to the sight of the homely red face of Christine by her bed, nodding,—jerking up,—nodding—

"Why, Grace!'' Because she was so thoroughly agitated she said it mildly. "Why, Grace, she saved our lives . . . yours and mine. . . .''

"I realize it, Mother. I've heard all that a hundred times. But, heavens . . . is the debt never paid?''

To keep herself cool and poised and her lips from trembling, Abbie rose and started into the next room. In the doorway she turned.

"Never!'' said Abbie Deal. "Never!''

Chapter 27

The same summer that Sarah Lutz went abroad with Emma, Abbie spent her spare time building the seat under the cedars. This was her sixty-sixth summer. She had almost finished her sawing and pounding on a warm August afternoon, when she looked up to see Sarah driving into the lane road in her electric car.

Abbie's gray hair was stringing over her face,—perspiration on her forehead.

Sarah piloted the car, which she had dubbed Napoleon, up to the Lombardys, where Napoleon, with his usual caution, refused to climb a little rise in the ground. Sarah looked "dressy." She had on a lavender summer silk, little amethysts in her ears.

"Well, Sarah . . . you've been to London. And what did you do there?"

"Abbie, I frightened a little mouse under the chair." Sarah kissed Abbie, held her close for a moment. What good old friends they were! And how they understood each other.

"Abbie Deal, whatever are you doing?"

"Sarah Lutz, I do hate to start anything I can't finish, but if old Asy Drumm was alive I'd have him here on the dog trot."

"But what *is* it?"

"It's a seat."

"For what?"

"To sit on. I suppose you've grown so high-faluting in your travel, Sarah, that you think a seat ought to be a

Louis-something *objet d'art,* as the magazines say. Well, it isn't. It's to sit on. I've been on the go for sixty-six years and now I'm going to sit down a little, and I can't think of a place I'd rather sit than here where I can look off to the fertile fields that have come out of the old rolling prairie."

"It *is* pleasant, Abbie. There's something about it, . . . after all my trip . . . the wide stretches of view . . . the way the rolling land meets the blue sky. . . . Well, it calls you back . . . the prairie does, just as the sea calls the fisher folk."

And then Christine Reinmueller turned into the driveway, trudging along in the inevitable blue calico, gathered full at the waist, her little greasy braids of hair plaited flat from ear to ear. Because she had looked so old when she was still young, Christine seemed to have changed less than the others. There was something ageless about her. As she had had no youth, she now had no age.

"Well, girls, here we all are."

For a long time the three "girls" sat under the trees and visited,—Abbie Deal and Sarah Lutz and Christine Reinmueller, —Abbie, the motherly home woman,—Sarah, who loved dress and travel,—Christine, with no thought but the accumulation of the land. Three varying personalities they were, —held together by a strange tie of memory,—friends, because on a long-ago hot summer day, three covered wagons in a long straggling line lurched over the prairie together.

When John's and Eloise's son Wentworth was nine, they welcomed a daughter, whom they named Laura, and whom Eloise proceeded to bring up by the ritual of a blue book, child training fads having changed, and the old red book of Wentworth's baby days having become a back number.

Abbie had six grandchildren now. Mack's sons, Stanley and Donald, were twenty and fourteen. Stanley, having graduated from an Omaha High School, was East, at Dartmouth, and Mack and Emma were talking of sending Donald to a select school for boys. "He needs culture and poise," Emma explained to Abbie.

"Dear, dear," said Abbie, "culture and poise! At his age, his father needed clothing and provender."

Emma laughed. That was one thing about Emma,—she was like Sarah, her mother, good-natured, ready to laugh at herself as readily as at another. Abbie felt as close to her as to her own girls.

Katherine, Mack's little daughter was eight,—an active child, always on tiptoe like some gay sprite, too full of the joy of living to settle down.

Fred Baker, Jr., was twenty-two, already taking a medical course, with that characteristic following of his father which a doctor's son seems so often to possess.

As for Abbie's sons, themselves, they progressed. Mack, who had been in the bank twenty-seven years, was now a heavy stock-holder. John did law work for half the county.

The old Weeping Water Academy, closed now in 1915, its usefulness over. High Schools, accredited to the University, were accessible to every boy and girl. The state owned nearly two million acres of school land, which, under the law, could not be sold. And it held first place in literacy.

The summer Abbie was seventy was the one in which the children planned an intensive campaign against her staying longer in the old home.

"We've just got to take things in our own hands," they told each other. "Mother's fairly well, but no woman of seventy ought to live alone like this on the edge of town."

"Why hadn't she?" Abbie Deal asked. "What's the difference . . . the *edge* of town or the *middle* of town?"

They talked it over,—she might have a room at John's in Cedartown. Then she would not be so far from old friends. "If she lives with me," Eloise informed them firmly, "I shall take it upon myself to see that she gets the right balance in her meals, and the right number of hours of sleep. I've always thought Mother Deal ate more protein and less carbo-hydrates than she should, and she gets up too early for a woman of her age."

"So I'm to be brought up according to a *green* book, I expect," Abbie Deal said grimly to herself.

"I think my home is the natural place," Margaret told them. "I'm the oldest daughter and Mother is as interested in my oil work as I am."

"We've got such a lot of room," Mack put in. "I don't know what a person wants so much for, anyway. But now that we've got it, I wish Mother would come with us and help fill it up. What do you say, Em?"

Good-natured Emma was willing, although she reserved certain secret doubts over the compatibility of Mother Deal and eleven-year-old Katherine.

Isabelle's Chicago apartment was permanently out of the competition. But there remained one other plan. Grace could give up her work and come home.

"I'll be willing to, Mother, if you just *won't* consent to leaving. I'd come right in and take charge of everything." Grace's sense of organization, like a pointer, was already scenting out a dozen little hidden plans. And her forty-horse-power energy was already tiring Abbie. "I'd turn the parlor into a room for Mother and take her bedroom for mine. Then I'd be down here close to her. I'd get a tea-cart in case she needed a meal in her room. . . ."

"And you could wheel the chickens in, on the wheelbarrow, for me to feed," Abbie retorted. Now she ought not to have said that, she was thinking. Why, she ought to be thankful they were so kind. How many mothers could have that number of good homes at their disposal? But she did resent being planned about and talked over. After all they were her children. In spite of their years, she was still their mother. She had never let them run over her and she wasn't going to now. When they had quite definitely decided on Margaret's home for her, she spoke up:

"I'll do nothing of the kind. I'll stay right here. And kindly let me alone. Because a woman is getting old, has she no rights?"

Eloise was almost openly relieved. Emma knew in her heart that the possibility of certain dramatic situations between the rather high-strung Katherine and her grandmother were now permanently avoided. Grace admitted to herself that it would have been more of a sacrifice for her to give up her work than the others could dream; and Margaret, with a slight sinking sensation, pondered for a moment over the mental picture of the marble-topped stand, the blue plush album and the patent swinging-rocker, rubbing elbows with the furnishings of her artistic house.

So they "let her alone." But from that time on they said among themselves that mother was childish, that you had to overlook an elderly woman's vagaries, and that they must drive in more frequently to watch her so that no harm would come to her.

When Wentworth was thirteen, and Laura four, John's and Eloise's third child was born. It was a boy and they named him Millard. John telephoned the news to his mother, who was now seventy-one. Abbie hung up the receiver, put on her hat,—a new one since the demise of the rusty black with the itinerant ornament,—and walked over to Cedartown. She could not wait longer to see the baby. She had borne six children, herself, and this was her seventh grandchild, but she experienced that same excited interest over its advent she had known at all of those other times. The first thing she saw when she entered the house was a new book on child rearing lying on the table,—a *brown* book.

"Mother, you shouldn't have done this," John was half-provoked. "I would have come out to get you."

"I am a little tired, I'll admit, but as long as I've got two good . . . well, we used to say limbs . . . but they're legs now, so I'll say 'legs,' . . . I'm not going to lose the use of them if I can help it."

She held the baby (to Eloise's discomfiture, for it said not to do so on page nineteen), turned it to the light . . . said she saw a little of Eloise about its mouth, John in the shape of its head, something of Laura, and even, by some wild stretch of imagination, a look of its great-grandfather Deal around the eyes.

Eloise, weak and nervous, was complaining about her help. The maid was cleaning and cooking all right but she did not know how to handle Laura.

Immediately Abbie was offering: "Let me take Laura home, Eloise. I'd like to so well. I'll take good care of her for a week or so . . . as long as you'll let her stay."

Eloise was a little dubious about the proposition and took no pains to hide it. "What do you think, John?"

"I'm wondering if Mother ought to. She's seventy-one, Eloise."

"Oh, it's not of your mother I'm thinking." No, it would not be of her mother-in-law that Eloise would be thinking.

"Well, you folks decide." Abbie slipped out into the other room. But Eloise was one of those quaint souls who think that because a woman is old she is also deaf, and her voice carried very clearly to Abbie:

"It's Laura, herself, I'm thinking about. You know, yourself, John, that your mother is terribly old-fashioned. And I don't know just whether to . . . well, *trust* Laura with her that long. She thinks every one ought to drink sassafras tea in the spring. She would still use goose-grease on a child's neck for colds and wrap a flannel around it."

Abbie heard John's low chuckle.

"And do you know what I heard her say?" She was earnest and serious. "She actually said, John, that a *red* flannel was better."

John laughed aloud. "Oh, Eloise, you never did quite understand Mother. That was a joke."

"Well, I must say I can't always tell when she's joking, then."

But, between the devil, rather mildly represented by the maid, and the deep sea, quite definitely represented by her mother-in-law's out-of-date notions about children, Eloise chose what seemed the lesser of the two evils, and packed Laura home with her grandmother.

Abbie and the maid and John picked out the things which the triumvirate thought Laura would need during the stay, materially assisted by the traveler, herself, who put in a few choice articles in the way of a one-eyed doll, some red beads in a bottle and a tooth of her dog which had been presented to her by the veterinarian and which had escaped the sanitary eye of her mother.

John drove out home with them, let them out under the Lombardy poplars, and took the little bag up to the screened-in porch. And if Eloise could have known the supreme faith and confidence with which her husband was looking upon the situation she would have been attacked by the little green god of jealousy.

Abbie led Laura by the hand up the steps of the porch. It was not possible to say which was looking forward to the visit the more,—the guest or hostess. For Abbie, with Laura's little warm hand in hers, was happy almost to the point of excitement. No, Abbie Deal would never get over being a mother.

"We'll gather the eggs first," Abbie's voice held all the notes of interest which an anticipated journey might have brought forth. "And feed the chickens and then we'll have a little supper."

"What will we have, Grandma?"

"Oh, we'll have . . . we'll have . . . What would you like . . . nice fresh eggs boiled in Grandma's new little kettle . . . or some creamed toast . . . or baked potatoes. . . ?"

"Mother doesn't let me eat potatoes at night."

"Oh, I see. That's all right. We'll do as Mother wishes."

"What are you smiling at, Grandma?"

"I guess I was just smiling to think how nice it is that you have so many things to choose from for your meals. You see when my children were little, it was so hard to get enough food for them, that *anything* agreed with them."

They gathered the eggs. ". . . in the very same egg pail your papa used to gather them," Abbie told Laura. And the child gazed with awe at the antique which had been saved from an age that seemed as remote to her as the one in which Noah's ark figured. They fed and watered the chickens. ". . . and see, . . . every time they take a drink they look up and thank God for it," said Abbie Deal, with a fine disregard for natural science and a sublime faith in her fowls' morale. They ate supper. ". . . and now, you'll wipe the dishes when Grandma washes them, . . ." with Laura excited beyond measure at the unusual confidence placed upon her close associations with chinaware.

Afterwards they went out on the porch and Abbie held the little girl on her lap. She cuddled her up and put her wrinkled cheek against the child's firm one. Oh, why didn't mothers do it more when they had the chance? What were clubs and social affairs and freedom by comparison? And what *was* freedom?

"Tell a story now, Grandma."

"A fairy one or a real one?"

"A real one about when you were little."

"Well, when I was a little girl . . ." Laura wiggled with contentment. "When I was a little girl I had a doll and you never could guess what it was made out of."

"No . . . what was it made out of, Grandma?"

A stone . . . and it had a little round stone head. . . ."

Yes, Abbie Deal was contented,—as contented as countless mothers, in a rather topsy-turvy world, are still contented.

Chapter 28

And now war again,—war, spreading its fear and heartaches like the circling ripples of a wave to the most remote farms beyond the tiniest village. And in the old farmhouse behind the cedars Abbie had said good-by to young Dr. Fred Baker and Stanley Deal, her two oldest grandsons, looking big and fine in their khaki.

"You know, Grandma, from the time Germany ran over little Belgium, . . ."

"You wouldn't want us to stand by and let a bully . . ."

Yes, yes, the words came back,—the same words,—the same spirit. How the clock hands went around.

She saw them drive down the lane road, saw them turn at the big gate, through which they had so often come to play, and wave their khaki hats gayly. The wind was blowing from the east and the cedars bent before it,—blowing from the east like the breath of the war god. And Fred and Stanley were waving their hats gayly back to her, while the cedars bent and the wind blew from the east. They were like her own boys marching off to war. Children of her children, she loved them as she had loved their parents. Did a woman never get over loving? Deep love brought relatively deep heartaches. Why could not a woman of her age, whose family was raised, relinquish the hold upon her emotions? Why could she not have a peaceful old age, wherein there entered neither great affection nor its comrade, great sorrow? She had seen old women who seemed not to care as she was caring, whose emotions seemed to have died with their youth. Could she not be one of them? For a long time she stood in the window and looked at the cedars twisting before the east wind, like so many helpless women writhing under the call from the east.

All during those following strenuous months she felt almost as though the very outcome of the struggle depended upon her individual efforts. So she knit at home and at the G.A.R. hall, bought a liberty bond whenever she could, and conserving everything, ate frugally. And prayed,—prayed that right would prevail.

Fate willed that Fred Baker, Jr., and Stanley Deal should come back to their people from overseas. Young Dr. Fred went into partnership with his father, immediately; and Stanley, after a three-month' period of recuperation, took back his old job in the bank.

Grace was teaching now in Wesleyan University. Life was still real and life was still earnest to Grace, splitting an infinitive one of its cardinal sins.

At thirty she received her second proposal of marriage from one of the younger college professors,—and refused him. Abbie was deeply concerned about it.

"Are you certain, Grace, you don't love him?"

"Quite certain, Mother." Grace was airily sure of herself.

"But Grace, . . . you're thirty . . . even if you don't look it."

"Yes, I'm thirty, Mother. And thank you for the implied compliment."

"Of course . . . if you don't love him. . . . But he is such a *nice* man . . . and your being thirty. . . ." Abbie's voice trailed off uncertainly.

Grace laughed. "Can't you conceive of a woman being happy, Mother, without a man at her heels?"

"But, Grace, it's so natural, . . . so . . . normal."

"Well, that sort of thing doesn't appeal to *me*."

" 'That sort of thing!' Why, Grace, it's the finest thing in the world when it's the right man."

Grace was impatient. "See here, Mother, I have my life all mapped out, and a man doesn't figure in it. I want to be free and independent. I want to do more research work in the East. And I'm perfectly satisfied with my lot. I have at present one hundred and twenty students in my classes, a large number of whom are fitting themselves to be teachers. If two-thirds of them go out to teach, that will be eighty new instructors. They, in time, will teach an average of forty students each and the result is, I have directly and indirectly influenced three thousand two hundred students.''

''Goodness sakes, Grace,'' Abbie said in exasperation, ''you sound like government statistics.''

And so Grace was not to be married and the pearls would still lie in the velvet box waiting for a Mackenzie bride.

But if there were no romance in the world for Grace, the little winged god was not without its victims in the Deal clan, for Stanley Deal and Dr. Fred Baker, Jr., were both married the same year, Stanley to an Omaha girl,—''popular in the younger set,'' as the papers unanimously agreed, and young Dr. Fred to a red-headed nurse with whom he had worked during the days in camp before going overseas.

The year that John was elected to the legislature, Mack was made a vice-president of his bank. John was forty-eight, tall, straight, his black hair showing two silver patches above the ear, his whole physique always reminding Abbie of his father.

Mack was fifty-three, and a bird's-eye view of him standing east and west, if the spectator chanced to be looking north, would resemble nothing in the world so much as one of the portly pigeons around his mother's old hay loft. He wore horn-rimmed glasses, went in for golf and Rotary and the Commercial Club, freely paid his church and associated charity subscriptions, thought a great deal of his first wife, who was also his last, and altogether was so decent and clean and so respected in the rather nervous business world, that he would have made an ideal target for the shots of any of the most weightily important and wordily devastating of the critics of our social structure.

Abbie took Lincoln, Omaha and Chicago papers, and with the same scissors that had cut out their homemade clothes, carefully cut out every item concerning her now rather well-known children. Sometimes she would run across one which gave her a few moments of almost wicked glee. One such was:

''Perhaps more through the influence of Mackenzie Deal than any other single person, this series of Shakespearean plays is being brought to Omaha, . . .''

For a few moments Abbie saw, in retrospect, a freckle-faced boy in a sod-house, hunching over a thick volume of plays and saying, "Aw, what's the sense in this?"

"Dear, dear," she said to herself, " 'There *is* a divinity which shapes our ends, rough hew them how we will.' "

After a year, Dr. Fred Baker, Jr., and his wife were parents of a sturdy son. Dr. Fred, Sr., and Margaret were grandparents. Abbie was a great-grandmother. Where had the time gone? Blown by the winds she could not stop,—ticked off by the clock hands she could not stay.

Tourists were flocking back now into war-torn Europe and one spring Grace began making plans to go abroad in the summer. She was thirty-three now. "Only four years younger than my mother was when we made the journey from Illinois," Abbie thought. "And Mother looked old enough to be her mother, if not her grandmother." What was the secret of it, she wondered.

One Friday night with the April buds bursting into pink froth on the peach trees, and the April moon caught in the top of a Lombardy poplar, Grace arrived home unexpectedly.

"Well . . . well . . . it's my baby." Abbie was as delighted as she was surprised. Life was full of nice things.

Grace, too, was happy to see her mother. "And why do you think I came?" She was sparkling, vivacious.

"You've got a beau," Abbie guessed right away. "You're not . . . oh, Grace, . . . you're not going to be married?"

"Oh, Mother." Grace laughed light-heartedly. "You're incorrigibly romantic, aren't you? Heavens, no! How you would enjoy tying me down for life. No . . . it's something about you."

"About me?"

"Yes." She seemed fairly exuding mystery and excitement.

"I never could guess, Grace."

"You're going abroad with me."

"Oh, no," Abbie was incredulous. "I don't think I could, Grace. You don't think I could, do you?"

"I certainly do. You know, Mother, I got to thinking about it in school and you are going, too. We'll take it very slowly. You're pretty well, you know, for a woman of your age. It just came to me as suddenly as a flash, . . . why couldn't

Mother go, too? I didn't write it because I was too anxious to talk it over with you. You will have to decide right away on account of reservations.''

"My! My! Grace." Abbie could not quite face the reality of the plan.

"Listen, Mother. How would you like to see the 'green coast of Ireland'?''

"My! . . . My! . . ." In moments of great emotion Abbie's words were few.

"And London Tower?''

Quite suddenly, to Abbie Deal, from somewhere out of the past there came a haunting melody. Its lilting notes wove in and out of the magical things Grace was saying. She could not quite catch its refrain, and the words, too, evaded her. In and out of her mind it danced with elfish glee, a little half-memory. Something about "having gold and having land.''

"And go to Scotland and look up the old Mackenzie estate?''

"My! . . . My! . . ." That old refrain,—what was it? It seemed to come to her out of the night.

"And Stratford-on-Avon with Ann Hathaway's cottage? . . .''

"My! . . . My! . . ." Little half-memory, singing tantalizingly near her,—something that was "dreaming visions longingly." It flickered ahead of her, a will-o'-the-wisp from out of the past, beckoning her to come and do this thing. She could not place it, could not catch it. Whether song or poem, story or scene, she was not sure. She only knew it was something that was mostly joyous, but a little sad.

Bewildered, incredulous, undecided, she went to bed.

"Will, what do you think?''

I think it would be fine.

All night she turned and tossed with the excitement and the responsibility of the decision. Once she got up and rubbed liniment on her knees. Toward morning she slept, but fitfully.

When she made her kitchen fire and cooked breakfast, all the high enthusiasm of the evening before had vanished. She hated to meet Grace and break the news, dreaded to see the eager interest fade from her face.

As soon as Grace came down the old enclosed stairway, Abbie told her. "Grace, I can't go.''

"Why, Mother! I thought last night you would."

"No, I can't, Grace. But you don't know how I appreciate your thinking of it, and wanting me. Don't I realize how much easier it would be for you to get around without me? Well, that makes me appreciate it all the more. It's one of the nicest, if not the very nicest thing you ever did for me,—to come home to talk it over. But I can't go."

"I think you're making a mistake, Mother. I'm quite sure you could get through the trip all right."

"No, Grace. I'm more disappointed than you can ever realize. I'm so disappointed that I almost wish you hadn't put it into my head. Isn't that childish? Last night I couldn't sleep for thinking about it. I was that excited . . . but when I woke up this morning from a little nap I had, I knew I couldn't go. I have pains in my knees sometimes until the tears come. And my spells of asthma are coming a little closer. I'm tied to a whole row of little bottles on the top pantry shelf. You wouldn't want me to have a spell of asthma in front of the Louvre or have to sit down on the Bridge of Sighs because I was all out of breath. It wouldn't be appropriate somehow. All the time my heart tells me to go, my mind says not. Desire says one thing and good sense another."

"I thought you would love it so."

"Oh, Grace, I would . . . when I was younger, *how* I would! Things just don't connect sometimes. When I was young I had no means or time, and now I have the means and time, I have no youth."

"Well, I don't want to be responsible about urging you against your judgment, of course. But I'm certainly sorry. I said to myself, 'I'll get half of my enjoyment from seeing Mother's enthusiasm.' "

"Thank you, dearie, for the thought, but I'll stay home and read about the trip. You write me from all the places you stop. And I'll just stay in my chair and travel with you. And if *anybody* could take a trip that way I know I can, for I've always thrilled over reading travels."

Grace was loath to accept the decision. "As I said, I'm sorry. You owe it to yourself, if you possibly can go. Your life has been so narrow, Mother . . . just here, all the time. You ought to get out now and see things."

Unwittingly, as so often she did, Grace had hurt her Mother's feelings. For a moment Abbie nursed her little hurt, and then she said quietly, "You know, Grace, it's queer, but I don't *feel* narrow. I *feel* broad. How can I explain it to you, so you would understand? I've seen everything . . . and I've hardly been away from this yard. I've seen cathedrals in the snow on the Lombardy poplars. I've seen the sun set behind the Alps over there when the clouds have been piled up on the edge of the prairie. I've seen the ocean billows in the rise and the fall of the prairie grass. I've seen history in the making . . . three ugly wars flare up and die down. I've sent a lover and two brothers to one, a son and son-in-law to another, and two grandsons to the other. I've seen the feeble beginnings of a raw state and the civilization that developed there, and I've been part of the beginning and part of the growth. I've married . . . and borne children and looked into the face of death. Is childbirth narrow, Grace? Or marriage? Or death? When you've experienced all those things, Grace, the spirit has traveled although the body has been confined. I think travel is a rare privilege and I'm glad you can have it. But not every one who stays at home is narrow and not every one who travels is broad. I think if you can understand humanity . . . can sympathize with every creature . . . can put yourself into the personality of every one . . . you're not narrow . . . you're broad."

Rather strangely, Grace was neither antagonistic nor argumentative. "You know, Mother . . . there's something to that thought. And another thing, Mother,—do you know, there's something about you at times that is sort of majestic and poetical. I believe if you had ever done anything with it, you might have written."

"No, . . ." Abbie Deal said wistfully, "no . . . I was only meant to appreciate it,—not do it."

At the close of the day Abbie went contentedly to bed. Her head was heavy. Her limbs ached. It seemed a little hard to breathe. But a warm feeling of comfort was upon her that she was to stay in the quiet backwater of her own home.

"I'm not going, Will."

That's too bad, Abbie. It would have been wonderful.

"I know it would have, Will. But you understand how it is."

I understand, Abbie-girl.

"I knew you would. Whenever I tell you things, Will, I always know you'll understand."

Chapter 29

At seventy-eight, Abbie had shriveled as the hazel-nuts near the old Iowa schoolhouse shrivel when the frost comes on. Her O'Conner body was shaped like her mother's had been,—a pudding-bag tied in the middle. Her shoulders were rounded. Her hair was drawn back into a small white knot at the nape of her neck. The girls were always trying to fix her up. They brought her dresses and shoes and gloves. But the feet that had carried her through nearly eight decades of activities had not kept their neat shape. The long Mackenzie fingers were as gnarled as they were tapered. Two of them twisted together grotesquely.

"Let me be," she said. "You can't make me over now . . . it's too late. I'll just keep on using plenty of soap and water. I like to see you girls look so nice. But there are too many things to do, to fuss with myself so much."

That summer the old settlers held a big picnic down on the Chautauqua grounds near Stove Creek. It was a gala occasion. Youth must be served,—but not on the day of an old settlers' reunion. Every one knew every one else. On all sides one heard the same type of comment: "Well . . . well . . . if it ain't Mamie Balderman. I'd never have known you. Heavier, ain't you?"

"That's Anne Jorden. I declare I believe she's carrying the same brown parasol."

"Yes, that parasol's as old as the schoolhouse."

"Your daughter, Lizzie? No . . . not *grand*daughter . . . you don't mean it? Why, it seems only a few years ago I was at your wedding."

Most of the old folks, who were there, had come into the
country as young married people. Some of them were bent
and gnarled and weather-beaten. Others looked sturdy and
clear-eyed. Many of the babies who had been wrapped in old
shawls in covered wagons or born later in the soddies were
there,—now farmers and attorneys, doctors, preachers and
bankers. By some peculiar thrust of Fate, that wag who plays
jokes on us all, it seemed that those who had been poorest in
the early days, were now the wealthiest,—those who had
been of least importance, now the most prominent. Some call
it the law of compensation,—others, luck. It is, of course,
neither one.

Standing about in twos or knots, they were all talking in
reminiscent mood. One heard snatches of life stories on all
sides,—a whole drama in every detached phrase:

"Yes, sir, when I got into Omaha, . . . I had ten cents.
Two men had just been drowned in the old Missouri, and I
made the coffins, . . . got ten dollars for them."

"When the Mormon train went by, women and children
were pulling carts. A child was crying . . . its foot painin'
from a loose laced shoe. Ma said she used to have a kind of
nightmare afterwards . . . 'n' in her sleep she would always
be tryin' to find that child cryin' . . . in a long train of
ox carts that kept goin' by 'n' goin' by."

"Shucks, we made *our* syrup by boilin' down watermelon
juice . . . *Sure*, it took an awful lot!"

"Yes, Uncle Zim's gone. He and Aunt Mandy used to say
if they ever saved a thousand dollars, they'd take it and get
back East as fast as they could go. Finally they made it, but
thought it would be lots nicer to have two thousand, so they
saved and accumulated and then set the amount to four
thousand. Never went back at all. Died four years ago, a few
months apart. Left several large farms and bank stock besides
ten thousand dollars to each of their seven grandchildren."

All of the groups were not of a peaceful character. Some
were having heated arguments over the trivial details of epi-
sodes a half century forgotten.

"No . . . you're wrong, Sam, . . . it was eighteen
seventy-one."

"No, . . . Joe, 'seventy-two. I remember because it was
the year the pie-plant froze."

Or, "I remember you coming just as well that day because I saw your wagons . . ."

"I don't know why you say 'wagons,' Celia. There was no plural number, when all we had was a bed and two chairs and a bob-tailed cow."

And then it was time for the speech of the day. The young county attorney made it, from the airy heights of the band stand, at his side a glass of water on Abbie Deal's marble-topped table.

It was a good speech. It flapped its wings and soared over the oaks and elms, and eventually came home to roost with: "You . . . *you* were the intrepid people! You, my friends, were the sturdy ones. Your days have been magnificent poems of labor. Your years have been as heroic stories as the sagas. Your lives have been dauntless, courageous, sweeping epics."

" 'Sweeping' is the word, Sarah!" Abbie said when the applause had faded away into the grove. "I wish I had a dollar for every broom I've worn out."

Sarah Lutz's little black eyes twinkled.

"How about it, Abbie, do you feel like a poem?"

"No, Sarah, I was always too busy filling up the youngsters and getting the patches on the overalls to notice that I was part of an epic."

It was after the speech that Abbie first saw Oscar Lutz, who, at eighty-four, a little bent but as hardy as any old hickory, had come from California to be present at the reunion. Of the four old neighbors, Will Deal, Henry and Oscar Lutz and Gus Reinmueller, Oscar was now the only one living. He was well-to-do with his bonds and mortgages, his land and his California home.

"How are you, Oscar?"

"How are you, Abbie? It's mighty nice to be back . . . mighty nice."

"We're glad to have you, Oscar . . ."

"Went down to Plattsmouth yestidy and found the post where the boats tied up fifty-eight years ago."

"My! My! Oscar! Is the post still there?"

"Still there, Abbie. Gettin' old like us . . . a little rotten . . . but still there . . . and a good mile and a quarter away from water. River bed's changed that much."

"I can scarcely believe it."

"Everything changes, Abbie . . . folks and rivers. I kicked the old post when I found it."

"What for, Oscar?"

"Don't know, exactly, Abbie. Kind of a ceremony, I guess." He had a far-away look in his eyes. "Remember how I told you I kicked it when Henry and I was waitin' for the boat to come bringin' Martha 'n' Sarah 'n' Grandpa?"

"Yes, I remember, Oscar, . . . you said you was so impatient waitin' for Martha you had to take it out on something."

"Well. . . ." He was silent so long that Abbie thought he had finished with the subject. ". . . Martha's been gone twenty-two years . . ." The old man fussed with his watch. "Twenty-two years! Went down to Plattsmouth yestidy 'n' kicked the post again . . . like I was waitin' for somethin' . . . a boat to come in . . . or somethin'. . . . Foolish, wasn't it? Kind of a ceremony, I guess."

After the old settlers' reunion, Abbie spent a few days with Margaret Baker in Lincoln. John Deal took his mother up in a big sedan. On the same road that Abbie had driven her team over thirty years before, stopping at Stevens Creek to eat her lunch, John took his mother now over the hard packed gravel in forty minutes. He growled a good deal at the county commissioners over a mile stretch in which he had to slow down a little.

The Bakers had one of the lovely new homes of the city, artistic in every point, from the dwarf evergreens in front to the Russian olives in the rear of the garden. Margaret had overseen every detail to the last door knob. Dr. Baker was a specialist now. "*Which* side of the heart is your particular line?" Abbie asked him in mock seriousness. "Dear, dear, you doctors have got our anatomy so divided up and pigeon-holed that nobody knows where to go if he just happens to feel bad all over. You're not as smart as our old Dr. Hornby. When he first came to Nebraska, he practiced medicine and surgery, fitted glasses and pulled teeth, was a notary public and sold sewing-machines."

Margaret Deal Baker was fifty-four now, gray-haired, calm-eyed, level-headed, one of the substantial women of the city, her name a part of every artistic and civic endeavor. " 'Poise' is Aunt Margaret's middle name," Katherine Deal, who was sixteen and given to expressing herself freely, would say. Democratic to the finger-tips, Margaret Baker, with her lovely home and her prominent position, refused to forget her humble beginnings. "When I was a girl . . ." she would say, and go off into a hearty peal of laughter over the memory of some funny episode out on the prairie when the state was new.

"Yes, I go to the beauty parlor every week," she would say frankly to a group of well-groomed women. "I have a shampoo and hot-oil massage and wave. And when I was a girl, I was thankful to wash my hair myself once in a while with water from a rain-barrel with drowned gnats in it."

Grace, lacking humor, was sometimes disturbed by her sister's attitude. "There's no use *parading* the fact that you once lived on beans and cornmeal," she would say.

"But plenty of use in parading the fact that it was your ancestor who hung the light in old North tower," Margaret would get back, with her mother's twinkle in her gray eyes. The Revolutionary ancestors on her father's side were a source of great pride and solace to Grace Deal.

"At least Aunt Grace believes in the D.A.R. part of the Darwin theory," was another of Katherine Deal's airy quips.

On this visit of Abbie's to Margaret, she found the latter just finishing a canvas with final loving touches.

"What do you think, Mother?" Margaret, in her studio smock, stood back to watch her mother's face.

Abbie came a step nearer to get the best vision. For some time she stood and looked at the unframed scene standing on the easel. When she turned, her wrinkled face was aglow. "You've got it, Margaret. It's there at last, . . . the light lying in little pools on the prairie. You've caught it . . . just as you said you wanted to."

"Yes, I believe I've caught it. But think, Mother, I've been trying for thirty years to get it as I wanted it. What was the matter with me before?"

"I don't know, dear. I guess it's always that way. There's no short-cut to anything. The Master demands full time of us before we are paid."

For some reason little Laura Deal continued to be Abbie's favorite grandchild. The little girl answered Abbie's deep love for her with an affection equally sincere,—or perhaps, it was the other way. Perhaps the fact that Laura held such admiration for her grandmother enkindled its answer in Abbie's heart. From the time Laura was five she had brought her grandmother little stories of her own composition. Abbie had them all in safe keeping, just as she had everything else which had ever come into her possession.

One of the first of these literary achievements, laboriously printed, was:

"A man once on a time had a poket-buk ful of munny he lost the munny and too this day he has to worck."

"Laura has the right idea," Abbie told the relatives in high glee. "She has the whole philosophy of life summed up in a short story. She'll be a writer some day."

At eight, she had brought her grandmother more lengthy compositions, running largely to an atmosphere of delectable foods, and over which the whole clan surreptitiously laughed: " 'Oh, no,' said the young lady, as she nibbled daintily at a piece of chocolate pie with whipped cream on it and a cherry on top of that and a nut on top of that."

At eleven, Laura had discovered what romance meant, and her writing leaned conspicuously toward that direction. Abbie was sitting on a bench under the cedars on a mild spring afternoon when Laura came out of the house bearing the inevitable pencil and notebook.

"Listen here, Grandma. Here's my new one. It's called 'My Dream of Imagination.':

> *"I was once a princess, a captive in castle grim*
> *And a dragon wanted to drag me to come and live with him.*
>
> *Now I had violet eyes and long yellow gleaming hair*
> *And people said I was beautiful with my pure white skin so fair."*

Abbie listened with undiminished interest to the twenty-six verses of dramatic, not to say gory, suspense, through:

> *" 'Twas a terrible sight to see prince after prince fall dead*
> *But the dragon only laughed with glee and said he'd have me to wed,"*

to the happy ending of:

> "*I gazed out of my turret,—it was my wedding day*
> *When suddenly I saw some one riding who was not far*
> *away*
>
> *I watched the shine of his armour glitter in the sun's*
> *bright ray*
>
> *Then nimbly and quickly I saw him dismount. He had*
> *stopped to pray.*
>
> *Then slowly arising I saw him make the sign of the*
> *cross*
> *While grasping his sword in his right hand, he mounted*
> *upon his hoss.*

"You know, Grandma, that worries me, to have to say 'hoss.' It isn't just right but neither is 'horse' with 'cross'."

And so they discussed it seriously, Abbie who knew that one may laugh *with* a child but not *at* him, and Laura, who knew that Grandma was one unfailing source of sympathy and understanding in a world which was beginning to be critical.

"Now, tell me about when you were young, Grandma . . . some of the things you've never told me."

"Well, there is something I never told one of my children . . . but now I'll tell it to you. Before I married your grandfather, another young man wanted to marry me. He was quite the catch of the community."

"Why didn't you, Grandma . . . why didn't you marry him?"

"I had a very pretty voice and he wanted me to marry him and go to New York to study music while he took some medical work. I was anxious to cultivate my voice and the whole thing was a very wonderful opportunity for me so I very nearly married the young man. But something happened that made me realize it was just the thought of the New York opportunity that was influencing my decision, rather than love for the young man himself."

"What happened, Grandma?"

"I saw Will Deal coming down the lane."

"Just coming down the lane, Grandma? Was that all?"

"Just coming down the lane."

"What became of the young man, Grandma?"

"He became a big New York surgeon . . . so . . . if I had married him . . . life would have been very different. I guess women have done that from time immemorial. A young man walks down a lane . . . and a whole life changes."

"And you had to tell the other young man you wouldn't marry him, Grandma?"

"Yes, . . . I told him."

"Was he sad?"

"A little sad . . . and a little angry . . and terribly surprised."

"Why was he so surprised, Grandma?"

Abbie Deal smiled reminiscently. "I think it had never occurred to him that any girl would refuse him."

"And what did he say?"

Abbie Deal pondered a moment. "That I cannot tell you."

"Because it was too romantic, Grandma?"

"No . . ." said Abbie Deal. And by this, quite suddenly she knew that she was an old woman. "No . . . because I have forgotten."

Chapter 30

You will remember that Basil Mackenzie, an aristocratic young Scotchman, of Aberdeen, riding to the hares and hounds, wooed and won Maggie O'Conner from the whins and silver hazels of Ballyporeen. But what you do not know is that several generations later, the good Saints, up in high heaven's court, gave that couple three chances each to mold the life of a descendant . . . a baby girl . . . just born upon earth. Basil Mackenzie first crowned her with hair like the mist around the mountains of Glencoe when the sun shines through, —and immediately Maggie O'Conner gave her eyes the color of the blue-black waters at Kilkee. Then the man, remembering sensibly that the outward appearance is not all, endowed her with a keen Scotch mind,—but the woman smiled and slipped an Irish heart into her. For a long time Basil pondered cannily, wondering how he might use his last chance and finally gave her the sturdiest of Scotch chins,—but Maggie O'Conner laughed and pressed a roguish V-shaped cleft into the center of it.

Practical folks there are, who will not believe this; but here, nineteen years later, was Katherine Deal with her misty Glencoe hair and her blue-black Kilkenny eyes and her gay great-granny's dimple in the middle of her daur great-grandfather's chin. Sure, and what more proof could a-body be needin'? Here she was,—Katherine, the only daughter of Mackenzie Deal,—this warm summer afternoon, stretched out in her Grandmother Deal's hammock on the screened-in sitting-room porch of the farmhouse, her slim lithe body in its

blue and white sport suit curved comfortably in the hammock's
old meshes, one slim silken foot rhythmically tapping the
floor.

"As free and irresponsible as any colt in a pasture," old
Abbie Deal thought, as she looked out at her granddaughter,
"and just about as untamed too."

Across the lane road, under the Lombardys, Abbie could
see the latest model of sport roadster, blue and white, a
special order of Mack's. Whether Katherine's dress had been
ordered to match the car, or the car to match the dress, Abbie
did not know.

Old Abbie Deal and her granddaughter did not have a great
many interests in common. They did not seem able to get
along comfortably for any length of time. Katherine had not
the slightest atom of her cousin Laura's interest in either the
grandmother's opinions or reminiscences. With her usual blunt
frankness, she had more than once announced before a group
of the relatives, including the object of her remarks: "Granny
Deal. . . ." (Incidentally, she was the only one of the seven
grandchildren who called her "Granny.") "Granny Deal and
I don't hit it off any too well." She said it with the air of one
who modestly announces an accomplishment.

But for some reason, she had driven in alone from Omaha
several times recently. The dashing new roadster had bitten
off the graveled miles between Omaha and Cedartown frequently this summer of Abbie Deal's seventy-ninth year. Rather
strangely, for her usual active self, the girl seemed to like to
sit quietly under the cedars or swing idly in the hammock on the
screen porch. This afternoon she had a book into which she
occasionally dived, and as often dropped back in her lap.

Abbie pulled her chintz-covered rocker up closer to the
screen door.

"What are you reading, Kathie?" she called.

"Michael Arlen . . . nothing but. He's delicious. Everything he says sounds silky. Listen to this, Granny:

'. . . love is like a hammer . . .'
'Oh, not a hammer!'
'A hammer, darling. It beats and beats inside him and
presently it doesn't beat so regularly, and presently it doesn't
beat at all. . . .'

"Doesn't that just melt in your mouth?"

"The words are very clever. But not all clever words are true."

"You said a bookful, Granny. And inversely most things that are true are not clever."

She seemed to have everything, thought old Abbie Deal, studying her attractive granddaughter. She had the Irish wit of the O'Conners, the Scotch canniness of the Mackenzies, the German self-interest of the Lutzes, the Yankee determination of the Deals. She carried everything before her. People did whatever she wished. She breezed in and out of every setting with self-assurance. She dominated every situation with poise. She told her parents what she thought of them and handed out indiscriminate advice to any of her relatives. And through it all she looked as lovely as a picture.

And now, Abbie, thinking of what the girl had just read to her, returned thoughtfully, "You can't describe love, Kathie and you can't define it. Only it goes with you all your life. I think that love is more like a light that you carry. At first childish happiness keeps it lighted and after that romance. Then motherhood lights it and then duty . . . and maybe after that sorrow. You wouldn't think that sorrow could be a light would you, dearie? But it can. And then after that, service lights it. Yes. . . . I think that is what love is to a woman . . . a lantern in her hand."

"Prosaic. . . . Granny, prosaic and uninteresting, albeit the romance chapter has possibilities. I choose to think of Mike's variety that 'beats and beats.' It's more thrilling."

"You'll see, Kathie, when it comes."

"Heavens,—the little grandmother speaks in the future tense,—and to me, Katherine Elaine Deal, wot has had several distinct and separate love affairs."

"Oh, Kathie, how can you speak so? . . . I doubt if one of those 'affairs,' as you call them, was love."

"Oh, but they *were, cher ami* . . . or *cher amie* . . . whichever you are. They were deep, thrilling, luscious love affairs while they lasted. *While* they lasted. . . !" She went off into a little rippling laugh.

Abbie Deal did not argue. She did not answer. She only sat and looked out at her granddaughter, flippant, sophisticated, wise, irresponsible, lovely. Because she had a deep-rooted clannish love for all her own people, Abbie Deal loved the girl,—but she did not understand her. They lived in two worlds. No, Granny Deal and Katherine did not hit it off any too well.

It was only a week later that Sarah Lutz came out to spend a few days with Abbie. Her seventy-seven years sat lightly upon Sarah. Her white hair, dressed rather elaborately, held a gayly colored, green jeweled comb in its coils and she had little emerald earrings in her small colorless ears. The natural pink in her cheeks of the early days had been replaced by natural pink from a box, and her small merry eyes behind their shell-rimmed glasses were still bright and twinkling. Her dress was of modern cut, and her dainty high-heeled slippers, by the side of Abbie's broad and altogether serviceable kids, looked, as they walked through the yard, like gay little yachts towing broad barges into harbor.

The two had just reached the sitting-room when they both jumped at the sharp sound of an auto-horn and looked out to see Katherine in the brilliant roadster turning into the lane road under the Lombardys.

"Honk . . . honk . . . the lark at heaven's gate sings," she called out breezily and slipped out of the car to run up to the house, her lithe young body aglow with health and energy.

"No?" she said in mock agitation at the sight of both grandmothers. "Not *two* old noble ancestors?" Katherine's reverence for old age was on a precise equality with her general timidity.

She gave them each a hasty peck and took immediate possession of the conversation. "I haven't seen very much of you lately, Sarah. But Abbie, here, . . . I have been cultivating her acquaintance this summer with malice. And the queer part, Sarah,—is that the little old dear doesn't have the slightest idea why I have been dropping in so solicitously."

Sarah laughed good naturedly, and Abbie asked, "Then it wasn't just because you wanted to see me, Kathie?"

"Oh, no," she admitted blithely, "it's all on account of Jimmie."

"Jimmie?"

"Jimmie Buchanan."

"Oh, . . ." Abbie remembered. "The young man in John's law office."

" 'The very same,' quoth the maiden, 'as a tear stood in her eye.' I've had a crush on him ever since I first saw him striding along with his little old textbooks across the campus. But I never dated him then. I suppose you can guess why?''

"No." Abbie Deal and Sarah Lutz gave up immediately, for the answers to Katherine's conundrums were usually as unique as they were varied.

"Because," Katherine said, mysteriously, "he was a barb."

"No," said Abbie. "Not that bad?" Abbie might not be conversant with half of Katherine's modern vernacular, but she did know that a barb was a non-fraternity man.

"Now . . . Granny . . . you're turning on the sarcasm. Don't you make merry with me. Yes, my loves, a barb, . . . *never* went into a frat." It was as though she spoke of Lucifer's fall or Napoleon's exile. "He probably washed his own shirts on Saturdays and ate at hamburger joints . . . and here I'm crazy about him. But he won't have me. I've done everything but fling myself on the cement walk in front of Uncle John's office and yell until he comes out and picks me up. Mother is getting a little discouraged about marrying me to the Prince of Wales. But she is still counting on some one of the Vanderastors . . . and here I am just foolish about Jimmie Buchanan and ready to throw myself at his re-soled Oxfords. He'll be Governor some day or Secretary of the Exterior. But in the meantime, he'll marry some neat little Jane that'll economize and have twins . . ."

"Kathie!" It was both grandmothers, simultaneously.

"Oh . . . very well . . . one at a time if you prefer," she went on unblushingly.

"He's a nice boy," Abbie Deal broke in to avert other verbal catastrophes. "John speaks so highly of him. I'll invite him out some night to supper when you're here."

"Oh, you needn't bother. I have already. It's tonight." She smiled at them cheerfully. "I'm going in to get him at six. You'll fix a nice little dinner, won't you, Granny?"

Abbie Deal sat down weakly. Flesh of her flesh was saying that. Blood of her blood was taking the initiative in a love affair. "Oh, Kathie . . . girls are so queer now-days. They do such *forward* things. It would have been nicer for me to."

"Girls now-days," said Miss Deal, "do things immediately . . . right off the bat . . . snap . . . just like that."

"So I see," said Abbie Deal dryly.

"Now, here's the idea," Kathie went on, unperturbed. "You two old baby-dolls get up a nice little dinner while I go after Jimmie. Then I'll come home with him and put on a fetching pink apron and set the table and bring in the provender . . . and Jimmie will begin to think *I'm* the neat little Jane." She smiled at them with gay nonchalance. She patted them both. She kissed them each a time or two. And they gave in.

"She's yours, Sarah, as much as she's mine," Abbie said, when they were starting the meal, "and I, for one, am ashamed of her."

"Oh, . . . she's all right, Abbie. She's just outspoken."

"At nineteen, Sarah, I was married, and had Katherine's father, and had washed and ironed and sewed and made soap and woven rag carpet . . . and . . ."

"Yes . . . but, Abbie, you just couldn't do anything else. I can think of a dozen things that Kathie could do right now if she set her mind to it."

They prepared the dinner . . . the two old belles of another generation.

A little after six, Katherine dashed into the lane road at a speed which jangled the nerves of a flock of stolid Plymouth Rock hens, and set the brakes a few inches from a gander that stuck out his neck and expressed disapproval of the blue and white monstrosity.

"Honk honk, yourself," Katherine called out to the offended dignitary, and then came into the house with a nice-looking, clean-cut young fellow. She came triumphantly. "Well . . . here's Jimmie. It took handcuffs and an anesthetic to get him but I did the deed. Jimmie, you know Grandmother Deal, . . . but I want to present you to Grandmother Lutz. Grandma . . . Jimmie Buchanan . . . the conquered. Well," she waved an airy hand at the two old ladies, "how do you like 'em, Jimmie? I could love either . . . 'were t'other dear charmer away.' "

Abbie Deal was embarrassed beyond measure. She was used to the girl's wild talk before her own people, but she did not dream Kathie would keep it up when the young man came. Abbie looked at him. He was not disgusted. He was looking at Katherine with approbation and liking . . . even admiration. He *liked* her flippant talk. The young man, himself, *liked* it. Well, she gave up. She washed her hands of the present generation. They were away beyond her.

Katherine put on a rose-pink apron which she had brought with evident forethought, and winked openly at her respective progenitors as she carried in the food.

They ate the palatable if simple dinner together,—this rather incongruous little group, after which Katherine said demurely, "Now, Jimmie and I'll wash the dishes, won't we, Jimmie?" Which was something of an astonishing innovation in itself, as, heretofore, dish-washing had not been one of Katherine's favorite indoor sports.

A half-hour later, Abbie and Sarah went into the kitchen, just as Katherine was hanging up her dishpan. "Everything all right, Granny?" she wanted to know.

"Why, I think so, Katherine. It looks very nice."

"Neat little Jane, am I not?" She grinned brazenly at Abbie Deal, who immediately reddened for her.

"Well, Sarah," said Abbie when they were alone, "my mother blushed and gave my father a rose by a well on the Scottish moors. I cried on Will's shoulder in an old honey-locust lane. Mack courted Emma after church and singing-school. And Kathie . . . Kathie goes out and gets her man."

Sarah Lutz laughed. "After all, Abbie, there's something honest about it and frank and aboveboard."

Abbie put the butter-crock back into the big white refrigerator. "Sarah," she said, "it may be honest and it may be frank and it may be aboveboard,—but it's not *subtle* and it's not *romantic* and it's not *artistic.*"

Sarah Lutz's bright black eyes twinkled behind her shell-rimmed glasses. "If you're not all wet, old lady," she said solemnly, . . . *"you've said a mouthful."*

Chapter 31

Abbie made her usual extensive preparations for Christmas that year. The daughters and daughters-in-law said a great deal against her using up so much energy. "But you might as well talk to the wind," Grace wrote to Isabelle. "There's something stubborn about Mother. She is bound to go through with all that mince-meat, doughnut, pop-corn-ball ordeal even if she's sick in bed afterward. Margaret wants us to come there to save her all that work, and Emma and Eloise have both offered their homes, too, but she won't listen. 'No,' she says, 'as long as I'm here, the Christmas gathering is here.' I've tried to tell her over and over that conditions have changed, that we don't live out on an isolated prairie any more; that she doesn't make one thing that she couldn't buy, but she just won't catch up with the times. 'They're not so full of the Christmas spirit when you don't fix them yourself,' she says. Isn't that the last word in old-fashioned ideas?"

So the clan came once more to the old farmhouse behind the cedars. Grace was the first to arrive in her own roadster, coming over the graveled highway from Wesleyan University. The others arrived at various times before Christmas eve. Mack and Emma, Donald and Katherine came. Only Stanley was missing from the Mack Deal family. Having married, Stanley had discovered that a wife's people must also be reckoned with. Margaret and Dr. Fred Baker, Dr. Fred, Jr., and his wife and two little boys came. Isabelle and Harrison Rhodes got in from Chicago on the afternoon train, the road boasting a flyer now instead of the old baggage-and-day affair of the time when the children were small. John and Eloise, Wentworth and Laura and Millard, who was eight now, all came over from their home on the other side of Cedartown in time for the evening meal. Every car was loaded to the doors with packages.

Abbie had an oyster supper. That, too, was a hang-over from the days when sea food was scarce and expensive. No matter that the bi-valves were on every menu placed before the various members of the Deal family these days, Abbie continued to have an oyster supper each Christmas eve,—bowls of crackers alternating down the long table with celery, standing upright in vase-looking dishes, like so many bouquets from the greenhouse.

Jimmie Buchanan came over later in the evening and brought Katherine a gift. Jimmie was rather astounded at the sight of so many relatives.

"Every one has to be here," Katherine told him. "In all the wedding ceremonies, whenever a Deal is married, the question is asked, 'Do you solemnly promise to spend all your Christmases at Granny Deal's, forsaking all others as long as you shall live?' And if you can't promise,—out you go before you're in."

Abbie Deal was embarrassed beyond words. To speak so to a young man with whom you were keeping company!

Katherine went on, "No, sir,—it wouldn't be Christmas without the wax flowers in the parlor and the patent rocking-chair and the painting of the purple cow and the *whut-nut*. Grandma makes us all animal cookies yet. Can you beat it? When I was big enough to read love stories by the dozens, she gave me 'The Frog That Would A-Wooing Go,'—not but that it had its romantic appeal, too. We always stay two nights and we have to have beds everywhere. Granny puts us in corners, on couches, sinks, bath-tubs, ironing-boards . . . and not one of us would miss it. Donald passed up a dance at the Fontanelle for it. You can't tell the reason, but the minute you see those old cedar trees and come up the lane under the Bombarded poplars with snow on 'em, you're just little and crazy over Christmas."

There were some very lovely presents the next morning, —the radio in its dull-finished cabinet for Abbie, jewelry, a fur, expensive toys and books,—an old musty smelling one for Emma, who had gone in for first and rare editions. Margaret gave her mother the painting of the prairie with the sunshine lying in little yellow-pink pools between the low rolling hills. "For I think you made me love it, Mother, when I was a little girl. I learned to see it through your eyes," she told her.

In the afternoon, Mackenzie Deal, the Omaha banker, in an overcoat and old muffler that had been his father's, spent a large share of his time out in the barn cracking walnuts on a cottonwood chunk. John Deal, the state legislator, went up into the hay-loft and potted a few pigeons with an old half-rusty rifle. Isabelle Deal Rhodes, the well-known Chicago singer, called her husband to help her get the old reed-organ out of the storehouse. She dusted it, and then, amid a great deal of hilarity, pumped out, "By the Blue Alsatian Mountains." One of the keys gave forth no sound at all, so that whenever she came to it the young folks all shouted the missing note.

By evening the younger members of the group had gone, —Fred Jr. and his family back to Lincoln, Donald and Wentworth to Omaha, while Katherine was off somewhere with Jimmie Buchanan. But the others, in the early dusk of the Christmas twilight, gathered in the parlor with the homely coal-burner and the lovely floor lamp, with Abbie's crude painting of the prairie and Margaret's exquisite one, with the what-not and the blue plush album and the tidy on the back of the patent-rocker.

"There was one Christmas we had, Mother," Mack said, "that I always remember more than the others. I can see the things yet,—my old brass cornet, a big wooden horse made out of logs, a tree that looked . . . well, I've never seen a tree since look so grand. Where in Sam Hill did you raise all the things in those days?"

"I think I know which one you mean," Abbie was reminiscent. "It was the year after the grasshoppers. Well, my son, your father and I made all of those things out of sticks and rags and patches and love."

It brought on a flood of reminiscences.

"Remember, Mack, the Sunday afternoon we were herding hogs on the prairie and that Jake Smith that kept the store at Unadilla, came along with his girl in a spring wagon, and threw a whole handful of stick candy out in the grass for us?'' Mrs. Frederick Hamilton Baker, well-known artist and club woman of Lincoln, was speaking.

"Do I? I can see them yet, red and white striped,—and looking as big as barber-poles to me. I wondered how any one in the world could be that rich and lavish," Mackenzie Deal, a vice-president of one of the Omaha banks, was answering.

"And do you remember, John, how scared you were . . . the time we chased the calf and you grabbed it by the tail when it ran by you and the tail was frozen and came off in your hands?''

When they had all laughed at the recollection, Isabelle put in, "But I'll bet he wasn't as scared as I was once, . . . the time a man came to the door and told Father he was drawn on the jury. You all stood around looking solemn, and I took a run for Mother's old wardrobe and hid in behind the clothes and cried.''

"Why . . . what did you think?" They were all asking.

"Well, I knew 'jury' had something to do with law and jails and penitentiaries. And I had heard of 'hung,' 'quartered' and '*drawn*' so the inference was that Father was going to be hung in the penitentiary.''

"I remember once when I wasn't scared but *mad*." It was Grace's contribution. "It was when Aunt Regina came to help Mother take care of Grandma. I was modestly effacing myself under the dining-room table and she scooped me out with a sprightly, 'So this is little Grace.' Then she took me on her lap and put her arms around me and pressed me to her bosom and apparently forgot me, while she and mother verbally married off and buried all the relatives over my head.''

"Why didn't you have the gumption to get down?"

"Too bashful, I suppose. That's where your ancient theories of child training come in. No modern child would stand it. But I just sat on while my legs went to sleep and my brain atrophied. I used to think I sat there a month. But I know now it couldn't have been more than a week.''

"That's as bad as I was." It was John. "Remember that preacher that used to stop at our house, the one with the beard that looked as though it was made out of yellow rope?''

"Who could forget it? He tied it up like a horse's tail when he ate." They were all answering at once.

"The first time he stopped, he said to Mack, 'What's your name, son?' Mack said, 'Mackenzie.' 'And what's yours, little man?' he said to me. I was so scared I said 'Mackenzie,' too. Can you beat it? I'll bet there isn't a kid living today as bashful as that."

"Do you remember," it was Isabelle, "the old milk-wagon, John, you rigged up to peddle your milk in? I can smell the inside of it yet, the damp, sweetish odor of warm milk. Remember how you used to ring an old cow-bell and the women would come out with their pans and pitchers, and have their aprons twisted up over their heads? Think of the evil-looking germs that must have perched on the rims of those pitchers when the dust swirled around!"

And so they went on, recalling their childhood days,—days of sunburn and days of chilblains, of made-over clothes and corn-bread meals, of trudging behind plows or picking up potatoes, of work that was interwoven with fun, because youth was youth. Prairie children never forget.

Far into the evening they sat around the old coal burner, talking and laughing, with tears not far behind the laughter, —the state legislator and the banker, the artist, the singer, and the college teacher. And in their midst, rocking and smiling, sat the little old lady who had brought them up with a song upon her lips and a lantern in her hand.

Chapter 32

The Mackenzie Deals were leaving the morning after Christmas.

"Can't you and Katherine stay longer?" Abbie asked Emma, a little wistfully.

"No, Granny," Katherine assumed the responsibility for the decision. "I've had a grand time, but now I must go, for I have a date tonight,—and a blind one at that, . . . a Minnesota U. Man."

" 'A blind date.' For goodness' sake, Katherine, what is that?"

"Blind, Grandmother mine, means 'not seeing.' A date is a man with whom to while away a boresome hour or two. There, you have it . . . a man that you have never seen with whom to while away an hour or two."

"Kathie . . . you mean you've never been introduced to him?"

"Not only never introduced to him . . . but have never set limpid violet eyes upon him."

"Kathie . . . how horrible! Why, it makes me think of veiled people in heathenish countries."

"Quite so, and a merry little gamble it is. But see the thrill of it! Is he going to be dark, light, short, tall, a keen looker, or a crock . . . interesting or a prune? Will he glide up in a high-powered machine or rattle up in an eggbeater?"

"Kathie!"

"If Jimmie were going to be there I wouldn't have made the date. But Jimmie's not going to be there . . . and a poor girl has to have somebody to love her."

"Kathie," Abbie looked at her granddaughter as at some queer museum specimen, "do you know, you just make me wonder whatever your great-great-grandmother would have thought of you. Isabelle Anders-Mackenzie, her name was. She was gentle and refined,—very lovely and very aristocratic. She lived on the beautiful Mackenzie estates . . ."

"Stop . . . stop right there!" Katherine sat up, alert as a young deer with uplifted head. "For heaven's sake, why has no one ever told me that before? Why, our sorority is just *keen* about family. That's our *line*. I've been sort of uncertain about the past . . . a little shy in mentioning some of our aunty-cedents and uncle-cedents . . . not ashamed of anybody, y'unn'erstan', but just supposing they were all this same kind, . . . out-of-the-soil-up-to-God."

"Kathie!"

"And all the time I had this keen ancestor. Now, say it again, and very slowly . . . 'Katherine, your great-great-grandmother was Isabelle Anders-Mackenzie, a beautiful, aristocratic snob. She *was* an awful snob, wasn't she, Granny?"

"Kathie!"

"Think how my marriage could read: 'The marriage of Miss Katherine Elaine Deal to Mr. James Worden Buchanan . . .' I haven't said anything about this yet to Jimmie, but as the Chinaman says, 'Can happen,' and there's nothing like taking time by the fetlock. Picture this in bold bad type in the Sunday edition: 'Miss Deal is a direct descendant of the Anders-Mackenzies of Aberdeen, Scotland, Knights of the Garters' . . ."

Abbie Deal's old eyes twinkled. "But don't forget the other side of the house, too, Kathie. There were knights of the suspenders, too. Don't forget old Grandmother Bridget O'Conner, Kathie. She was an Irish peasant woman and she lived in a shack at the side of a hill on the edge of the moors. The chickens and the pigs ran in and out of the thatch-covered hut. She couldn't read a word and she couldn't write her name, and she smoked a black pipe. But if it wasn't for the sturdy plebeian blood of her daughter, Maggie (my mother, Kathie) you wouldn't be here."

Katherine waved it aside. "We'll pass lightly over the O'Conners. It's the Mackenzies that intrigue me. What more do you know about them?"

Abbie Deal told all that she could remember hearing from her sister Belle,—the story of the lovely lady,—of her reddish-brown hair and tapering fingers, and of the picture that hung on the landing of the stairway in the great hall.

"That settles it," Katherine arose. "I'm going right up to Jimmie and bring matters to a climax, by revealing to him just who I am. Right into the office I go and say, 'Jimmie, here comes the Lady Katherine Elaine Anders-Mackenzie Deal, great-great-granddaughter of Isabelle Anders-Mackenzie, who had flowing white fingers and a long reddish-brown nose that tapered at the end.'"

When the door had closed behind her, Abbie sighed and said, "Whatever are you going to do with her, Emma?"

"Oh, she's all right, Mother." Emma was always like Sarah, her mother, good-natured, easy-going. "She's just breezy. She tells me everything." Mrs. Mackenzie Deal temporarily disregarded the recollection of some of the things Katherine had told her.

When they had all gone, Abbie took a great deal of comfort with her new radio. The dull-finished, beautifully-polished cabinet put a new interest in life for her. At first in the wonderment of the thing, she rubbed the Aladdin lamp all day long. Sermons, jazz bands, market reports, monologues, she listened to them all with equal interest and amazement. A sermon from Denver, a talk on fruit tree culture from Lincoln, a dance orchestra from Omaha, interested her with equal intensity. Preaching and pruning and prancing, they were all the same to her. And when "The Ring of the Piper's Tune" came in, she shut her eyes and saw her Irish mother lift her skirts and do the Kerry dance as lightly as a thistledown.

"My, I wish you could hear the music, Will."

I've heard wondrous music, Abbie.

"There's nothing more now, Will, that can be invented."

There are things undreamed of, Abbie-girl.

And then Abbie had a letter from Isabelle. She was to sing from a Chicago station on February third.

"Find the station beforehand, Mother," Isabelle wrote, "so you'll not have any trouble that night or lose time trying to locate it while the program is on."

On the night of the third, Abbie sat up later than was her custom, so that she could hear Isabelle. Even then she experienced a little trouble in getting the station. "I suppose nothing's just perfect," she thought. "We always have to have some little grief to make us . . ." Suddenly she had them. But the program had begun. Isabelle's voice came forth in an aria as plainly as though she were in the room. When she had finished, the announcer spoke. "Mrs. Rhodes will sing her second number especially for her mother, listening in at Cedartown, Nebraska."

The piano, with violin accompaniment, played a few notes and then Isabelle's voice came again, full and clear:

> *"Oh, the Lady of the Lea*
> *Fair and young and gay was she*
> *Beautiful exceedingly*
> *The Lady of the Lea."*

And then it came to Abbie Deal. That was it,—the little half-memory! That was the old strain that had haunted her and which she could not quite remember.

> *"Many a wooer sought her hand*
> *For she had gold and she had land . . ."*

That was the forgotten melody,—the song of her youth.

> *"Everything at her command*
> *The Lady of the Lea."*

She was young again, singing on a grassy knoll, with the future all before her, with the years of her life still unlived.

> *"Oh, the Lady of the Lea*
> *Fair and young and gay was she . . ."*

Where had they gone, those years? Blown away by the winds you could not stop,—ticked off by the clock hands you could not stay.

> *"Dreaming visions longingly*
> *The Lady of the Lea"*

Isabelle finished the last verse of the song. Abbie turned off the radio, performed all the little nightly duties about the house, and undressed for bed. When she had turned out the lights, she stood for a few minutes at the bedroom window looking out at the night. It was moonlight and cloudless and very still. The trees stood etched in black against the white of the snow, their shadows as real as their substance. For some time Abbie looked out at the cedars standing silently there in the snow and the moonlight, like old women listening for something,—perhaps the strains of a song of their youth, and the dreams of desire.

Chapter 33

In the spring, Katherine's affair with Jimmie Buchanan culminated in an engagement, duly announced on the part of Mr. and Mrs. Mackenzie Deal, by way of an elaborate luncheon and the Sunday papers,—the wedding to take place in the early fall. The immediate effect upon Abbie was to have her begin a quilt for the bride-to-be, on Monday morning, as soon as the chickens were fed and the dishes washed. For some time she pondered whether to do "The Basket of Flowers" pattern, "The Rising Sun," or "The Rose of Sharon," eventually deciding on the rose pattern, done in pink and white. Grace came home to find her in a puddle of pink and white blocks, her blue-veined fingers trembling a little over the stitches.

Grace scolded. "Mother, whatever are you doing that for? You can walk into any department store now and buy these very same old-fashioned patterns."

"They cost an awful lot."

"Maybe they *are* expensive. All nice hand work is. But *think* of the labor! Please, Mother . . . I'll be glad to get it for you . . . any pattern you say . . . if you'll just put the thought about doing it yourself out of your mind."

"No . . . it's more like a real gift if you do it yourself."

"But, Mother, Katherine wouldn't *care*. And there'll be *thousands* of stitches in it."

"And a thousand thoughts of love caught in the stitches, Grace."

No, you could not do much with old Abbie Deal when she had made up her mind.

Sometimes when she had sewed all afternoon· she would walk over to Christine's "to get the cricks out of her back." On a cool April evening she found Christine sitting up close to her cook-stove cutting up potatoes for the morrow's planting. She wore the inevitable faded blue calico dress gathered full at her portly waist line. Her little greasy braids, neither white nor gray, nor yet any particular color, were wound flat from ear to ear.

"Oh . . . So it's you. Come in. Shall I make a light?" Christine wanted to know. And then added, with characteristic frugality, "If we sit up close the stove by, we not have to make it. Ya?"

Abbie looked around for Anna, Christine's granddaughter, who had been living with her for several years. "Where's Anna, Christine?"

"Huh!" Christine was evidently disgruntled about something. "Anna, she's gone to Omaha up."

"Omaha?"

"Ya. To vork . . . until she some money earn." She was excited. Her broken words came tumbling over each other. "I give Anna land all the same to her . . . eighty acres. Eighty acres to every child I give, I tell you. I give Anna the land from her dead mother. What keep I? Three eighties. Ya! Out of all that eleven eighties, for myself three I keep. Maybe I starve. Maybe I go the county house by. How they like their old mother go the poorhouse by? Anna care nothing. She come by me and say, 'Grandmudder . . . I haf it . . . the land . . . but I haf taxes to pay. Can I haf money the taxes to pay?' How you like? Huh? The land I gif her . . . do you hear . . . Abbie Deal? Eighty acres I gif her and she come already yet and say, 'For taxes no money I haf.' I say, 'Better you get and money earn for taxes then. Nein?' "

"Oh, and she's gone?"

"Ya, she's vent."

"But, Christine, Omaha is such a city. Don't you know about her . . . where she first went?"

"Oh, I guess herself she take care. She svill pigs and corn shuck. You learn 'em svill and shuck, and demselves they take care."

"Christine, why don't you sell some of your land and use the money for yourself? The three eighties you kept for yourself are worth a lot of money now. Sell one of the eighties and have more comforts and conveniences."

"Ya . . . and go the poorhouse by. How long I know I live? Only eighty-two I am. A man I know a hundred-and-four was when he die. Maybe like dat I live. Maybe twenty year I live yet already. I guess dey not all my land get. Ya . . . when I die, over it quick dey fight. Not while here I stay."

Abbie Deal sighed. Well, she thought, one gets out of life largely what one puts in. Christine had put all her time and thought on the land and for reward she had . . . land.

As soon as the Cedartown school was out that summer, Laura came over to spend a few days with her grandmother. Abbie still found pleasant companionship in this particular grandchild, an understanding and sympathy deeper than the usual twelve-year-old girl possessed. The two seemed to hold a oneness of thought, a kinship of mind as well as of body. With none of Katherine's sophistication, the child yet seemed mature.

On this visit she would help her grandmother with the morning's work and then fly to the pencil and tablet which she kept hidden under the bench by the long double row of cedars. It was on a late June morning that the two were seated there under the big trees which, toy-size, the Deals had planted a half-century before. Laura took out her portfolio from the box under the bench, with, "Listen, Grandma . . . listen to this that I wrote this morning. It's about you and Grandfather Deal:

"*I know not if 'twas beating rain,*
That lightly tapped the window pane,
Or if the dying embers flare
Shone softly on my old arm chair.

"*But in the scent of dusky gloom,*
That stole within my chamber room,
It seemed that from the shadowy wall
I dreamed I heard you softly call.

"Maybe it was only the book I'd read,
But I heard your voice,—you, who are dead.
You called me by a name most dear
And then I knew that you were near."

There were tears in Abbie Deal's eyes. "Why, Laura,
—you didn't do that yourself?"

"Yes, I did."

"But how could you . . . a little girl like you . . . how
could you have the feeling?"

"Well, I don't know . . . I can't quite tell you. But I get
to thinking about a thing and it almost hurts me . . . kind-of
in my throat or somewhere . . . and then when I work away
and get it all written down, I feel sort of happy afterward. I
don't suppose you'd undertand it."

"Oh, yes, I would," said old Abbie Deal. "I'd understand."

"I like to read my things to you, Grandma."

"And I like to have you, Laura. They seem splendid to
me. I suppose they are not what critics call technically correct,
but that can come with the years. It's the feeling you show."

For a long time they sat there in the morning sunshine
under the cedars that had grown old. The flyer went through
town, its thick black smoke writing spiral-shaped figures
across the blue slate of the sky. To the east, the wide rolling
prairie held on its breast the young corn and wheat and the
grass of the pastures. The Reinmueller boys, grandsons of
Christine, were plowing corn, with a new type cultivator. To
the south and west, Cedartown with its comfortable homes
and its paved streets overhung with elms and maples, sat
astride the great highway that was once a buffalo trail. To the
north, behind the curving arch of a wide graveled driveway
lay the silent city of the dead,—on a knoll in the center, the
monuments of the Deal and Lutz families.

"What are you thinking about, Grandma?"

"That your life is like a field-glass, Laura. When you look
into the one end, the landscape is dwarfed and far away,
—when you look into the other, it looms large as though it
were near at hand. Things that happened seventy years ago
seem like yesterday. But, when I was a girl, eighty years
seemed too remote to contemplate. And now, it has passed.
The story is written."

"You sound as though you were sorry about something, Grandma."

"I didn't mean to, but I was thinking that when I was a little girl, my sister Belle used to tell me about our grandmother . . . that would be your great-great-grandmother. Her name was Isabelle Anders-Mackenzie. She was wealthy and beautiful and accomplished for her time. I used to think I would grow up to look just like her. I pictured her as an ideal and I would say to her in my mind, 'You'll be proud some day of the things I am going to accomplish.' All my girlhood I always planned to do something big . . . something constructive. It's queer what ambitious dreams a girl has when she is young. I thought I would sing before big audiences or paint lovely pictures or write a splendid book. I always had that feeling in me of wanting to do something worth while. And just think, Laura . . . now I am eighty and I have not painted nor written nor sung."

"But you've done lots of things, Grandma. You've baked bread . . . and pieced quilts . . . and taken care of your children."   •

Old Abbie Deal patted the young girl's hand. "Well . . . well . . . out of the mouths of babes. That's just it, Laura, I've *only* baked bread and pieced quilts and taken care of children. But some women have to, don't they? . . . But I've dreamed dreams, Laura. All the time I was cooking and patching and washing, I dreamed dreams. And I think I dreamed them into the children . . . and the children are carrying them out . . . doing all the things I wanted to and couldn't. Margaret has painted for me and Isabelle has sung for me. Grace has taught for me . . . and you, Laura . . . you'll write my book for me I think. You'll have a fine education and you will probably travel. But I don't believe you can write a story because you have a fine education and have traveled. I think you must first have a seeing eye and an understanding heart and the knack of expressing what you see and feel. And you have them. So I think you, too, are going to do one of the things I wanted to do and never did."

Abbie Deal thoroughly enjoyed talking to this grandchild. Any of the rest of the family would have been a little impatient with an old woman's musings. The others were always so alert, so active, so poised for flight. Of them all, only little

Laura Deal wanted to sit and talk and dream. She told her that now.

"You are a great comfort to me, Laura. You are something like me . . . a part of me. We think alike . . . you and I. Between you and me, I think my reminiscences bore the others. Well, well . . . old people used to bore me when I was young."

"They don't bore *me*, Grandma. They interest me."

Abbie smiled across at her. No longer could she look down upon Laura. The twelve-year-old girl was larger than her little grandmother.

"And we old pioneers dreamed other things, too, Laura. We dreamed dreams into the country. We dreamed the towns and the cities, the homes and the factories, the churches and the schools. We dreamed the huge new capitol. When you walk under its wonderful tower, you say to yourself, 'My Grandfather and Grandmother Deal dreamed all this . . . they, and a thousand other young couples dreamed it all in the early days . . . and the architect had the imagination to catch the dream and materialize it. It is their vision solidified. They were like the foundation stones under the capitol . . . not decorative, but strong. They were not well-educated. They were not sophisticated. They were not cultured. But they had innate refinement and courage. And they could see visions and dream dreams.' "

"How does it feel to be old, Grandma?"

Abbie laughed. "Laura, it doesn't *feel* at all. People don't understand about old age. I am an old woman . . . but *I* haven't changed. I'm still Abbie Deal. They think we're different . . . we old ones. The real Abbie Deal still has many of the old visions and longings. I'm fairly contented here in the old home. . . . There was a time when I thought I never could be . . . but . . . some way . . . we get adjusted. I've never grown tired of life as some old people do. I'm only tired of the aches and the pains and the inability to make my body do what I want it to do. I would like to live a long time yet . . . to see what can still be invented . . . to read the new things that will be written . . . to hear the new songs that will be sung . . . to see heavy foliage on all the new shrubbery . . . to see all the babies grow into men and women. But there comes an end . . ."

"Don't talk that way, Grandma. It makes me feel like crying."

"Why, it ought not, Laura . . . not when Grandma has happy memories to live over."

"What memories do you have, Grandma?"

"I have many . . . my little girlhood days when Chicago was a village . . . the three weeks' journey from Illinois into Iowa . . . the fun in the Big Woods behind my sister Janet's house. I can shut my eyes and smell the dampness and the Mayflowers there. The old log school and then the new white one with green shutters . . . my wedding . . . the trip from Iowa into Nebraska. . . . There are many memories. But I'll tell you the one I like to think of best of all. It's just a homely everyday thing, but to me it is the happiest of them all. It is evening time here in the old house and the supper is cooking and the table is set for the whole family. It hurts a mother, Laura, when the plates begin to be taken away one by one. First there are seven and then six and then five . . . and on down to a single plate. So I like to think of the table set for the whole family at supper time. The robins are singing in the cottonwoods and the late afternoon sun is shining across the floor. Will, your grandfather, is coming in to supper . . . and the children are all playing out in the yard. I can hear their voices and happy laughter. There isn't much to that memory is there? Out of a lifetime of experiences you would hardly expect that to be the one I would choose as the happiest, would you? But it is. The supper cooking . . . the table set for the whole family . . . the afternoon sun across the floor . . . the robins singing in the cottonwoods . . . the children's merry voices . . . Will coming in . . . eventide."

"I think it's a nice memory, Grandma, but something about the way you say it makes me sad."

"But it's not sad, Laura. My memories are not sad. They're pleasant. I'm happy when I'm living them over. You'll find out when you get old, Laura, that some of the realities seem dreams . . . but the dreams, Laura, . . . the dreams are all real."

Chapter 34

That summer,—the one in which Abbie Deal was eighty,—was the summer of the Great Harvest.

Nebraska was favored of the gods. Ceres' throne was in Nebraska. It was as though she chose the state from all others upon which to lavish her goods,—as though the bulk of her fortune had been given to a favorite child. From the old Missouri to the foot of the sand-hills,—from the Kansas border to the land of the Dakotas, the wheat fields, like the sun's reflection, lay ripe under the July sky. In every direction one saw a thrasher belching out its yellow breath of wheat straw.

The fields were springs from which never-ending brooklets of yellow wheat, pouring into the thrashers, rolled forth in golden streams to form a mighty river of grain.

The barley, rye and oats yield was also heavy. The beet sugar output was to be of gigantic proportions. A bumper corn crop loomed in promise for the fall,—three hundred million bushels were being predicted. Those who juggled with figures said that it would bring four hundred million dollars. The combined sum of all the grain figures was almost beyond comprehension. Poor conditions in many of the neighboring states, and a shortage in production in the east and south, added to the fancy that Nebraska seemed to hold the gifts of the gods in her lap that summer.

The crop moved to market in an unprecedented volume. The various transportation systems had prepared for their part in this great procession of the grains. Tens of thousands of workers had bent their backs to the task. Tens of thousands of freight cars had been assembled at various points, awaiting the signal to move. And the grain came in,—and the cars moved. To the east and to the west they moved for weeks, carrying new life blood to the nation.

It filled old Abbie Deal with an overwhelming pride. "Do you know, John," she said to her attorney son, "it makes me happy . . . proud and happy. When I think of all those early lean years . . . the droughts . . . the grasshoppers . . . the crop failures . . . and then this! 'Poor Nebraska' people said. They looked down on us . . . as though we were a lot of destitute relations. They sent us old clothes and seeds and dried apples. And to think we're sending grain in great trainloads."

"Mother," John chuckled, "to hear you, anybody would think you owned the state."

"I do, John. She's mine in spirit. I feel as though she had been on trial before a world court and the trial dragged out over many years. We, who loved her, had faith to believe she would come through unscathed. And in these later years she's acquitted . . . and vindicated. And to think she's one of the wealthiest states in the union . . . the only one, I guess, with no bonded indebtedness! I wish your father might have lived to see it. He was so loyal . . . and so faithful . . . and so hopeful. He didn't live to see all his hopes fulfilled . . . but he did his part in making them materialize. They were prophets, John . . . prophets in a strange country . . . those hardy young men who ferried across the Missouri and forded the Platte and the Weeping Water and the other streams. What a legacy they've left you all,—farms and cities . . . cattle on a thousand hills, . . . manufactories, . . . great educational institutions . . ."

"Mother, that sounds quite oratorical. You can put all that into a speech up at Lincoln on the twenty-ninth. That's what I came over to see you about. They told me in Lincoln today that they wanted you to come up and speak at the unveiling of the Donovan Marker. That's the sixtieth anniversary, you know, of choosing the site of Lincoln for the capital. They want those present who were here then."

"Oh, but I wasn't here, John. That was almost a whole year before we came. I've only been here fifty-nine years."

"Fifty-nine years is quite a while, Mother, and you're getting to be one of the few left, who came that long ago. They want you to make a little talk."

"But what can you say in a few words, John, that will cover fifty-nine years? I guess 'Behold what God hath wrought,' is the most condensed statement I can think of."

And then it turned out that there were to be two big events for Abbie Deal in July. Katherine's wedding, which was to have been in the fall, was suddenly set for the twentieth. John was sending Jimmie Buchanan east on business, and in spite of the off-season time of year, the wedding was to take place so that Katherine could go with him. Already Katherine was being dined and fêted and showered by the friends who were still in town. Sarah Lutz was in California and was not coming back. "So *you* must be careful and not get sick, Granny," Katherine told her, "or we wouldn't have either of you at the big doings." She and her mother had driven down one afternoon to see Abbie. They brought her a lavender silk dress and a real lace cape-collar which Emma had bought in Vienna.

"You must be all dolled up, Granny," Katherine told her. "You must be massaged and manicured and you ought to have a permanent. I believe you would take a lovely one." She bent low over her grandmother's head and examined a strand of snow-white hair. "It looks as though it might have had a bit of natural curl in it once."

Oh, why couldn't they know? Why did an old woman seem always to have been old? Abbie was back on the knoll near the Big Woods, singing . . . her head thrown back . . . her thick hair curling and rippling over her creamy white shoulders. Why couldn't they understand that once she had kept tryst with Youth? Why didn't they realize that some day, they, too, must hold rendezvous with Age?

"Yes," said old Abbie Deal, simply, "it used to be quite curly."

It was just before they left, that Abbie said, "I have two presents for you, Kathie."

"Two, Granny? How lovely! Why two?"

"Well, one I am making myself so that you will always have something of Grandma's hand work. The other . . . the other, Kathie, is an heirloom, a string of little pearls. I want you not to plan for anything else for your neck. They're beautiful. Even you, with all your nice things, will be proud to own them."

"Fine . . . Granny! Fine!" Even so, it was said half carelessly. Things had come so easily to Kathie.

In the next two weeks, Abbie worked hard to finish the pink and white quilt with its rose-shaped blocks rambling up the borders. On the nineteenth, Grace came from summer school where she was teaching, and left immediately for Omaha in her roadster, as she had some shopping to do before the wedding. Early on the morning of the twentieth, Christine Reinmueller came over to receive her instructions from Abbie for caring for the place. The chickens were to be fed. Abbie gave minute directions for the ceremony,—the laying hens in the chicken-yard, whole corn out of one box, —the fries so-and-so out of a certain can. If it looked like rain, Christine was to turn the water-spout into the cistern. But if it rained too long, it ought to be turned out before it started to run over. And Christine was to pick the sweet-peas and nasturtiums.

John and Eloise Deal, with Wentworth and Laura and Millard, came for Abbie in the big sedan. Abbie had on her black silk with white collar and cuffs, and a new hat with a noble-appearing pom-pon on one side, which the milliner had told her looked "chic." Above Abbie's old wrinkled face it looked as chic as a painted one would have looked atop the portrait of Whistler's mother.

She had the quilt done up in a big flat package, and she put her feet on it in the car, as though it might, from sheer naturalness of the roses, ramble out of the sedan window. The pearls in the little box she held tightly in the bag in her hands.

The big car shot out over the graveled roads. Wentworth was at the wheel. Abbie wished John would do the driving. As a matter of fact Wentworth, born to the wheel, with all the younger generation, was the more alert driver, but Abbie could not think so.

"You know, Wentworth, I wish you wouldn't go so fast. Can't we go a little slower and see the country better?"

"You're sort of cracked about the country, aren't you, Grandma?"

"Yes, I guess I am, Wentworth. But if you'd gone over these same roads in a covered wagon, when there wasn't even a trail in the grass, you'd be, too."

At the top of a hill, John said something to his son, and the big car slowed down and stopped. "Take a drink, Mother," John waved his hand to the panorama before them, "but don't get intoxicated."

In the distance the Platte sprawled out lazily in the morning sun, the thick foliage of its tree-borders green against the sky's summer blue. There were acres of yellow wheat stubble where once the buffalo had wallowed, fields of young corn where once the prairie grass had grown, great comfortable homes and barns where once the soddies had stood. There were orchards and pastures and cattle, and a town nestling under the sheltering shade of huge trees. And soft white languorous clouds slipped into the east.

As they looked, there was a humming sound, and like one of the dragon-flies from the old creek bed, an aeroplane came out of the southwest. As direct and as fast as the southwest winds, it shot toward Omaha, back over the road that the Deals' and Lutzes' and the Reinmuellers' plodding oxen had come. From the hilltop near the Platte, Abbie Deal watched the mail plane go back over the road that the plodding oxen had come.

They slipped into Omaha at ten o'clock,—the Omaha that had been the raw frontier town, but was now a city of nearly a quarter million.

Mack, at home from the bank, came out to meet them when they turned into the driveway. The Mackenzie Deal place, a huge brick structure, with its clipped lawn and its sunken garden and its lily pools, was lovely in the morning sunlight. And it belonged to a man who had lived in a soddie until his thirteenth year, and to a woman whose first home on the prairie was hung with burlap to keep out the cold.

"Let me take your bag, Mother."

"Take the package, Mack, but I want to carry this myself." And they all laughed that Mother would trust no one with the pearls. She got slowly out of the car, her limbs a little numb. For a few moments she could not walk steadily, so that Mack put his arm around her and helped her up the wide steps.

In the house, Abbie asked at once for Katherine. The

moment had come. It had been sixty-two years coming and now it was here. The winds had blown it by . . . the winds she could not stop. The clock hands had ticked it off . . . the time she could not stay.

Old Abbie Deal, with her snow-white hair, and her eighty years beginning to set heavily upon her, climbed the mahogany-railed stairway with its imported carpet. A ladder with sapling cross-pieces . . . bare pine steps . . . a mahogany-railed stairway with thick imported carpet.

Katherine was in her room. Abbie knocked and went in, the little bag tightly clutched in her hand.

"Well . . . Granny?" Katherine did not seem flippant today. She was gentle, a little tender. She kissed her grandmother with genuine affection and sat down beside her.

"Here they are, dear." Abbie laid the pearls in Katherine's lap, her blue-veined hands trembling.

It was as though they had brought everything to Katherine, —had heaped their all into her lap,—the fruits of their labor, the results of their pioneering. The price of the prairie had been paid. The debt was canceled. For Katherine they had fought the prairie fires, split open the prairie furrows, and planted the corn. For Katherine they had set out the trees and made the roads and built the bridges.

Katherine took the pearls out of the little velvet box.

"Thanks, Granny, dear. They're darling."

There was no great surprise. She had spoken in a matter-of-fact way. "Thanks, Granny, dear. They're darling."

Well, she could not sense it. She was young and had never wanted for a thing in her life. She could not realize all the hardships which had been undergone since Abbie Deal's wedding night,—all the privations which had been endured while the pearls lay in the box for sixty-two years waiting for the time to come when a Mackenzie bride could wear them.

"I want to tell you about them. Could you . . . for just a few minutes, Kathie? I don't want to take your time . . ."

"Sure . . . Granny . . . tell me about them."

"They were Isabelle Anders-Mackenzie's, Kathie. After her death they became my mother's and then she gave them to me in the old log-cabin on my wedding night. They always seemed to me a sort of symbol . . . standing for everything that was fine and artistic and lovely. You probably don't

understand, but the work on the land in our early days was so
hard that it took all of our time and strength to keep body and
soul together. There was neither time nor opportunity for the
things that many of us wanted, with all our hearts, to do. But
we kept our eyes on a sort of gleam ahead, a hope that our
boys and girls could have all the things we could not have.
And so the pearls became a symbol to me of those things. I
said Margaret could wear them at her wedding, thinking we
would have everything to go with them. But you can't always
do with life as you wish. Sometimes life does things to you.
And so we didn't have much to do with, and Margaret was
married without them. Isabelle was married suddenly on the
eve of war, and Grace never married . . . and now they're
yours, the first granddaughter to marry. They've gone in a
sort of circle, from wealth, through hard times, back to
prosperity."

"I'll love them, Granny." Katherine kissed her grandmother again. Then she rose and slipped her arm through
Abbie's. "Now, Granny, I want you to come in and see the
spoils of war."

Out in the upper hall, with Persian rugs hanging over the
mahogany-railed balcony, most of the relatives seemed
gathering. Margaret and Dr. Baker had just driven in. Isabelle
and Harrison Rhodes had arrived the previous evening. Stanley's
and young Dr. Fred's wives were both there with their children.
One room had been converted into a receiving room for the
gifts, and it was into this one that the whole clan gathered.
Dainty gifts from exclusive shops were there. Many countries
had contributed their loveliest to Katherine Deal. Abbie,
wandering among the tables, made little clucking noises of
delight. "My, my, Kathie, whatever can you do with them
all? How beautiful! And to think that I was happy to get some
quilts and plain dishes and an old rooster and six hens!"

Mack came in and wandered aimlessly about. Every one
was there in the room, now,—Mack and Emma, Isabelle and
Harrison, Margaret and Doctor Baker, Grace, John and Eloise,
Laura, Wentworth, Stanley's and Fred Jr.'s wives, Katherine
and Jimmie Buchanan—— Suddenly it seemed to Abbie that
there was some concerted plan that they should all gather.
Two or three were whispering mysteriously.

"Are you ready, Daddy?" It was Katherine. "There's

something else we want to show you, Granny. We're too anxious for you to see."

Abbie turned toward Katherine who was holding the cord of a silken drape in her hand. Katherine's head was thrown back. Her eyes were merry. She was excited about something. "All set. Eyes front and guide right, Granny."

She pulled the silken cord and the drape parted. Behind the soft folds there hung a huge painting in a wide dull gold frame,—the painting of a lovely lady in velvet draperies, her reddish-brown hair curling over her shoulder, and a string of pearls at her neck. A hat with a sweeping plume was in one hand,—held by long slender fingers that tapered at the ends.

Katherine waved an airy hand. "Here she is, Granny. Allow me to introduce to you Isabelle Anders-Mackenzie, painted with my pearls on her . . . the little wretch."

Abbie Deal stared. The faint coloring of excitement under her old cheeks slipped away. One hand went up to her wrinkled throat and the other above her pounding heart. She turned to Mack. "You don't . . . not really, Mack? It isn't . . . ?"

"Yes, it is, Mother . . . your grandmother . . . my great-grandmother . . . Kathie's great-great-grandmother. It's the original and it cost like the old Harry, but Katherine has been after me ever since she heard you tell about it. I had the deuce of a time getting it, too. The agent traced it from Aberdeen to London and then to Edinburgh and back to London."

Abbie turned to the picture again.

"Can you beat it, Granny?" Katherine was laughing and calling to her. "All in one fell swoop I get six tons of china, nine carloads of silver, a darling new house, a homely new husband, *and* a snobocratic ancestor and her pearls."

Abbie Deal stood in front of the picture with Katherine's flippant words rippling past her. Old Abbie Deal, with her snow-white hair in its neat little knot at the back of her head, with her dumpy pudding-bag figure and her long, gnarled fingers that tapered at the ends, stood and stared at the picture. And standing there, looking up at the lovely lady, old Abbie Deal began to cry. They are the most painful tears in the world . . . the tears of the aged . . . for they come from dried beds where the emotions have long burned low.

Mack put an arm around his mother and patted her shoulder awkwardly. "Why, Mother, dear! Katherine, we shouldn't have . . . I never thought, Mother . . . only the pleasure . . ."

They all closed around her, making comments. Jimmie Buchanan and Wentworth stood off, a little embarrassed.

The others all explained it volubly to each other.

"It was too much of a surprise . . ."

"Yes, she's too old to have a surprise sprung . . ."

"The trip up here was too much for mother at her age."

"It's those weeks of sewing. I told her that quilt was too much . . ."

"No,—it's the whole excitement together."

Laura Deal came through the little knot. "It isn't *any* of those reasons, is it, Grandma?" she said. "I know what it is . . . but I don't know how to say it."

Abbie dried her eyes. "I'm all right now." She even smiled at them. "My, my, Kathie, tears on your wedding day. Whatever will you think? How selfish of me,—I'm that ashamed! But when I saw . . . when I saw the lovely lady that I used to dream about . . . it just came over me . . . in a sort of wave . . . all the wonderful things I planned to do when I was young . . . and never did."

Chapter 35

Abbie was back in her bedroom and dressed, now, for the wedding, in the lavender silk with the lace collar from Vienna. Margaret had dressed her hair and Isabelle had manicured her nails and Grace had powdered her skin,—with Abbie a little uncertain of the outcome as though, in her excitement, Grace might have purchased gunpowder by mistake.

She loved the beauty of everything connected with the affair, but she was tired. It was queer how much more she could stand around home than when she was away. The work in the house, the care of the chickens and flowers,—the whole responsibility of the home place was not so tiring as something unusual and out of the ordinary like this.

It was nearly time to go to the church when there was a little movement outside the door and she heard Katherine's voice, "I want to see grandmother."

The door opened and Katherine stood on the threshold, in the exquisite whiteness of filmy lace, her eyes luminous, her face softened.

"My . . . my!" Abbie Deal raised her hands in admiration, "you take my breath away. You look like *her*, Kathie . . . but you're even lovelier."

With a swift little movement of the short lacy skirt, Katherine was across the floor and down by her grandmother. She caught Abbie Deal's wrinkled old hands in her firm young ones. "Granny . . . I wanted to see you a minute. You've not liked me a lot of times, I know. We've been miles apart most of the time . . . but I wanted to come in and tell you

that nothing really counts but Jimmie. Oh, Granny, I'd go
with Jimmie . . . just as you did with grandfather. I'd live on
pumpkin seeds, you know.'' She was laughing a little, with
moist eyes. ''And dig a house in the side of a tree, just as you
did . . . you know . . . all those things I've heard you tell
about . . . Oh, heavens, I'm going to cry and I'm all made
up, but Granny . . . I wanted you to know . . . that, after
all, I'm just a lot of things you think I'm not . . . Oh, you
won't understand . . .''

Abbie Deal patted the lacy shoulders and with gentle old
fingers touched the upturned face. ''Why of course, Kathie,
. . . of course, dear, . . . Grandma understands. The clock
hands go round . . . and Grandma understands . . .''

The wedding was all that the wedding of Mackenzie Deal's
daughter would be,—a thing of extravagant simplicity. There
were beribboned pews, soft lights, and chaste white tapers in
silver candelabra against green palms. There was the organ's
mellow voice and the rich contralto one of the bride's aunt,
Isabelle Deal Rhodes, the well-known Chicago singer. There
was Mackenzie Deal with his bald head and his horn-rimmed
glasses and a lump in his throat. There was Mrs. Mackenzie
Deal in her orchid and silver lace, a little too concerned over
the details of the affair to think of her emotions. There were
all the Deal relatives, well-groomed and prosperous-looking.
And there was old Abbie Deal, sunk down low in the pew,
the lavender silk dress with its lace collar from Vienna over
her pudding-bag body, a knot of white hair at the nape of her
neck, her tapering, gnarled fingers trembling with age in her
lap.

The bride was at the altar now,—lovely Katherine, in her
white lace and satin, with the heirloom of pearls around her
neck. Old Abbie's thoughts went over the cycle of one hundred and thirty-five years. Satin and pearls in a Scottish
mansion,—a peasant dress and a head-shawl in an Irish hut,—a
wine-colored hoop-skirted merino in a log cabin,—a navy-
blue silk in a cottonwood and pine farmhouse,—white lace
and satin and the pearls again in their beautiful modern
setting.

''Do you take this man . . . for better . . . for worse . . .
death do you part?''

''I do.''

The same solemn question, solemnly answered. Would it be as faithfully kept? Abbie wondered.

And now it was all over. Katherine and Jimmie had left for the east. The big house had been quietly put to rights by two soft-footed maids. The whole Deal clan was gathering in the sun-room with its striking green and black and orchid English chintz hangings, and its fountain spraying over cool ferns and rocks.

Emma was bustling about hospitably, seeing that every one was comfortable. "Come on in, Donald. Sit here, Grace."

Standing in the doorway, Abbie heard Margaret coaxing Fred Jr.'s youngest with "Come to Grandma, Baby." It was still hard for Abbie to remember that two of her children were grandparents.

Then they saw her standing in the doorway.

"Come in, Mother."

"Sit here, Mother."

"No,—over her, Mother."

Mack brought a cushion, Isabelle a stool.

"Are you comfortable, Mother?"

How they thought of her bodily comfort,—always her physical needs. Not one ever said, "Are you sad, Mother?" or "How does your mind feel?" or "Does anything hurt your heart?"

Abbie, sitting in the big ivory chair with cushions at her back, found herself slipping away from the group, standing apart from it, looking at the members of it in a detached way. How efficient they all were,—and how smart,—and how easily they did things. They went hither and yon, either for business or pleasure affairs,—into Chicago, down south . . . sometimes abroad. Mack, now, was saying something about going down to New York the last of the week.

"*I* had a chance . . ." For the first time Abbie Deal spoke. Her voice cracked a little because of its age. From the depths of the big chair it cracked in its earnestness. "*I* had a chance to go to New York once."

Grace looked up quickly and then walked over to Isabelle. She spoke very low and turned her head so that her mother might not hear: "See! That's what I've been telling you. I've noticed that in her quite a little lately. Just detached sentences like that with no special meaning. It would just *kill* me if her mind . . . at the last. . . . But she does that quite often, now. 'Well, well, the clock hands go 'round,' she'll say, right out of a clear sky. Or, 'Dear, dear, the winds blew it all away.' And now this one, '*I* had a chance to go to New York, once,' . . . childish, that way.''

In the big chair, Abbie Deal was chuckling a little to herself, shaking with silent laughter.

''What's the joke, Mother?'' Mack spoke from across the room.

''Nothing much. I was just wondering about all of you . . . now . . . if I had gone.''

''See . . . ?'' Grace was grave in her anxiety, ''. . . like *that*.''

Abbie Deal sat looking out at the family gathered there in the beautiful sun-parlor, sat there with half-closed eyes like an old Buddha looking out on the generations. Eighty years of living were behind her,—most of them spent in fighting, —fighting the droughts, the snows, the hot winds, the prairie fires, the blizzards,—fighting for the children's physical and mental and spiritual development, fighting to make a civilization on the raw prairie. Bending her back to the toil, hiding her heart's disappointments, giving her all in service, she was like an old mother partridge who had plucked all the feathers from her breast for the nest of her young.

Old Abbie Deal, so near the borderland now that she held intercourse with both worlds, sat there looking out through half-closed eyes at the children and the grandchildren and the great-grandchildren.

''Well, Will . . . there they all are. What do you think of them? I did the best I could.''

You did well, Abbie-girl.

Chapter 36

Grace Deal, in her roadster, went back to summer school early in the morning. John Deal and his family left about the same time for Cedartown. Isabelle and Harrison Rhodes were remaining in Omaha for a few days' visit at Mack's, before making the rounds of the other homes. Abbie rode back with Margaret and Dr. Baker.

On the way, Margaret asked: "Don't you want to go on up to Lincoln with us for a few days, Mother?"

"No. Oh, no," Abbie said hastily. "I'm tired and I'll be real glad to get home again."

When the big car stopped under the Lombardy poplars near the sitting-room porch of the old farmhouse, Margaret got out with her mother and helped her up the short walk to the house.

"I just can't bear to leave you here alone, Mother. Don't you want me to stay all night with you? Fred could run out and get me to-morrow or I could go in on the morning train."

"No. Oh, no. I'm all right. I'm just tired from the excitement. When you're used to being alone you don't mind it a bit."

"Promise me you would call some one on the phone the first minute you didn't feel well."

"I promise. I would call Christine. She's got a phone in now, but she certainly begrudges the money. Anyway, I won't be alone much more this summer. Isabelle will be here next week, and Grace will be home again soon, and Laura is going to come and stay a few days."

When they had gone, Abbie Deal opened some of the windows to air out the house. She had a whimsical notion that the things seemed glad to have her back,—the table where old Doc Matthews had rolled his pills, the walnut cupboard, Will's corner what-not. There was something human about them as though they shared her thoughts,—as though, having come up through the years with her, they held the same memories.

She fed her chickens, watered the sweet-peas, picked the dried leaves off her geraniums, and went over the whole yard as though to greet every bush and shrub after her absence.

For the next few days she went slowly about her household duties with the same little sense of pleasure she always experienced after she had been to one of the children's homes. How could old women bear to sit around with folded hands? What mattered it that the children all had such nice houses, there would never be any real home for her but the old wing-and-upright set in the cedars and poplars.

By Friday night she had accomplished a lot of extra small tasks, setting an old hen that was foolishly wanting to raise a family out of season, gathering some early poppy-seeds and putting fresh papers on her pantry shelves. At five-thirty she started her supper. As she worked she tried to hum an old tune she had known when she was young, an old song she had not thought of for years and years, until Isabelle had sung it over the radio in the winter:

> "Oh . . . the La . . . dy of . . . the Lea,
> Fair and . . . young and . . . gay was . . . she"

She had to make long pauses between the syllables to get her breath.

> "Beau . . . tiful . . . exceed . . . ingly
> The La . . . dy of . . . the Lea."

Her voice cracked and went up or down without her volition, so that even though her mind heard the song, her ear scarcely recognized the melody.

"Many . . . a woo . . . er sought her . . . hand
For she . . . had gold . . . and she . . . had land,
Every . . . thing . . . la la . . . la la"

She had forgotten what the words were right there.

"The La . . . dy of . . . the Lea."

She was completely out of breath, so that she had to sit
down a few minutes before starting to put her dishes on the
kitchen table. As she sat looking at the old table, she suddenly wished that she could pull it out, put in all the leaves,
set the places for the children and then call them in from
play,—not the prosperous grown people she had been with so
recently in Omaha, but just as they were when they were
little. Queer how plainly she could see them in her mind:
Mack's merry round face with its sprinkling of freckles,
Margaret's long dark pig-tail, her gray eyes and her laughter,
Isabelle's reddish-brown curls and her big brown eyes, Grace's
square little body with her apronstrings always untied, John's
serious face,—a sort of little old man who did not want to be
hugged. How real they seemed to her. One could almost
imagine that it was they who were playing, "Run, Sheep
Run" out there now instead of the neighbor children.

Abbie Deal had never forbidden the north-end children
access to her yard, and their high-pitched voices calling
"Going-east . . . going west . . ." came to her now from
the region of the cottonwood windbreak. Yes, it sounded for
all the world like her own children out there.

As she got up and went about her supper, putting a little
piece of meat on to cook, her mind slipped to the fact that she
had promised to make a short talk on the following week at
the sixtieth anniversary of the founding of the city of Lincoln.
She must begin to think of what she could say. There was
plenty to talk about but she dreaded the speaking. She hoped
her voice wouldn't quaver and break. That was the trouble of
being old. Your body no longer obeyed you. It did unruly and
unreasonable things. An eye suddenly might not see for a
moment. Your knees gave out at the wrong time, so that
when you thought you were walking north, you might find
yourself going a little northwest. Your brain, too, had the

same flighty trick. You might be speaking of something and
forget it temporarily,—your mind going off at a little to the
northwest, too, so to speak.

She glanced up to see what time it was, and discovered that
the clock had stopped. Whatever had happened to the faithful
old thing? It must be wearing out, for she was sure she had
wound it.

She opened the door with the little brown church painted
on the glass, and reached for the key. Suddenly,—so suddenly that it was like a flash,—a queer feeling came over
Abbie Deal. It was unlike any she had ever experienced—a
tightening of the throat and chest as of cold icy hands upon
her. She tried to take her arms down from their stretched
position, but it was almost impossible to move them for the
pain. In a moment the icy hands released their hold upon her
as quickly as they had clutched at her, but they left her so
weak and shaken that she started into her bedroom holding
onto the backs of the chairs.

She lay down on her bed to get herself in hand. There was
a sharp pain now in the back of her head and it seemed a little
hard to breathe. For a moment she wondered if it could be
that her time to die had come. No, that could not be. She was
a little sick, but she had been so many times. "I never *do*
die," she said to herself and smiled a little at the humor of it.

The sun's rays slanted along the floor from the west sitting-
room windows. The meat was cooking, for the air was filled
with the odor of it. Robins were singing outside in the
poplars. The neighbors' children ran across the yard with
cries of "All's out's in free." They would trample the grass a
little, but children were worth more than grass anyway. She
must not get sick, for she was planning to go to something in
a few days. For a few moments she could not think what it
was, and then she remembered. It was the old settlers' meeting in Lincoln. There would be a lot of old folks there and
they would tell their reminiscences all day. No doubt she
would be bored to distraction. Old people usually bored her.
No, that was not right. Something was wrong with that
thought. She was not young. She was *old*. She, herself, was
one of the old settlers. How strange! Well, she would go. Her
mind seemed not quite under control. She tried hard to think
whether she was to go in the big shining sedan on the straight

graveled roads or in the creaking wagon through the long swaying grass. *Blow . . . wave . . . ripple . . . dip. Blow . . . wave . . . ripple . . . dip.* She felt ill. It was the swaying of the prairie grass that made her ill.

If she were taken sick she had promised to do something,—something with the little brown box at the side of the bed. Suddenly, she remembered . . . call Christine. That was it. Good old Christine! . . . Old friends . . . were best. Maybe she ought to call Christine in the little brown box. Her arm slipped around the rolled silk quilt at the foot of the bed. Such a soft silk quilt . . . and an old patched quilt in front of a sheep-shed for a door. There it was again,—her mind going northwest.

The sun slanted farther across the carpet. Whoever was frying that meat, was letting it burn. The children shouted very close to the house: "Run, sheep, run." It was nice to know the children were all well and out there playing,—Mack and Margaret, John and Isabelle, Grace and the baby. She hoped they were taking good care of the baby,—the baby with a face like a little white rose. She would let them play on until she got to feeling better, and then she would get up and finish supper.

That queer thought of death intruded itself again, but she reasoned, slowly and simply, with it. If death were near she would be frightened. Death was her enemy. All her life she had hated death and feared it. It had taken her mother, and Will and the baby and countless old friends. But Death was not near. The children playing outdoors, the sun slanting over the familiar carpet, the meat frying for supper,—all the old simple things to which she was accustomed, reassured her. A warm feeling of contentment slipped over her to hear the children's happy voices. "All's out's in free," they called. It was almost time for Will to come in to his supper. It was the nicest part of the day—the robins singing in the poplars—the meat cooking—the supper table set—every one coming home—the whole family around the table—all—Will—the children. She must wind the clock before they come in. You—couldn't —stop—Time—

It was hard again to breathe,—the icy pain—in her chest— *Oh . . .*

Immediately the children were quiet. The robin had stopped

singing. Whoever had been frying meat had removed it from the stove, and some one must have pulled down all the shades. It was strange to have all those things happen at once,—the robin cease singing, the children stop playing, the meat taken from the stove, and the shades pulled down. For a moment it was as though one could neither see nor hear nor smell. At any rate she felt much better. The pressure in her chest and in the back of her head was gone. That was nice. It seemed good to be relieved of that. She breathed easily,—so very easily that she seemed not to be breathing at all. She sat up on the edge of the bed. She felt light, buoyant. "I'll wind the clock and finish supper now and call them in."

Through the semi-darkness of the house there was no sight or sound. But as she looked up, she saw Will standing in the doorway. For a moment she thought he was standing under honey-locust branches in a lane, but saw at once that it was only shadows.

"Well, Will!" She stood up. "I'm so glad you're home. You've been away all day, haven't you? Where were you, Will? Isn't that stupid of me not to remember?" She moved lightly toward him, but suddenly stopped, sensing that for some reason there was a strangeness about his presence. She stood looking at him questioningly, a little confused.

Will was looking intently at her, half-smiling. She would have thought he was joking her—teasing her a little—if his expression had not been too tender for that.

"I don't quite understand, Will. Did you want something of me? . . ." That was a way of Will's,—always so quiet that you almost had to read his mind. There was no answer, but at once she seemed to know that Will was waiting for her.

"Oh, I must tell the children first. They *never* want me to go." She turned to the window. "Listen, children," she called, "I'm going away with Father. If some one would pull up the shades I could see you, but it doesn't really matter. Listen closely . . . I'm only going to be gone a little while. Be good children . . . You'll get along just fine."

She turned to the doorway. "It seems a little dark. You know, Will, I think we will need the lantern. I've always kept the lantern . . ." Her voice trailed off into nothing. For Will was still smiling at her, questioningly, quizzically,—but with something infinitely more tender,—something protecting, enveloping. Slowly it came to her. Hesitatingly she put her hand up to her throat. "Will . . . you don't mean it! . . . Not *that* . . . not *Death* . . . so *easy?* That it's nothing more than *this* . . .? Why . . . *Will!*"

Abbie Deal moved lightly, quickly, over to her husband, slipped her hand into his and went with him out of the old house, past the Lombardy poplars, through the deepening prairie twilight,—into the shadows.

It was old Christine Reinmueller, who came in and found her.

"*Ach . . . Gott!*" She wrung her hard old hands. "Mine friend . . . de best voman dat efer on de eart' valked."

The children all came hastily in response to the messages. In the old parlor with the what-not and the marble-topped stand and the blue plush album, they said the same things over and over to each other.

"Didn't she seem as well to you last week as ever?"

"Do you suppose she suffered much?"

"Or called for us?"

"Isn't it *dreadful.* Poor mother . . . all alone . . . not one of us here . . . as though we had all forsaken her just when she needed us most . . . and after all she's done for us . . . ."

It was then that little twelve-year-old Laura Deal turned away from the window where she had been looking down the long double row of cedars and said in a voice so certain that it was almost exalted:

"*I* don't think it's so dreadful. I think it was kind-of nice. Maybe she didn't miss you. Maybe she didn't miss you *at all*. One time grandma told me she was the very happiest when she was living over all her memories. Maybe . . . ." She looked around the circle of her relatives,—and there was a little about her of another twelve-year-old Child who stood in the midst of his elders in Temple,—"maybe she was doing that . . . then."

Stories of Courage from Vista